A Fatal Accounting

Jack Mallory Mysteries - Book 3

William Coleman

A Fatal Accounting

Dedicated to my lovely wife, Vicki, who has supported me every step of the way through each of my novels by allowing me the time to write, being my first beta reader as well as my main editor. By being my biggest fan and my sharpest critic, she has helped me produce final manuscripts for you to enjoy.

1

Richard bolted upright in full panic. He had been dead asleep, and he searched the darkened room for whatever had woken him. What little light breached the blackout curtains offered no clue as to what it may have been. He rubbed at his eyes trying to push the sleep away.

Looking at his phone where it lay charging on his nightstand, he could see that it was 2:21 am. Maybe it had just been a bad dream, something he hadn't experienced since childhood. There didn't seem to be any other explanation.

He started to lie back down when he glanced at his wife's side of the bed. She wasn't there. Had she gotten up and woken him as she left the room? The pillow and sheets looked undisturbed as if she hadn't been to bed at all.

He heard a thumping sound from outside the room and Richard realized two things; someone was at the door, and it was the knocking that had awakened him to begin with. Stephanie must have forgotten her keys. The doorbell had not worked in over a year, something he kept saying he would fix but hadn't.

He threw back the covers and swung his legs over the side of the mattress, his calves sore from taking his Cannondale for a ten-mile ride the day before. He slid to the floor where his slippers dutifully awaited, grabbed his phone out of habit, and dropped it into the pocket of his pajamas.

As he opened the bedroom door, the knocking came again, much louder, the door reverberating in its frame. She was pissed. He wondered how long she had been out there. 'Patience is a virtue,' his mother used to tell him. Ironic coming from the most impatient woman he had ever known.

He was still a bit groggy from being yanked from sleep. But by the time he reached the top of the stairs, he was good to go and took them down at a healthy pace. Reaching the front door, he turned the knob and pulled it open.

"Did you forget . . ." It was not Stephanie. Two uniformed officers were standing on the porch in the dark. Richard slid his hand along the wall and turned on the exterior light. His mind raced with the possibilities that could have brought them to his door. "Can I help you?"

"Mr. Ellison?" the officer on Richard's left asked. He was tall, thick with muscle. His name plate identified him as Walters.

"What's this about?" Richard turned to him.

"Richard Ellison?" Walters asked again.

"Yes." Richard nodded. "What's going on?"

"Mr. Ellison." The officer on his right, Mendez, stepped forward. He was shorter but just as thick. "There has been an incident."

"An incident?" Richard furrowed his brow. "What do you mean?"

"Your wife was found in Evergreen Park," Mendez said. "She has been transported to St. Peters Hospital."

"What?" Richard shook his head to clear the fog that was threatening to take over. "She was where? What happened?"

"Evergreen Park," Mendez repeated. "We only know that she was attacked."

"Attacked?" Richard stared at the officer. "Who?"

"Maybe a mugging," the officer said. "We don't know. We're hoping she can tell us more when she recovers."

"Recovers?"

"We can take you there, if you want to follow," Walters offered. "Or is there someone you can call?"

"Call?" Richard was having trouble processing his thoughts. He knew he was repeating what the officers were saying. He just couldn't seem to stop. "Yes. I can call our friends. But I would like to follow you. If I can change and get my keys?"

"We'll wait," Walters nodded.

Richard left the door standing open, turned, and ran up the stairs back to his room. As he climbed, he pulled out his phone and sent a text to Wendy and Brent, their closest friends, telling them to meet him at St. Peters when they could. Five minutes later he was backing out of his driveway and following the police cruiser out of the neighborhood.

2

Richard sat in the waiting room with his elbows on his knees and his face buried in his hands. Even with the police escort, he had been too late to see Stephanie before she was taken to surgery. She had experienced blunt force trauma, a doctor explained, leaving her brain swollen, and they had to relieve the pressure as soon as possible to avoid permanent damage. Immediately after delivering him that news, the doctor's name was called over the intercom, and he excused himself.

Officer Walters, the taller of the two who had broken the news to him, was sitting directly across from him with notepad in hand. He had waited for the doctor to give his report. But he had a job to do.

"Mr. Ellison," the officer grimaced. "Do you have any idea why your wife would be at the park so late?"

"What?" Richard raised his head, his dark bangs falling into his eyes, a reminder that Stephanie had recently suggested he get a haircut. "No. I didn't even know she was at the park. I've never known her to go there."

"Didn't you wonder where she was?" Walters asked. "She wasn't home when you went to bed. Does she often stay out?"

"She called me from work this afterno-... ," Richard looked at his watch. "I guess it was yesterday, now. She told me she would be late. Some problem at work. It happens sometimes. But she's usually home by eleven."

"But last night she wasn't." Walters jotted in his notepad. "Didn't you worry? Try to check on her?"

"I, uh . . ."

"Richard."

He looked up to see his long-time friend, Brent Meadows, rushing into the room. Close on his heels was his wife, Wendy. Brent sat heavily in the seat next to Richard and wrapped his arm around his friend's shoulders. Unlike Richard, Brent kept his hair military short and looked every bit the part, though he had never served.

"My God," Brent said. "What the hell happened?"

"Is she okay?" Wendy looked sincerely worried. The petite woman was Stephanie's closest friend. "Have you seen her?"

"She's in surgery." Richard closed his eyes and took a deep breath. Having their friends there suddenly made everything seem more real. "I haven't heard anything."

"But she's okay," Wendy leaned in. "Isn't she?"

"I don't know," Richard's voice caught in his throat. "I don't know anything."

Officer Walters slid to the front of his seat. "Mr. Ellison. We can finish this later."

"Are you sure?" Richard straightened himself. "I mean, I would appreciate it. But . . ."

"Sure." The officer stood. "I'll catch up with you in a while. These are standard questions. Nothing you can't answer later."

Walters stretched and turned away in search of a cup of coffee. He was nearing the end of his shift, and he was dragging. A nurse walked by and the tall man gave chase, hoping she could point him in the right direction.

Richard watched him walk away before turning his attention back to the Meadows. "I guess you got my text."

"Yeah, about that," Brent leaned in close and whispered, "Wendy is pissed that you didn't call instead."

"I didn't have time," Richard defended.

"Hey, I get it," Brent raised his hands in surrender. "But she doesn't see it that way."

"She'll have to." Richard grimaced.

Down the hall, the doors marked 'personnel only' opened and a grey-haired man in scrubs walked out. He glanced around to be sure there was no one else, then walked toward the three of them.

"Mr. Ellison?" he inquired.

"I'm Richard Ellison," Richard stood. "Is she out of surgery?"

"Can we talk alone?" The man looked at him over his glasses.

"No." Richard stood his ground. "Whatever you tell me, I'm just going to tell them. How is she?"

"I'm Dr. Jeffries. I was the one performing your wife's surgery," he introduced. He took a deep breath. "We did everything we could. But her injuries were just too severe."

Richard's knees buckled and he started to fall. Brent caught him and guided him to a seat. Wendy burst into tears, almost wailing. Brent reached for and took her hand. He was staying strong for them.

"Do you understand?" the doctor asked.

Richard nodded, his head spinning. "My wife. She's gone."

Richard lowered his gaze to the floor and stared at his shoes. He noticed that the shoe on his left foot was black. On his right was a brown one. Any other time, it would have been funny. If Stephanie were there, she would have had a big laugh. Richard's eyes filled with tears and he cried.

3

Richard wasn't sure what was expected of him. Were there papers for him to fill out? Was Officer Walters coming back to question him? Was he supposed to stay, or could he go home? Did he even want to go home?

It was almost six o'clock and the three of them decided they needed to get out of there. The police knew where Richard lived and could find him if needed. Everything else could wait.

Richard knew the answer to one of his questions. He didn't want to go home. He didn't want to be alone. He wasn't ready. Not yet. Like he followed the police to the hospital, he followed the Meadows home, to their home. They promised company and fresh coffee, an offer he couldn't refuse. The Meadows pulled into their garage and Richard watched the door close as he parked in the driveway.

Exiting his truck, the first rays of sunlight were cresting the eastern horizon promising a brand-new day, and Richard cursed it. The thought of a day beginning without Stephanie being in it made his heart ache. He numbly climbed the steps to the Meadows' front door where his friend waited to let him in.

"Wendy's making coffee." Brent held the door open.

"Stephanie and I have coffee together nearly every morning." Richard wasn't talking to anyone in particular. He was barely aware that words were escaping his lips.

The two men walked to the kitchen where the coffee was just starting to brew. Brent sat Richard at the dining table, patted his back then joined his wife at the kitchen sink.

"I can't tell if he's in shock," Brent leaned in and whispered to Wendy. "Or if he's plotting revenge."

"If it's revenge, I'm in." The anger in her voice surprised him. More softly, she said, "My money is on shock. I still can't believe she's gone."

"I know." Brent wrapped his arm around his wife and pulled her close, kissing the top of her head. "I know how close the two of you were."

"I just talked to her." Her emotions built up again. "She said she had something to tell me. Now, I guess I'll never know what it was."

"It probably wouldn't mean anything now anyway." He squeezed her. "Best to focus on the time you had together. Celebrate her life and all."

Wendy stared at Richard. He had his face buried in his hands as he had at the hospital after learning of Stephanie's death. "I'm worried about him."

"I know," Brent said. He let Wendy go and poured two cups of coffee. "I'll sit with him for a while."

"He's lucky to have you," Wendy wiped at her eyes.

"You may be overestimating my ability to comfort him." He lifted the coffee. "I don't know how to deal with this kind of pain."

"Just be there for him." She patted his arm as he walked around the island that dominated their kitchen. "I'm going upstairs for a minute."

Brent set one of the cups in front of his friend and took the chair next to his. Richard didn't react. Brent sat back in the chair and sipped from his own mug as he tried to figure out what to do. Before he could think of anything, Richard raised his head.

"What happens now?"

"Now, you need to make arrangements," Brent said. "Wendy and I will help you. If you want us to, that is."

"No." Richard shook his head. Brent was taken aback. "I don't mean that. I mean what happens with the police? How do they find her killer? It had to be random. No one would want to hurt Stephanie. How do they find him if it was just a random stranger?"

"They'll do the best they can," Brent assured him. "But you're right. They may never catch who did this."

"That's not what I want to hear." Richard looked his friend in the eyes. "I want to hear that they're going to catch the bastard and make him pay."

"That's what we all want." Brent picked up his coffee and looked at the reflection of the overhead lights on the surface of the dark liquid. "But you need to face reality, Richard. You need to prepare for the worst."

"Worse than Stephanie being murdered?"

"Worse than that."

"What could be worse?" Richard asked.

"The police always look at the husband," Brent lowered his voice. "They're going to look at you. Where were you when she was attacked?"

"I was home." Richard insisted. "In bed."

"Alone?"

"Of course, alone," Richard said. "If I wasn't alone, Stephanie would have been home instead of in some park."

"So you don't have an alibi," Brent informed him.

"An alibi?" Richard said a little too loud. "Why do I need an alibi?"

"Did you do this?" Brent asked.

"No," Richard said. "You know I didn't."

"I know you didn't because I know you," Brent said. "I know the relationship you and Stephanie had. The police don't know you. And if they can't come up with another suspect, and you don't have an alibi, where else are they going to look?"

"What are you saying?" Richard asked.

"I'm saying as long as you're a suspect," Brent patted his shoulder. "They aren't going to be looking for the real killer. They're going to focus solely on you."

"But I didn't do anything," Richard insisted.

"It would be better if you had an alibi."

"Well I don't have one." Richard snapped. "I didn't know I was going to need one."

"I know." Brent put a hand on his friend's shoulder. "I just wish we had been together, you know. So I could be your alibi. Then they could focus on finding whoever killed Stephanie."

Richard looked at his friend. They had known each other most of their lives, nearly inseparable since they met in third grade. Brent and Wendy had introduced him to Stephanie. And Stephanie deserved better than what happened to her. She deserved justice. And he didn't deserve to be wrongfully accused of her murder.

"Maybe you could say you were," Richard said, absently.

"What?" Brent asked.

"You could say we were together," Richard clarified. "You could say I was at your place."

"Your place," Brent suggested. "I was at your place until after midnight, say 1:00 a.m. It sounds better. That way we don't have to get Wendy involved."

"Won't she know you weren't at my place?" Richard asked.

"She went to bed early," Brent said. "I watched a movie in the basement. I had just gotten into bed when your text came. I've had almost no sleep."

"Yeah, okay." Richard nodded. He looked his friend in the eyes. "You sure about this? Lying to the police?"

"I would do anything for my best friend." Brent wrapped his arm around Richard's shoulders and squeezed. "You know that."

Wendy appeared and walked over to sit across from them. "What are you two talking about?"

4

On warm, sunny days, Evergreen Park was a popular destination for families and dog owners. The large open fields of grass made perfect picnic grounds as well as providing plenty of room to run and play. The walking trails offered options for varying distances and skill sets.

When the sun set, it was a different place entirely. A meeting place for bands of teenagers, causing mischief at different levels of seriousness, and unsavory types, participating in activities at different levels of illegality. It was not the type of place the victim should have been.

Jack Mallory arrived at the scene just before sunrise, hours after the woman had been found. The police had spent that time investigating an assault. Now that it was a homicide, it became Jack's case.

The victim had been found on one of the easier, paved walking trails near a park bench, with a light post directly behind it. The light was necessary because the path ran through a dense thicket of trees and brush, blocking all view of the rest of the park. Jack had a flashback of his last major case where women walking their dogs were abducted in the same type of place.

Yellow crime scene tape cordoned off the area. He was glad to see that. The scene was already contaminated. The person who found the victim, the police and paramedics, and the police investigator would have all tracked through. Granted, their main focus was on trying to save the poor woman's life. But it left Jack a mess to deal with.

One officer remained, standing just outside the tape. Everyone else cleared out as soon as the woman passed away and the case was kicked to homicide. Jack walked up to the officer who had watched him somberly for the last quarter mile.

"Detective Mallory," he greeted.

"Officer Franks." Jack read the name off his tag. He knew the man, just couldn't remember where from. "Did you draw the short stick?"

"Nah," Franks said. "I volunteered."

"Really?" Jack's eyebrow rose. "I guess it is a nice day to be in the park."

"Yes, sir," Franks smiled.

"You weren't first on scene were you?" Jack asked.

"No, sir." Franks shifted his stance. "That would be Walters and Mendez."

"And where are they?"

Franks looked at his watch. "Shifted out."

"When you arrived, was it still dark out?" Jack scanned the surface of the ground for anything that may have been missed. He raised the yellow tape and stepped past it and the officer.

"Yes," Franks confirmed.

"Was that lamp lit?" Jack pointed at the light post behind the bench.

"Sure was."

Jack circled the scene, almost following the tape all the way around. As he walked, he looked down at his feet, glancing toward the epicenter from time to time. Usually, when he arrived there was a body, sometimes fresh, sometimes not. But a body. This victim had been rushed to the hospital, though it was easy, by way of the blood on the ground, to determine where she had been found. A few feet from the bench and just off the path. Her killer had not been worried about her being found, and may not have even known she was so close to death.

Jack tilted his head to look at the bench. It could easily have been a random attack on the woman as she sat on the bench. She tried to run but did not make it far. A thrill seeker? A mugging? A man who hated women and saw an opportunity to express it? In each of those possibilities, it would be difficult to find the perpetrator.

"Do you know if they found her purse?" Jack looked at the blood-stained grass again.

"I don't know." Franks was directly behind him, outside the tape. "Want me to call someone to find out?"

"Not necessary." Jack pulled his phone out and started taking pictures of everything. "How long were the techs here?"

"About an hour," Franks said. "Left about a half hour before you arrived."

Jack stood and walked to the bench. "What were you doing out here at that hour?"

"What was that?" Franks twisted his neck.

"Nothing," Jack said. "Just thinking out loud."

The detective took some pictures of the bench before turning around and sitting in its center. He quickly took a series of pictures from where he sat to show the view in every direction. There was nothing special about the location, at least nothing that Jack could identify.

Putting his phone away, Jack sat back and tried to imagine what Stephanie Ellison would have seen with only the lamp post supplying light. It was unlikely there would be much to see. The lamp would flood the area around the bench with a bright light, essentially creating a blanket of darkness to cover anything outside its glow. Of course, just because she was attacked next to the bench, it didn't mean she had to be sitting on it. She could just as easily have just been walking by. It could be that the attacker was sitting there, waiting for his opportunity. Or maybe they weren't waiting, just happened to be there when she passed by and reacted.

Random attacks were difficult cases to solve. Unless the perpetrator left behind DNA that could be matched to someone in the database, there was little chance of tracking them down. Jack took a deep breath, let it out slow, and stood. He informed Officer Franks that he was done and followed the path back to the parking area where he had left his car.

He imagined the killer following the same path, only faster in order to flee the scene. If the crime was planned, they would have been parked close, so they could make a quick getaway. If it was a crime of opportunity, they could have been anywhere. He reached the edge of the asphalt and scanned the almost empty lot. The city crews came through regularly to keep it clear of trash, but they hadn't been there yet today. There were several paper and plastic cups, along with discarded water bottles and miscellaneous papers, and other trash.

Jack walked along the perimeter looking for anything significant. Concrete posts were evenly spaced to prevent visitors from driving into the park. A short distance from the path he had emerged from, he found a thick piece of red plastic from a taillight at the base of one of the posts. He bagged it and wrote on the bag where and when he found it. A short distance farther, next to another post, he found a second piece of taillight that did not match the first. And farther still a clear piece of plastic headlight. He bagged and labeled each. In his younger days, he would have been surprised by the number, but he had been around long enough to know some people just shouldn't be allowed to drive.

When he finished his stroll around, he looked out into the parking area itself. There were only five vehicles in the lot, his department issue sedan, Franks' cruiser, and three others.

Jack pulled out his phone again and selected a number from his contacts. "This is Mallory. On the Ellison case, was the victim's car recovered?"

There was a pause before they came back. "No, sir."

"Check with the DMV and let me know what vehicles are registered to the Ellisons." Jack turned away from his car and headed directly for the nearest civilian car, a silver BMW. He was just peeking into the driver's window when the response came.

"There are two. A blue 2014 Chevy Impala and a black 2012 GMC Sierra 1500."

Jack stepped away from the BMW and looked at the other two. One of them was a blue Chevy parked directly under a light post. He walked toward it. "What is the plate number on the Impala?"

They gave him the number. He circled the car and checked the tag. It was a match.

"I've got the car here." Jack shook his head. "Call the lab and tell them to get someone down here to pick it up."

He disconnected the call and stepped up to the driver's side window. Inside, the car was clean with the exception of a to-go cup in the center console. He could see a shoulder strap laying on the passenger seat, that appeared to belong to something on the passenger side floorboard. The console blocked his view, so Jack walked around to the passenger side. From there he could see a laptop bag and a purse.

Jack leaned against the light post to wait for the lab. He looked up at the light over his head. Had she arrived after dark? Parking here for a sense of security? Or had she known she would be there long enough to need the light when she returned? With every question that crossed his mind, Jack kept coming back to the same one: Why was she in the park so late?

5

Richard Ellison was on his third cup of coffee by the time he remembered to call his employer. Already more than an hour late by that time, his manager was upset, going into full rant mode about absenteeism, proper notification, and the amount of work to be done. After Richard was able to explain the situation, his boss backpedaled and told him to take all the time he needed.

"Sorry for your loss, Richard." The man cleared his throat. "We'll all miss her."

"Thanks." Richard was numb and didn't know what else to say. There was an awkward moment of silence, and they both stammered over ending the call. Richard stood staring at the blank screen of his phone wondering how long it would be before he could have a normal conversation.

Moving to the living room, Richard sat in a plush armchair opposite his best friend's wife, Wendy Mcadows, sitting on the sofa. He exchanged looks with the woman whose eyes were red and puffy from crying. They sat in silence, having no words that would make the situation better. Anything they might say would simply sound hollow.

They both heard the groan of the garage door opening and turned to the kitchen door in anticipation. About eight o'clock in the morning, Brent suddenly announced that he had to go take care of some things. It was unusual, given the circumstances, but Richard was more than happy to have Wendy keep him company. He just didn't want to be alone. Now, almost two hours later, Brent had finally returned.

Wendy rose to her feet and met her husband as he came through the door. He was about to greet her but stopped himself when he saw the expression on her face.

"Where have you been?" she demanded.

"I told you I was running errands." He raised his hand to show the bags of groceries he held there.

"Your best friend just lost his wife," Wendy rasped. "My best friend, I might add. And you choose now to go shopping?"

"I picked up some coffee and donuts." He set the bags on the counter. "Eggs. Bacon. Bread."

"It doesn't take two hours to get groceries," she scolded. "Why are you avoiding him?"

"I'm not avoiding him," Brent whispered a little too loud. He looked up at Richard who sat staring off into darkness. Brent leaned closer to his wife and lowered his voice. "I'm not avoiding him. I just don't know what to say."

"How about, 'Hey, Richard, I'm here for you.'," Wendy suggested. "The two of you have been friends for a lifetime. Be his friend."

"You're right." He pulled her into his arms and hugged her. "How are you holding up?"

"I'm not," she blurted, pushing away from him. "Richard first. Then me."

"Okay. Okay." Brent looked over to where his friend sat. "I've never seen him so broken. He's usually the strong one."

"And today," Wendy said. "You're the strong one."

Brent inhaled deeply and nodded. Sitting in the seat Wendy had just vacated, he looked at his friend. "How are you doing?"

Richard, who had been staring off to a point beyond the walls of the house, turned. "Really?"

"Stupid question," Brent shrugged. "I know. I just . . . I don't know what to say."

"How about you just sit there?" Richard suggested. "You don't have to say anything."

"I can do that."

Richard turned back to search for the same distant point that only he could see. Brent settled into the cushions and fell silent. Wendy joined her husband on the sofa and pulled her knees to her chest. She was crying again, just couldn't seem to stop. She wondered how long it was going to go on.

They sat in silence for about an hour before Richard broke his gaze and looked over to where Wendy sat. Tears streaked her face, though they had finally stopped. She raised one corner of her mouth in an attempt to smile. It looked more like a twitch to Richard. He thought about smiling back, but it didn't come. Instead, he just stared at her eyes until she eventually lowered them.

Richard then looked at his best friend, Brent, who was sound asleep, curled up in the corner of the leather furniture. Richard couldn't help but wonder how he could sleep after what had happened. But then, his wife was okay. Richard's eyes drifted back to Wendy. If Stephanie was okay, he would probably be sleeping too.

He pulled himself to his feet and stretched. Wendy took his cue and did the same. When he turned to leave the room, she followed, almost like a puppy looking for attention. In the entryway, he stopped and rubbed his eyes. He, too, had shed some tears and his eyes ached.

"I need to get back to the house," he whispered, so as not to wake Brent.

"I understand." Wendy nodded. She tried again to give him a smile for support, but it came off more like a grimace. "I'm so sorry, Richard."

"Me too." He sucked in air and closed his eyes. "I still can't . . ."

He felt her arms wrap around his chest, and he opened his eyes and returned the hug. He hadn't realized how much he needed it.

"Tell him to call me when he wakes up." He looked over her to the sleeping form.

"I will."

She let him go and wiped her eyes as she stepped back. He gave her a reassuring nod before walking out the door.

Richard had taken a couple of steps away from his friends' house before turning back. Even though they were just inside, he had a sense of emptiness. He shook it off and continued to his truck.

The drive to his house was not long but seemed to last forever. Twice he was honked at when he failed to go after the light turned green. He was relieved when he finally turned onto his street, only to be deflated again when he saw a police car parked in front of his home. His mind flashed back to the conversation he had with Brent just hours earlier, about needing an alibi.

Pulling into his driveway, he parked in his usual space, so Stephanie could have access to the garage. It hit him that she would not be parking there ever again. And he suddenly wondered where her car might be.

Richard locked up his truck and started for the front door, glancing occasionally at the police car on the street. It occurred to him that the neighbors wouldn't know what had happened to Stephanie and would probably be wondering and speculating why the police were at his house. Since they weren't getting out of their vehicle, he was wondering as well.

Inside the house, the silence overwhelmed him. It wasn't that he had never walked into a quiet house before. It was just that sense of emptiness he felt at the Meadows' house tenfold when he walked in and realized he would never hear her voice again.

Richard stood, unmoving, for the longest time, unsure what to do next. Showering, changing clothes, fixing something to eat; it all seemed pointless. When he did move, he made his way to the kitchen. He couldn't do one more cup of coffee. And though it took convincing, he decided it was too early for alcohol. His head spun and Richard walked on through the kitchen, through the French doors, and onto the deck. He collapsed into his favorite seat and stared out at the trees in the wooded lot behind their house. Their house? His house? What was it now?

That is where he remained for the next half hour until he heard knocking coming from the front door. The events of the night before flooded his mind, and he couldn't bring himself to move. When he finally did open the door, a man stood on his porch, wearing a suit and tie and holding a badge out in front of him.

6

Detective Jack Mallory," Jack introduced. "Mind if we talk?"

Richard stared at the badge as if in a trance. He absently stepped aside to allow the detective in. They walked into the living room, but Richard would not sit. Confused, Jack followed him to the deck where they sat in matching patio chairs. Richard returned to the almost comatose state he had been in before the detective had arrived. Jack sat back and looked out into the trees, absorbing the sound of nature, allowing Richard a moment to get comfortable. It took a long time.

"Sorry about that," Richard finally said.

"How's that?" Jack turned to him.

"The living room," Richard explained. "I just can't . . . It was Stephanie's favorite room in the house. I just couldn't get myself to sit in there."

"I understand."

Richard nodded as if they had reached an agreement. "Do you have a family, detective?"

Jack wasn't sure why Richard had started asking questions. But if it would help get him talking, he would play along. "My job isn't really conducive to relationships."

Richard furrowed his brow. "How can you say you understand? If you don't have a wife, you couldn't possibly. There's this hole inside me that is suddenly empty and can never be filled."

"As much as I would like to debate the experience of loss with you." He really wouldn't. "I'm investigating your wife's murder. I need to ask you some questions."

"I know." Richard looked down at his feet. "What do you need to know?"

"Where were you when your wife was murdered?"

"I was here." He looked over his shoulder toward the house.

"She was out awfully late," Jack commented. "Weren't you worried?"

"Looking back, I suppose I should have been." Richard turned in his chair and watched a squirrel running along a tree limb. "Honestly. I didn't think anything of it. She had called to say she would be working late."

"Is that something she did often?" Jack asked. "Work late?"

"Sometimes." Richard seemed to drift into thought. His gaze continued to follow the squirrel. "I wouldn't say often."

"But she did last night?" Jack wrote in his notepad.

"She said there was a problem at work." Richard lost track of the squirrel and searched the limbs for it. "I assumed that was where she was."

"So, not often," Jack said. "But on those occasions that she worked late, did she usually work that late?"

"I don't think so."

"You don't think so?" Jack sat up. "You don't know? This woman's death has left a hole in you that can never be filled, but you don't know if she ever worked until midnight before?"

"No," Richard said. "She never worked that late before."

"Yet, you weren't worried?"

"I may have been." Richard closed his eyes and tried to will the detective away.

"You may have been?"

"I thought she was at work," Richard snapped.

"But she wasn't," Jack pointed out.

"Apparently not."

"She was at the park," Jack said.

"So it seems."

"Why?"

"Why what?" Richard made eye contact with Jack for the first time since opening the front door.

"Why would your wife be at Evergreen Park that late at night?" Jack asked the question slowly.

"I have no idea." He looked down at his feet again.

"Is it possible she was having an affair?" Jack asked.

"No." Richard was quick to answer.

"Are you sure?" Jack pressed. "She wasn't where she said she was. Could she have been meeting another man at that park?"

"No." He was adamant. "Stephanie loved me. She wouldn't have cheated on me."

"Maybe she wasn't cheating." Jack nodded. "Maybe she was angry. Were the two of you fighting? You know. Something that made her want her space?"

"No."

"Maybe it was something you considered inconsequential?" Jack asked. "Sometimes men have fights with their significant others without even knowing it. We men can be clueless. Maybe a disagreement that you didn't think much of. Something that infuriated her?"

"We weren't fighting, detective," Richard sighed.

"Okay." Jack looked out at the trees. "So, your wife, who you weren't fighting with, told you she would be at work, but was at Evergreen Park, while you were here alone, not wondering where she was."

"Not exactly." Richard squeezed his eyes shut. This was his moment of truth, or rather his moment of not truth. He was going to lie to the police to throw suspicion off of him, so they would look for the real killer. If he was found out, he realized, it would probably convince them of his guilt. But Brent was right. He needed to keep them from focusing on him.

"Not exactly?" Jack turned. "What does that mean?"

"I wasn't alone." There it was. The lie was out. There was no turning back.

"You weren't?" Jack was surprised. "Were you having an affair?"

"No." Richard shook his head. "What is it with you and infidelity? I wasn't having an affair. I was with my best friend. Or rather he was with me. He was here until about midnight."

"Doing what exactly?"

Richard froze. The lie had just rolled out like it was something he did every day. But he hadn't anticipated questions. If he said one thing and Brent said another, he would be found out. He would lose his alibi. He would become the main suspect and someone out there would get away with murder.

"Beer and sports," Richard said.

"Beer and sports?"

"Yes."

"Sports?" Jack repeated. "In the middle of the night?"

"We watched a game I had recorded," Richard said. "Surely you've watched a game that you've recorded."

He had. In Jack's line of work, he often had to record games if he wanted to watch them. "And this friend. He has a name?"

"He does," Richard said. "It's Brent Meadows."

Jack wrote the name and his contact information in his notepad.

"You said Stephanie was having a problem at work."

"She said there was a problem at work," Richard clarified. "Not that she was having a problem."

"What did she do?"

"She is an Accounting Manager for Havencroft Financial Group." Richard choked up. "Or was."

"You said she told you there was a problem at work," Jack corrected. "Could that problem be an individual? Someone she works with?"

"No," Richard said. "They are like a family down there. They treat each other so well. Oh, God. I have to tell them. Unless Brent already has."

"Your friend, Brent?" Jack asked. When Richard nodded, he continued. "Why would he tell them?"

"Brent works there too," Richard explained.

"And what does Brent do there?"

"He's an Account Manager."

"He has the same job Stephanie had?" Jack looked at his notes.

"No." Richard shook his head. "Stephanie was an Accounting Manager. She works with the company financials. Brent is an Account Manager. He works with the clients."

Jack wrote in his notepad, marking through a couple of lines and rewriting them to fit what Richard had said. "Which of her coworkers was she closest to?"

"Uh, that would have to be Lacey Novak," Richard answered. "She's an accountant, too."

"And outside of work?" Jack continued writing. "Who is she close to?"

"Wendy," Richard blurted.

"Wendy who?"

"Sorry." Richard's face flushed. "Wendy Meadows."

"Meadows?" Jack wrote it down. "Related to Brent?"

"They're married," Richard confirmed.

Jack tilted his head while he added that detail to his notes.

"Now comes the hard part," Jack warned. "Can you think of anyone who might have wanted to harm your wife? Or even wanted her dead?"

"You think this wasn't random?" Richard sat forward. "She was targeted?"

"Until I have something solid," Jack said. "All options are on the table. I am going to exhaust every possibility before I rule it out."

"Everyone loved Stephanie," Richard drifted. "I mean everyone. People I never met would stop to talk to her in the grocery store. There wasn't anyone who . . ."

"What?" Jack pushed him to continue. "You thought of someone."

"I mean, it couldn't be." Richard stood and then sat again. "It couldn't, could it?"

"Let me determine that." Jack put a hand on his shoulder. "Who came to mind?"

"Old man Johnson." Richard pointed to one side of the house. "Our neighbor. He wasn't fond of Stephanie."

"Why is that?" Jack prompted.

"Stephanie didn't like him," Richard said. "He can be grumpy. So, she bought some shrubs to plant along that edge of our yard so she wouldn't have to see him. Only Mr. Johnson decided they were partly on his side of the property line and hacked the hell out of them. They've been feuding ever since. But surely he didn't do this?"

"I'll talk to him," Jack informed him. "You never know what might trigger someone to do something they might not otherwise do."

"Okay." Richard nodded. "I guess."

"Anyone else come to mind?"

"Not that I can think of," Richard grimaced. "I'm sorry. I never dreamed I would have to scrutinize people to determine who might have killed her."

"No need to apologize," Jack assured him. "Mr. Ellison? Did your wife keep a diary or a journal?"

"Not that I know of." Richard looked around the room as if to look for a journal he had never noticed before.

"Mind if I take a look around?" Jack asked. "Maybe the master bedroom? Where did she spend her time?"

"She has the desk over in the corner." Richard twisted and pointed. "It's her space. I never messed with her space."

"Is that something you learned the hard way?" Jack grinned. "Or did she give you a warning?"

Richard chuckled. "She warned me. But I didn't truly learn until I crossed the line. She has a system. And you don't want to mess with the system." His face slid back to the sad expression he had before. "Guess it doesn't matter now."

"Can I take a look?"

"Be my guest." Richard waved his hand toward the corner of the room.

Jack walked over to the small desk and started looking through the small pile of papers neatly stacked on top. They were spreadsheets one might expect an accountant to have, nothing more.

He sat in the chair and opened the center drawer. It contained an array of well-organized office supplies. The drawers on the left were filled with documents and ledgers. Jack pulled the ledgers out one by one and looked inside hoping he might find a journal. All he found were columns of numbers, page after page. It gave him a headache.

The drawers on the right side were locked. Jack looked at Richard, who was sitting on the edge of a chair bent forward with his head in his hands. "Do you have the key for the drawers?"

"Key?" Richard raised his head and looked at Jack with a confused look. "It's locked?"

"Don't worry about it." Jack decided it would be best to open the drawer with a warrant in hand, just to be safe. "Where's the bedroom?"

"Upstairs." Richard pointed. "Straight back."

"Okay. You want to show me?" Jack started for the stairs. "In case I have questions?"

"Sure." Richard rose to his feet and followed the detective up.

The two men walked in silence down a hall dominated by photos of the happy couple. Jack studied the images as they passed. They showed a progression of their lives together and Jack saw no sign of discord. Of course, they were photos, and staged. They could have easily faked smiles that disappeared the moment the camera was lowered.

The bedroom featured a king-size bed in the center of the back wall. One side was made with crisp edges, the way Jack made his bunk in the military. The other was a chaotic mess of sheets, blankets, and pillows. Despair or a guilty conscience? The detective glanced at Richard before moving to the unused side of the room.

Jack pulled the drawer to the nightstand open and examined the contents. A romance novel, a pair of reading glasses, a small package of tissue, a bottle of prescription pills, a notepad, and a pen each in its place. It had to be the tidiest drawer Jack had ever seen.

He lifted the prescription and examined it. Take one pill before bedtime as needed to sleep. What kept Stephanie awake at night? He put the bottle back where it had been and removed the notepad. Flipping through the used pages, there were grocery lists, to-do lists, and notes to self. There was nothing suggesting troubles or other people in her life. He put the notepad back and opened the drawer below it.

Unlike the first, the second drawer was anything but organized. A number of romance novels with broken spines were thrown in among discarded cellphones, charging cables, watches, and used notepads. Jack pulled a couple of the pads out and thumbed through the pages. Each contained more of the same information as the current one had. Nothing useful.

"Closet?"

Richard pointed at the door on the left wall. "Through there. Closet's on the left as you enter."

Jack twisted the knob and pulled, revealing a short corridor leading to the master ensuite. As promised there was an opening immediately to the left that was a deep walk-in closet. Clothes hung on the right side while shoe cubbies and shelving filled the opposite wall. The first few feet of what hung were men's suits and shirts. The rest of the closet was dedicated to the wife's clothing.

Jack moved hangers to look behind. On the closet floor, leaning against the wall were various framed photos, prints, and paintings. Only one of the cubbies did not contain a pair of shoes. The shelves were piled with scarves, sweaters, and shoe boxes. Dozens of shoe boxes. Jack wondered if they all contained shoes.

He tested a couple by lifting the edges. They seemed to contain what they advertised. The third box however was much too heavy. With a little hope, Jack pulled the box down and lifted its top. Inside were months of receipts rubber-banded together. With disappointment, he returned the box to its place at the top of the stack. There were too many to search through, and he again had the feeling he should use a warrant to assure there would be no misunderstanding should something be found.

"I think I'm done for now," he announced.

Richard nodded and led the detective back through the house to the front door.

Jack stopped, pulled a card from his wallet, and handed it to Richard. "If anything comes to mind, don't hesitate to call."

Richard held the card with both hands "Find them, detective. Find the bastard responsible for killing Stephanie. Make them pay."

"I'll do my best, Mr. Ellison." Jack turned to leave, stopping on the front porch and turning back. "One more thing. Did Stephanie have an insurance policy?"

7

Richard stared at the card in his hands. Detective Jack Mallory was printed boldly across its center. The interview had gone as expected. All the right questions were asked, including the ones that needed to be asked if he was suspected of killing his wife. Richard couldn't help but wonder if that were the case and Brent had been right all along.

He pulled out his phone. He had to tell Brent what he had told the detective. It wouldn't help if Brent told him they were watching a movie. He stopped for a moment and took a deep breath to clear his head.

He couldn't believe he had lied to the police. And now he was coordinating his story. It made him feel guilty. He would never have hurt Stephanie, but he now had something to hide. And people who had things to hide usually had a reason. Sure, his was to convince the police to look for her killer elsewhere and not waste time looking into him. But if he or Brent slipped up, they would make him their number one suspect.

"How are you doing, Bud?" Brent answered.

"A detective was here." Richard ignored the question.

"You knew there would be," Brent said. "No matter who they think did it, they're going to talk to the spouse."

"I know," Richard acknowledged. "I was just caught off guard."

Brent didn't respond for a minute. "Did you tell them what we talked about?"

"Yeah," Richard said. "That's why I'm calling. He asked what we were doing."

"What did you say?"

"I told him we were drinking beer and watching a game I had recorded."

"That's good," Brent said. "What game?"

"What game?" Richard asked. "I don't know. Why does it matter?"

"It matters because he might ask me what game," Brent explained. "What's a game still on your DVR?"

"Can't I just tell him I deleted it?" Richard ground his teeth together. Lying was so stressful.

"Do you have old games that you've watched and haven't deleted?"

"You know I do," Richard growled.

"Then why did you delete the one we watched the night your wife was killed?" Brent demanded.

"Fine." Richard took a deep breath. "I'll look at the DVR and pick one. I'll text you later."

"Call," Brent corrected. "They can subpoena texts."

"It's kind of scary how much you know about this stuff." Richard kind of laughed but not quite.

"I know." Brent laughed as well. "Watching all those true crime shows over the years is really paying off."

They were silent for a moment.

"And you told him I left around one?" Brent asked.

"Oh," Richard sighed. "I told him midnight."

"Midnight?" Brent questioned. "Okay. That'll work. Listen, Richard. You stick to this story and they'll think you're innocent."

"I am innocent," Richard insisted.

"I know." Brent lowered his voice to a calming level. "Now they will think so too. And they can focus on finding her killer."

"It just seems wrong," Richard said. "Lying to the police."

"It is wrong," Brent said. "But not as wrong as the killer getting away with what he did while you spend the rest of your life in prison."

"I know you're right." Richard ran his hand over his face. "Hey. I think I'm going to take a shower. I'll talk to you later."

"Sure thing," Brent said.

Richard disconnected the call, sat back, and stared at the trees.

8

After Richard shut his front door, Jack strolled down the steps to the sidewalk where he had parked. As he went, he read through the notes he had just taken to be sure he had the facts straight in his mind.

The spouse of the victim was always scrutinized in cases like these. It was always a good sign when they cooperated as Richard had. That, paired with the alibi he supplied, would suggest he was not involved. Jack would have to verify the alibi, but it seemed straightforward enough. So that left Jack to track down and interview possible witnesses and suspects, including the ones Richard had just named.

As good a place as any to start would be the neighbor with whom Richard said Stephanie had been feuding. He turned away from his car and followed the sidewalk to the next driveway. As he passed the property line he looked at the butchered shrubs that were the source of their disagreement. He had to hand it to Mr. Johnson, his side of the bushes was cut almost perfectly vertical.

Jack followed the driveway to the walkway that took him to the front door of the brick ranch with its perfectly manicured lawn. The detective pressed the doorbell and listened to it chime inside the house. He stood in front of the door with his hands clasped together before him. After what seemed to be an excessive amount of time, he reached up and knocked loudly, resuming the position.

Time passed and no one came to the door. Jack was concluding no one was home, pushing the doorbell one more time before retreating to his car. Almost immediately the door opened in a rush and a short man in his eighties sporting a receding hairline and what appeared to be a permanent scowl stepped into the opening.

"Can't you read?" The man growled. He pointed to a small plaque mounted above the doorbell that Jack had not even given a thought to. The no soliciting sign was black with white lettering.

"I can." Jack did not waver.

"Then why are you ringing my bell?"

"I'm not soliciting." Jack pulled out his badge and showed it to the man. "Are you Benjamin Johnson?"

"What's this about?" He squinted at the object in Jack's hand. "Did that woman call again?"

"What woman would that be?" Jack played dumb.

"That next door lady." Benjamin pointed past the no soliciting sign toward the Ellison's house. "I told her to keep 'em off my property."

"By them, I assume you mean the shrubs," Jack said.

"So it was her." Benjamin's face scrunched up into a wrinkled mess of anger and hate. "Why can't she just let it go?"

"Did you?"

"Did I what?"

"Did you let it go?" Jack asked.

"What does that mean?" Benjamin put his hands on his hips. "I don't have anything to let go. Her bushes were over my property, so I cut them back. End of story. Until she started calling you guys."

"So when she called us, it wasn't the end of story anymore?" Jack looked the man up and down wondering if he was strong enough to beat the woman to death.

"That's what I said."

"So what's the new end of story?" Jack asked.

"What?"

"The end of story," Jack repeated. "What is the new end of story?"

"I don't know," Benjamin sneered. "It's a figure of speech. It is whatever it is."

"Was it when you smashed in her skull in Evergreen Park?"

"I what?" The man's face softened, his eyes widened. "Did you say smashed her skull?"

"Where were you last night, Mr. Johnson?"

"She's dead?"

"She is," Jack confirmed.

"So you're not here about the bushes?"

"I'm not," Jack nodded. "Now, where were you last night?"

"Had I known, I would have been out celebrating," the man said. "But I was just here watching the TV with Lucy."

"Celebrating?" Jack frowned. "A woman died."

"Don't get me wrong," the man held up a hand. "That's awful business. Wouldn't wish it on anyone. But I can't say I'm going to miss her."

"Can I speak with this Lucy, to confirm your alibi?"

"If you want." The man turned to face into the house. "Lucy, come here."

Jack waited. A moment later a graying Black Lab lumbered into view. The dog strolled up to Benjamin and sat heavily on the floor at his feet.

"This is Lucy." Benjamin reached down and rubbed the dog's head.

Jack looked the man in the eyes. "So, no alibi?"

"You callin' Lucy a liar?" Benjamin met Jack's gaze.

"She's a dog. I'm not calling her anything," Jack said. "Do you still drive, Mr. Johnson?"

"Of course I still drive," Benjamin scoffed. "I'm old, not dead."

"If I search for video, am I going to see you driving to the park last night?"

"No." Benjamin shook his head. "I wasn't there."

"I'm going to have to advise you not to leave town in the next few days," Jack said. "We may need to talk to you some more."

"Unlike me," Benjamin pursed his lips. "Anyone I would want to visit is dead. I'm not goin' anywhere."

"Okay." Jack stood on the porch and looked over the butchered shrubs. "You didn't happen to see anything last night?"

"Anything is a lot of things," Benjamin looked up at the detective.

"Mrs. Ellison coming home? Mr. Ellison leaving?" Jack suggested. "Something along that line."

"I don't make a habit of watching the neighbors," Benjamin informed the detective. "So, no."

"Here's my card." Jack handed one to the man. "If you remember anything, give me a call."

Benjamin hesitated before taking the offer from the detective. He held the card tentatively by one corner. "We done?"

"For now," Jack nodded.

Benjamin took a half step back and the door swung shut almost as fast as it had opened, leaving Jack to wonder if all of the man's visitors received the same treatment.

Walking back to his car, Jack took another look at the property line, and the row of shrubs cut perfectly in half from the ground up. Under different circumstances, it would be amusing.

9

"Thanks for having me." Richard sat in the living room of Brent and Wendy Meadows. "I just couldn't be there any longer."

"Of course." Wendy gave him a sad smile. "You know our home is always open to you."

"I just can't believe she's gone." He buried his face in his hands. "You know?"

"I know." Wendy's blonde bangs fell into her eyes and she shook her head. "None of us can believe it."

"I don't understand why." Richard looked at her. "Why was she there? Why would anyone harm her? It makes no sense."

"Everyone loved Stephanie," Wendy said. "No one who knew her could have hurt her."

"That's just it," Richard lowered his eyes again. "If this was random, some senseless attack, they may never catch who did it."

"You don't know that," Wendy comforted him. "Bad people, people who do things like this, they get caught eventually. Their DNA will show up and they'll be caught. We will get justice for her."

"I hope you're right." Richard sighed.

The door from the kitchen to the garage opened and Brent walked in carrying a bag that he set on the counter. "I thought that was your car."

"Hey, Brent," Richard said. "I hope you don't mind. I needed someone to talk to and your wife was gracious enough to listen."

"No problem, bud." Brent rounded the island and walked over to where his friend sat and took the seat next to him. "How are you holding up?"

"I'm not." Richard took a deep breath to fight back his emotions.

"I guess not." Brent put a hand on Richard's shoulder and squeezed. "You know, if you need anything, we're here for you."

"I appreciate that," Richard nodded. "I really do."

"Where were you, babe?" Wendy asked.

"Needed to clear my head, you know." Brent tapped his forehead with his finger. "So I ran to the store to pick up a few more things."

"You were gone a while," Wendy said.

"Clearing my head, like I said," Brent said. "Drove a bit."

"It's just, Stephanie was Richard's wife and my best friend," Wendy pressed. "We could both use you right now."

"You think her death doesn't affect me?" Brent frowned. "She was my friend, too. I'm hurting just like you are."

"I know," Wendy said. "I just thought . . ."

"You thought I didn't care?" Brent cut her off.

"I wasn't going to say that." Wendy crossed her arms and fell back in her chair.

"Guys?" Richard spoke calmly. "Could you not do that?"

"Do what, bud?" Brent turned to him, his expression softening.

"Argue about who hurts the most, who cares the most." Richard turned to Brent. "It's not what Stephanie would want. It's not what I want."

"You're right," Brent said. "I'm sorry. My emotions are just all over the place right now. Don't really know how to react to anything."

"I get it." Richard gave a weak grin. "I don't think I'll ever know how to react again. Stephanie always told me what to do."

"Classic Stephanie," Wendy smiled. "You ever notice she gave advice better than she took it?"

Richard smiled. "I did. Tried to advise her on something once, what was that? Anyway, it didn't go well. Gave me a twenty-minute lecture on why her method was better."

The three of them laughed briefly and fell silent. Brent's phone buzzed. He pulled it out of his pocket and looked at the screen.

"This is work," he stood. "I have to take it. I'll be right back."

He walked toward the room that served as his office at home, answering the call as he went. When he shut the door, Richard and Wendy looked at one another.

"I can't believe they're bothering him today," Wendy grumbled.

"The rest of the world keeps going," Richard sighed. "Even if it feels like they shouldn't."

The office door opened. "Sorry about that. Clients don't know what's going on."

"I understand," Richard said.

Brent sat next to his wife again. The three sat silently. Wendy was fighting back tears that she thought she was done with. Richard was sullen and couldn't bring himself to take his eyes off the floor. Brent leaned forward.

"I remember, shortly after you two started dating, you went to the restroom, and these two," Brent pointed at his wife. "She and Stephanie lean together and start whispering. Didn't stop until you got back."

"Of course we didn't," Wendy defended. "She thought he was cute as hell. I told her everything you had ever told me about him so she could get his attention."

"She had my attention already." Richard thought back. "I had to go splash my face with water to be sure I wasn't dreaming. I knew that night that I was going to marry her. I just had to figure out how to convince her of it."

"And you did." Brent patted Richard on the back.

"I did, didn't I?" Richard sighed.

"You did," Wendy said. "Stephanie loved you very much, Richard. She was always telling me how lucky she was to have you in her life."

"I'm the lucky one," Richard choked up. "I was, anyway."

"You were both lucky." Brent slid to the front of his chair. "And it would be tragic if you were to go down for this."

"Brent!" Wendy scolded him.

"I'm serious." Brent put a hand to his chest. "They always look at the husband. They don't know him like we do. I'm just saying you need to be ready for when the police question you."

"They already questioned me," Richard reminded him.

"That was an initial questioning." Brent brushed him off. "Unless they find the real killer, and soon, they will question you again. And when they do, it won't be as the grieving husband. It will be as their number one suspect."

"Brent, are you trying to scare him?" Wendy put a hand on her husband's arm.

"Not scare him," Brent denied. "Prepare him."

"Prepare me?" Richard turned to face him. "Prepare me for what?"

"You need to be ready for when they come at you." Brent clenched a fist. "You have to be strong because they will try to break you."

"But I'm innocent."

"I know that and you know that," Brent said. "But they don't. And without another answer, they will be convinced you had a hand in it."

"They can't prove something I didn't do," Richard argued.

"Like nobody innocent ever went to prison," Brent scoffed. "You have to be realistic."

"What do you propose?"

"Stick to your story," Brent said.

"So, the truth?" Wendy asked.

"That's what I said," Brent shrugged.

"Your advice for him is to say what he would have said anyway?" Wendy shook her head. "No wonder he went to Stephanie for advice."

"What I mean is," Brent said. "They will try to get you to say things that fit their narrative, to admit things that didn't happen. You have to stay strong. You have to stick to your truth."

"The truth," Richard said.

"The truth. Your truth. What's the difference?" Brent held his hands up.

"Well, one sounds like the truth," Richard explained. "The other sounds like my version of the truth."

"Just don't change anything you've said up to this point." Brent put his hand on his friend's shoulder and squeezed. "No matter how hard they push you, don't let them break you."

"I won't." Richard brushed Brent's hand off. "I think I should go. I wanted to get my mind off of what's going on, and this isn't doing it."

10

Havencroft Financial Group was located on the third floor of a twelve-story building, sandwiched between a law office above and a software startup below. For more than two decades they had invested millions and millions of dollars in various business ventures, the stock market, and real estate. They had made small fortunes for most of their clients and large fortunes for a few. For five of those years, Stephanie Ellison had been their Accounting Manager.

Jack sat in an expensively decorated, although surprisingly bland lobby waiting to see the Chief Financial Officer. A receptionist sat behind a very modern desk answering and transferring phone calls. The detective checked his watch. He had been waiting for more than fifteen minutes.

A tall brunette in a navy blue pinstriped pantsuit walked in, an aura of strength and power about her. She quickly focused on Jack, approaching him in two long strides with her hand extended.

"Detective Mallory, is it?" She shook his hand with a firm grip. "So sorry to keep you waiting. It's just . . . it's awful. We just can't wrap our heads around it. I'm Beverly Wallis, Stephanie's boss. I understand you have questions. If you'll follow me."

Jack nodded and fell into step behind the woman as she led the way through their halls to her office. They passed dozens of people, each far more sharply dressed than the detective, each staring at the man who had come to disrupt their day to investigate the murder of their friend and colleague. Jack made eye contact with every one of them, trying to read whether they felt sadness for their loss or fear of being discovered. None presented themselves as an obvious suspect.

Beverly's office was one of the coveted corner spaces, larger than Jack's living room and better furnished. Windows lined the two exterior walls providing a more than sufficient amount of natural light. The shelves were covered with decorative pieces and framed photographs. There was a picture of her with what Jack assumed was her family. Another showed her receiving a first-place ribbon. Another still showed her accepting her black belt. She was an achiever. She set goals and made them happen through work and dedication.

The CFO circled her large desk and sat in her executive chair while gesturing for Jack to take one of the two chairs facing her. He chose to stand.

"How long have you known Stephanie?" Jack asked.

"Oh." Beverly seemed caught off guard by the question. "It must be seven or eight years now. I had her job when I hired her as an accountant. Promoted her when I was promoted five years ago."

"She was good at her job?"

"The best." Beverly smiled for the first time. "She had a mind for numbers. We're going to miss her."

"Were you close?" Jack found himself staring at an out-of-place strand on her otherwise perfectly kept hair. "Were you friends?"

"We were friendly," Beverly said. "I wouldn't say friends. We never went to dinner or out for drinks except for business functions."

"Were there many of those?" Jack asked. "Business functions outside of work?"

"Occasionally," Beverly straightened herself in her seat. The wild strand of hair fell into her eye and she used her hand to sweep it back to where it belonged. "For celebrations or to schmooze with clients."

"Did she ever get close to clients?" Jack wrote in his pad.

"Oh, no," Beverly quickly shot down the idea. "She was far too professional for that. Besides, even if she wasn't she wouldn't do anything with Brent here."

Jack's eyebrow rose. "Brent?"

"Brent Meadows." Beverly seemed surprised the detective didn't know the name. "He's one of our Account Managers."

"Another accounting manager?"

"No," Beverly corrected. "Account Manager. He manages client accounts, just like the name implies."

"And he would stop her from getting close to his clients?" Jack asked.

"No. I mean yes." Beverly shook her head. "But not because they were clients. Because he was friends with her husband."

"Ah." Jack flipped through his notes. "That's right. Mr. Ellison's alibi."

"That sounds about right." Beverly grimaced. "From my understanding those two are inseparable."

"And that bothered you?"

"You know," Beverly spoke softer. "Grown men behaving like boys. Not my thing."

"I see," Jack nodded in understanding. "What about friends at work? Did Stephanie have anyone she confided in? Spent time with?"

"Most everyone liked Stephanie." Beverly seemed lost in thought for a moment. "As far as friends go, I would say Lacey Novak. She's one of our accountants. I think they were friends."

"Mr. Ellison gave me her name as well," Jack said. "I'll need to speak with her. Along with some of her other colleagues."

"Of course."

"You said that most everyone liked Stephanie," Jack walked up to one of the windows and looked out. "What about the others?"

"I just meant that some people aren't as friendly as others, detective," Beverly said. "No one disliked her."

"She wasn't having any problems with anyone?"

"Not that I'm aware of."

Jack turned back to the CFO. "I understand she stayed late yesterday. Do you know what she was working on? Or perhaps what time she left?"

Beverly's expression shifted to confusion. "Stephanie didn't stay late yesterday. She asked to leave early. She left for lunch at noon and took the rest of the day."

"Are you sure?" Jack stared at the woman.

"Positive," Beverly said. "I approved the time myself."

11

Richard sat in his car staring at the red light. His mind drifted to the last conversation he had with Stephanie. Just a day ago. It seemed so much longer.

She had called him from work. At least he thought she was at work. She had told him she was going to have to stay late, but she hadn't. Was she even at Havencroft? Is it possible she never went in? Could she have lied about everything? Was she having an affair? Could her lover be her killer?

A car horn jerked him into the present. He blinked and saw the light had turned green. He accelerated through the intersection wondering what he would do if he learned she had not been faithful. Did it even matter anymore?

He turned right at the next cross street. Three blocks later he pulled into the parking lot of The Law Offices of Carter, Burns, and Wellington. It was the law firm that had drawn up all their legal documents over the years, including their wills. That wasn't why he was there. He knew their contents in and out.

He entered the front doors and looked grimly at the receptionist.

"Mr. Ellison," the receptionist smiled. "I haven't seen you here for some time. How is Mrs. Ellison?"

Richard looked at her like he hadn't expected her to be there. "Is John in?"

"He's with a client," she said. "Could Mr. Burns help you?"

Richard inhaled deeply and let the air out slowly, closing his eyes. When he opened them, the receptionist was looking at him with a mixture of concern and confusion. "I'll wait for John."

He sat in one of the chairs in the lobby. He had known John Carter since they were young. The two of them and Brent Meadows had all been on the high school basketball team. John had been a year older and went to college on a basketball scholarship, ultimately getting his law degree before returning home. Brent had also received a scholarship for the sport, although to a local college. Richard had received multiple academic scholarships and had gone to the same university as John.

Richard and the future attorney had not been close while in high school but ran into each other at the university gym where they both played ball for fun and exercise. After that, it became a weekly event.

Richard's phone rang, and he took it out to check the screen. The number was unknown to him, so he rejected the call and dropped the phone back into his pocket. Leaning forward, he rested his arms on his legs, clasped his fingers together, and stared at the floor.

He sat motionless for a quarter-hour until he heard a door open and voices in the hallway. A tall lean man in a suit was escorting an elderly woman with a walker as she made her way to the lobby. He nodded to Richard as he passed and held the door open for the woman as she left. All the while he made pleasant conversation with her. With one last wave, he closed the door and turned back.

"Richard?" John smiled genuinely at his old friend. "What a surprise. I wasn't expecting you today. How's Stephanie?"

It was the kind of small talk everyone participated in nearly every day of their lives. Richard's dull eyes focused on the man. "She's dead, John. Stephanie was murdered last night."

"Oh my God." John put a hand on the other's shoulder and steered him toward his office. "Janet, hold all my calls."

The receptionist's mouth hung open, her eyes wide. "Of course, Mr. Carter."

Richard followed the attorney to his office where they sat across from one another behind closed doors. He sat in the comfortable client's chair and stared at his hands as they shook.

"What happened, Richard?" John prompted.

"The police don't know." Richard dropped his hands to his knees and looked up at John. "She was in the park at night. No one knows why she was there. And someone just killed her. Don't know who. Don't know why. I just know that she's dead."

"No witnesses?"

"None that I know of." Richard cocked his head to one side. "Would the police tell me if they had a witness?"

"Depends," John gestured with his hands. "If the witness says they saw you kill her, they probably wouldn't. If they say they saw someone else do it, then maybe. But they aren't usually going to share too much with anyone."

"Do you think I should have a lawyer?" Richard asked. "Brent says they're going to consider me a suspect."

"Brent is probably right," John grimaced. "As for getting a lawyer. You might want to talk to someone and have them ready, just in case."

"What about you?"

"I've done criminal law," John sighed. "Years ago. But I'm a corporate lawyer, specializing in contracts. I did your wills because we're friends. You need a criminal lawyer. I can get you some names if you want."

"That would be helpful." Richard nodded. "Of course, the reason I'm here may not be your area either."

"If not, I'll know someone." John smiled. "What do you need?"

"I've never had to make arrangements before."

"Funeral arrangements?"

"That and whatever else needs to be done at this point." Richard let his head fall back onto the chair and stared up at the ceiling. "I don't even know how to get her to a funeral home."

"Don't be in a hurry," John pulled a large yellow notepad to him and took a very expensive-looking pen from inside his jacket, and began writing. "In murder cases, it would be unusual to have the body released before the investigation ends."

"You're telling me I may not be able to bury her?" Richard looked appalled.

"Not for some time," John said. "But you can make the arrangements so things are ready."

"Which brings me back to not knowing what to do." Richard sighed.

"What about your grandparents?"

"My parents took care of things."

"And your parents?"

"Still alive," Richard said. "At least I assume my dad's alive. Don't know for sure."

"And your mother didn't offer to help you with things?" John asked.

"Oh, crap." Richard sat up straight. "I haven't called her. I haven't called Stephanie's mother. Her sister. I . . . oh, my God."

"Richard," John said his name sternly. Richard focused on the attorney. "You're in shock. Catch your breath. When we're done, call her parents first, or they won't forgive you. Then her sister, unless her parents offer to do it. Your parents are last. They'll understand. And ask them to help you."

Richard nodded. John tore off the paper he had written on and handed it to him.

"This is a criminal lawyer I've recommended to some other clients." He sat back. "You wouldn't believe how often businessmen need the services of criminal lawyers."

Richard stared at the name on the paper without seeing it. "Thanks."

"Listen," John said. "I'll make some calls. See if I can find out about getting her to a funeral home for you. If nothing else, they might give me an idea of how long you'll have to wait. Meanwhile, make your calls. Make your arrangements."

"How much do you think it'll cost?" Richard hated himself a little for letting his mind go there.

"Don't worry about that." John shook his head. "If you need, I can loan you some money until the insurance pays out."

"Insurance?" He looked at the lawyer. "I completely forgot about those policies. They were supposed to pay off our mortgage and go toward our kid's college fund in case something happened to one of us. When we decided to wait to have kids, I completely put them out of my mind."

"Richard," John lowered his voice. "When the police find out about the policy, and they will, it's going to look like a motive."

"A motive?"

"Money is always a motive," John explained.

"What do I do?"

"Make sure you tell them about the policy," the lawyer advised. "You don't want to look like you're hiding it from them."

"What?" Richard furrowed his brow. "I should call the detective?"

"No." John shook his head. "But the next time he talks to you, tell him about it."

"I don't even remember how much we made them for." Richard looked even more lost than he had before.

John typed into his computer and scrolled through files, clicking repeatedly. "Here they are. Two identical policies for. . . one million each."

12

At Jack's request, Beverly showed him to Stephanie's office. Just a couple of doors down, it was less than half the size of the CFO's spacious corner office. Several book shelving units contained binders dating back to the beginning of the business's incarnation. One shelf was dedicated to binders on the current tax laws and regulations.

Inspirational posters decorating the walls seemed out of place. He wondered if they were there for Stephanie or for her employees. Her desk was an organized mess of papers. Most were financial documents that left a bad taste in Jack's mouth. In school he had hated math, accounting in particular. Maturity had not softened his feeling about the subject. If it came down to it, he would have a forensic accountant wade through the documents to see if there was anything that would explain the "problem at work" that Stephanie had mentioned to her husband.

With gloved hands, he set the financial documents aside and started sifting through the notes on her desk, looking for an appointment notation for the time she was at the park. He found nothing. Dozens of phone messages requesting calls back were stacked next to the phone with no indication whether she did or did not respond. There were numerous callers, but the name appearing on more of the messages than any other was "Andy G.". It could easily be a work colleague with whom she exchanged several calls throughout any given day. Just as easily, it could have nothing to do with work at all. Jack used his phone and snapped photos of all the messages.

In the center of the desk and the bottom of the piles was a desk blotter calendar that was from three months ago. He checked it out anyway, searching for repeated names, and possibly Andy G. The name did not present itself, however, three names repeated at least twice in the month.

To the side was an appointment book that lay closed, but was tabbed to the current month. Jack opened it and checked the day before. There were two morning meetings written in. For the afternoon there was only one entry, at three o'clock. A single "B" was penned in red ink where everything else was black. An omen perhaps. Or was this Stephanie's way of telling herself there was danger.

Jack stared at the red letter then looked at the pencil holder on the desk. He opened every drawer and quickly searched through the contents. When he was finished, his eyes were drawn back to the appointment book. Where was the pen?

There was a soft knock on the door and Jack looked up. A man in his early thirties stood there in khaki pants and a polo. To the detective, he looked more like a man ready for a game of golf than one ready to work.

"They said you wanted to see me?" It was a statement the man turned into a question.

"Have a seat." Jack directed the man to one of the chairs opposite him. "And your name?"

"Paul." The man entered the office and sat. "Paul McIntosh."

"Like the computer?"

"Spelled differently." The man pulled up his name badge for Jack to see before letting it drop back to his chest.

The detective wrote down the name in his notepad. "And what do you do here?"

"I'm an accountant?" He sounded unsure. "Didn't they say you wanted to speak with the accountants?"

"I did." Jack nodded. "And who do you answer to?"

"Stephanie Elli . . ." Paul trailed off. "It was Stephanie. I don't really know, now."

"How many of you reported to Mrs. Ellison?" Jack focused on Paul's face. The man seemed confused by every question but the one about his name.

"Three." Paul glanced out the door as if to count his coworkers.

"Three?"

"Yes."

"Yourself and two others?"

"No." Paul's brow furrowed. "Me and three others. So I guess that makes four."

"Yourself and three others?" Jack wondered how this man could possibly work with numbers.

"Four," Paul declared. "I'm sorry. I'm still in shock by what happened."

"Understandable," Jack sympathized. "So, who is next in line for her job?"

"Next in line?" Paul tilted his head.

"Yes," Jack said. "Who will take her place? Who benefits most by her death?"

Paul's eyes went wide. "You think one of us did this?"

"Mr. McIntosh." Jack lowered his voice to a gentle tone. "I'm investigating a murder. I have to look at all options, all possibilities. I'm not accusing anyone of doing anything at the moment. So, tell me who is in line to take her job."

Paul nodded his head. "Assuming they promote from within, I guess it would be Lacey."

"Lacey?"

"Lacey Novak."

"Stephanie's friend, isn't she?" Jack checked his notes.

"I suppose," Paul said. "They do spend a lot of time together."

"Outside work?"

"I don't know." Paul shrugged. "They're together a lot here."

"Where they work together?" Jack asked. "Wouldn't they have to be together?"

"Some," Paul confirmed. "They were just always together."

"Am I sensing a little jealousy?"

"Jealous?" Paul sat up straight. "Of what?"

"Of the attention Stephanie gave Lacey," Jack said. "That you didn't get."

"That's not the case at all," Paul defended. "I have no reason to be jealous."

"You never wondered if Stephanie was showing Lacey favoritism?" Jack asked.

"No," Paul said. "I mean, I wasn't. I am now."

Jack sat silent for a moment staring at the man in front of him. "I have to ask you, Paul. Where were you last night?"

"Last night?" Paul shifted uncomfortably. "Home."

"Can anyone confirm that?"

"What?" Paul asked. "I mean no. Am I a suspect?"

"Until I have more information," Jack said. "Everyone is a suspect."

13

Richard sat in his driveway staring at the house where he and Stephanie had lived for nearly a decade. They found the place just before they married, despite not being able to afford it at the time. But Stephanie fell in love with the house and Richard could not say no. He worked a second, part-time job for a year until they both received raises that made their expenses doable.

For the next decade, they put aside a little money each year to make changes that put their personal touches on each room. From that point forward it was upkeep and update. But it was the decorating that Stephanie had done over the years that turned the house into a home.

As he sat looking at the house, he wondered if he would be able to stay there. On the one hand, there were reminders of the love of his life in every room, and leaving would feel like a betrayal. On the other, for the same reason, he wasn't sure he could get past the pain if he stayed.

He suddenly smiled, remembering their first argument which took place on the front porch shortly after moving in. He had just gotten home from his second job to find her cutting down a shrub that was impeding access to the front door. She was trimming one limb at a time. He was furious. It was one of his favorite elements of the landscaping and insisted it could have simply been sculpted. She made the valid point that she had asked him to do something about it weeks before and couldn't wait another day. He was exhausted from working both jobs that day but realized she was right and said he would finish what she had started.

Her response was to say, "Fine," while pushing the clippers into his hands. The combination of being exhausted, unprepared, and standing on the very edge of the top step sent him off the porch and into the shrub she had been butchering, with its jagged branches. Richard suffered multiple cuts and abrasions including one twig that pierced his forearm and caused them to spend the rest of the day in the ER. While the doctor worked on his arm, they promised one another they would never argue again. It was a declaration that the nurse found sweet and the doctor wished them 'good luck with that one'. In the end, arguments came, but they were always mindful of just how far they went.

Richard could not bring himself to go inside, knowing she would not be there. He backed out of the driveway and drove away. He was dreading what was to come, but it was past time to talk to Stephanie's mother.

His mother-in-law was a kind, thoughtful woman who had been very supportive throughout his marriage to her daughter. Although about three years ago when she lost her husband, Stephanie's father, things changed. He had been diagnosed with cancer, and it had been a very rough regression and her ever-pleasant personality all but vanished. It was only recently that they had begun to see signs of her return to normal. The news Richard was about to share with her would undoubtedly set her back. He would give almost anything not to have to give it.

It was only about a ten-minute drive from Richard's house, but he found it difficult to make the turns he needed to take. It was nearly an hour before he pulled up in front of her home and Richard found himself wishing it was further still. He parked his truck on the street and sat for the longest time trying to get up the nerve to get out. Somehow, he knew that once he talked to Stephanie's mother, there would be no going back. Stephanie would be gone forever. It was irrational, he knew. She was already gone. He just wasn't ready to face that fact head-on. But he knew he had to deliver the news, to allow her family to start their grieving process.

The walk to her front door was one of the longest he had taken in his life. He reached his destination and stood staring at the door. It was solid oak, with inlaid glass that his father-in-law built in his workshop out back. Richard had helped him hang it, which took everything he had. It was so heavy and awkward to get into position. But it looked remarkable.

He made a fist and knocked loudly on the wood. Hearing the rapping sound made him anxious. He wanted to turn and run, though he knew he couldn't. He shifted his weight from leg to leg and perspiration dripped down his forehead. He wiped at it, amazed that he could be perspiring on such a cool day with a slight breeze. He closed his eyes and took a deep breath. Opening them again, he saw movement through the glass. Stephanie's mother pulled the door open.

"Richard?" she said. She leaned to one side to look behind him. He knew she was looking for her daughter.

"Faith," he replied.

Her gaze came back to him, and she looked him over. "Is everything okay? You look awful. Where is Stephanie?"

He remained silent, unable to say anything. Unable to acknowledge what needed to be said. Unwilling to break the woman's heart.

"Richard?" She prompted him. "You're scaring me."

"It's not okay." He began to sob, his body shaking violently. He had talked to Brent and Wendy, to the doctor, the detective, their attorney. But until he heard Faith's voice, so similar in many ways to Stephanie's, he had not allowed himself to break.

"Richard?" The panic in Faith's voice was evident. She reached out and put a hand on his arm. "What is it, Richard? Is Stephanie okay?"

"No." He forced the word through his tears. "She's gone, Faith. She's gone."

"Gone?" Her voice cracked. "Gone where?"

"She's dead, Faith," Richard said, barely above a whisper. He forced himself to lock eyes with hers. "I'm so sorry."

"What?" Faith exclaimed, her hand clasping over her mouth. "When? How?"

"This morning." He inhaled deeply. "Or last night. She was murdered, Faith. Someone took her from us."

"What?" She wailed and doubled over. Richard stepped into her space and wrapped an arm around her shoulder, guiding her into the house. "How could that be? Who would do such a thing? My poor baby?"

He sat her in the first seat they came to, a decorative armchair in the front hall that she used when changing or tying her shoes. Richard knelt next to her, a hand on her shoulder. With his other hand, he wiped at the tears that were streaking his face. "The police don't have a suspect yet. Or at least not that they've told me about."

His mother-in-law sobbed without speaking. He wasn't sure she had heard what he said but decided not to repeat it. He simply propped himself on one knee and patted her back while they cried together.

After a time, he left her as he went in search of tissues. He found them next to her favorite recliner and handed her the whole box on his return. The tears had stopped flowing, but she pulled out several tissues and wiped at her face. Then she sat staring at the wall opposite her, looking like a lost soul. He excused himself and slipped out of the house.

14

Nettie Huber was a plump woman in her early fifties, wearing a checkered print dress that did not compliment her shape. She sat heavily into the chair across from Jack and wiped sweat from her brow with a small cloth she carried loosely in her hand.

"You a detective or something?" she asked.

"I am," Jack answered. "May I call you Nettie?"

"Everybody does."

"Okay, Nettie," Jack held his hands apart, palms up, non-threatening. "Can you tell me your role here?"

"I'm an accountant," Nettie ran the cloth over her face.

"Can you tell me about your relationship to Stephanie Ellison?"

Nettie got a disgusted look on her face and wagged a finger in his face. "I ain't no lesbo."

"No." Jack turned his hands, so the palms were toward her. "You misunderstand. Not that kind of relationship. Just how well did you know her? How closely did you work together?"

"I didn't really know her." The woman moved the cloth to the back of her neck.

"I thought she was the head of your department?" Jack was confused.

"Oh, yeah. She was," Nettie sighed loudly. "She was the boss, such as she was. She gave me assignments. I completed them and gave them back."

"Not a fan?"

"Look." She waved her cloth toward Jack who instinctively leaned away. "I've been in this business for almost thirty years. I know a thing or two. And they bring in these young go-getter types who don't know much of anything, and then they wonder why things aren't going right. I could tell them why they aren't going right."

"Then why don't you?"

"What?"

"Why don't you tell them?" Jack locked eyes with hers.

"Well, I . . .," Nettie stammered. "I can't just tell them."

"Why not?"

"It's not how things are done," the woman said.

"Then tell me," Jack suggested.

"Well, I can't do that," she was adamant.

"Why not?"

"Because you don't work here," she said. "And frankly, I am uncomfortable with you even asking."

"Fair enough." Jack nodded and wrote in his pad.

"What are you writing?" Nettie sat forward and stretched her thick neck in an attempt to see the paper.

"I take notes." Jack strategically lowered his hand to block her view. "Did Stephanie have problems with any of the other accountants?"

"What kind of problems?" Nettie pushed her face forward. Sweat was running down her forehead, but this time she did not wipe it away.

"You would have to tell me." Jack looked from her forehead to the cloth in her hand. "Even the smallest, seemingly insignificant confrontation could be important."

"That's rich," Nettie said, finally raising the cloth to wipe her face.

"What is?"

"You think one of these nimrods killed her," Nettie laughed. "They can barely make coffee."

"Seems to me, those would be two different skill sets," Jack said.

"True." She wagged her finger. "But the coffee is the easier of the two."

"So who makes the coffee?"

"I do," she said.

"And where were you last night?" Jack narrowed his eyes.

"Wait a minute," Nettie dropped her cloth and reached to the floor to retrieve it. "I didn't kill her. Why would I?"

"That's what we're here to determine." Jack thought the woman was sweating even more than before. "You want to tell me where you were last night?"

"I was at home all night." Her cloth in hand, she readjusted herself in the chair.

"Alone?"

"Just me and the cats."

"Anyone who could vouch for you?" Jack asked. "A neighbor, maybe?"

"No." Nettie shook her head. "But I told you, there is no reason for me to want to kill Stephanie."

"You said you weren't a fan," Jack reminded her.

"I know." Her head bobbed as she talked. "But I don't like much of anybody. Doesn't mean I'm going to kill them."

"That's good." The detective glanced at his watch. "But I'm going to need more than that. Have the two of you had any issues lately? And remember if you lie to me, I will probably hear the truth from one of your coworkers. It would not go well for you."

She pursed her lips and sat silently contemplating her answer. "Well, if I must tell you." She turned her head from side to side as if looking for eavesdroppers. "As the others will probably tell you, we were usually at odds."

"But it's accounting?" Jack questioned. "What in the world could you be at odds at? Either the numbers are right or they aren't."

"Our problems were never about the numbers, detective." The woman wiped her forehead. "I didn't like the way she ran the department. She didn't like the way I challenged her authority."

"So, you wanted her job?"

"Of course I wanted her job," she said. "You think I don't have ambitions?"

"How bad do you want it?"

"Not bad enough to kill her." Nettie shook her head. "I would never kill anyone over a job."

"Many people have killed for less." Jack looked her in the eyes.

She shifted uncomfortably. "Well, not me."

15

Leaving his mother-in-law's home, Richard drove home the longest way he could think of without leaving town. It reminded him of being a newly licensed teen being sent to buy groceries by his mother. The store was only two miles from his house, but it would take him a half hour to get there. His mother knew what he was doing and didn't mind as long as he was picking up something like ice cream he didn't take the same route home.

He pulled into his driveway as he had done earlier that day and stared at the house. Richard knew he had to go in and if he didn't simply rip off the bandage and go, he may never do it. He slid out of his pickup to the ground and walked to the front door with key in hand.

Entering the house, he went straight to the makeshift bar they had created using an old rolling table. One of the wheels was cracked which caused it to wobble slightly when used, but Stephanie had been so excited to find it in a garage sale about three summers back. She had spent countless weekends stripping the old paint, sanding it smooth then repainting it.

He set a tumbler on the corner and filled it halfway with scotch. The table shifted, reminding him he had never fixed the problem as he had promised Stephanie he would time and time again. He stared at the table a moment then lifted the glass to his lips and downed the brown liquid in one gulp. He refilled while holding the glass in his hand.

With the drink topped off, he stood in the middle of his house wondering what he would do next. He had not planned on a solo journey through life. He wasn't sure he knew how to do it alone. And he was pretty sure he couldn't do it with anyone else. But this was not the time to be thinking of that.

His gaze fell on the small desk in the corner where Stephanie would work from home on occasion. Detective Mallory had searched it earlier, looking for a journal, but hadn't found anything. He had not been looking over the detective's shoulder, had not been looking his way at all. He had not seen what was or was not in those drawers.

Richard made his way across the room, sipping as he went. Sitting in her chair felt strange to him. He couldn't remember ever sitting there before. It had always been her desk, her chair. He felt like an intruder.

Stephanie had lied to him, telling him she had to work late. If not at work, where had she been? Was this the first time she had lied to him about where she was? Or was it a regular occurrence that he was not aware of? Was she cheating on him? He wondered if she did indeed have a secret journal with all the answers inside. He wondered if she kept it in the desk. He also wondered if there were any other secrets his wife had kept in the very same drawers. Did he even want to know?

With his hand on the pull handle of one of the drawers, he was interrupted by knocking on the front door. He felt relief that he had a reason to postpone going through Stephanie's things. At the same time, there was a twinge of anger that someone had chosen to bother him at home. He considered not answering but knew that if it was the detective, it might seem suspicious.

He pulled himself up and started for the front door, setting his drink down on a coaster on the way. The knocking started again, more persistent, and by the time he reached the door, he opened it without hesitation.

"What?" Richard snapped.

Standing on his porch with mascara streaking her face was his sister-in-law. He had forgotten. Faith must have called her after he left.

"Ashlyn?"

She stepped forward, hands balled into fists, pounding on his chest as he moved backward away from her attack. "What did you do?"

"Ashlyn," Richard repeated her name like he was still trying to work out who she was. "I . . . I need to talk to you about Stephanie."

"You bet your ass, you do." She struck at him again. This time he used his arms to try to block her blows. "What did you do to her?"

"She's gone," Richard said. "She died last night. Murdered."

"If you killed her, I'll kill you!" She changed the focus of her assault to his face.

"I didn't." Richard suddenly understood the anger. "I didn't kill her. I would never hurt her. You know that."

"Do I?" Ashlyn suddenly stopped. She stood in front of him, weeping. "She was fine when I talked to her yesterday. And now you're saying she's been murdered."

"You talked to her yesterday?" Richard took over the conversation. "When? What did she say? Where was she?"

She stood silent. She looked confused, her head tilted as if thinking through his questions.

"Ashlyn?"

"She said she was with you when we talked." Her voice was less harsh, less angry.

"With me?" Richard was taken aback. Absently, he thought aloud. "Why would she say that? Why would she lie to you, her own sister?"

"She wasn't with you?"

"No. She didn't come home," Richard said. "She told me she had to work late. But that was a lie. Apparently, she told her boss she had to leave early. I don't know where she was, but she wasn't with me. She didn't give you any clue as to where she was?"

"Just said she was home." Ashlyn's emotions started to build. "How do I know you aren't the one who is lying? I mean if you killed her, it's not like you would admit it."

"That's true, but," he sighed. "I'm not lying. She didn't come home. I wasn't with her. Did she call you for a reason? Did she want something? Tell you anything?"

"I called her," Ashlyn said, flatly.

"Oh." Richard seemed genuinely disappointed. "And she didn't tell you anything?"

"She told me she couldn't talk because the two of you were about to have dinner."

"She said she and I were having dinner?"

"She said, 'I can't talk. We're about to have dinner.'," Ashlyn quoted.

"So, she didn't say my name?" Richard let his mind drift. "She could have been with someone else."

"What?" Ashlyn became combative again. "Now you think she was cheating on you?"

"I didn't say that," he defended. "I just want to know who she was with, because whoever it was either killed her, or possibly saw something that would help me figure out what happened."

Ashlyn fell silent again. Her shoulders fell as the anger gave way to grief. As she started to cry, Richard put an arm around her shoulder and pulled her to him. He held her for what seemed an eternity as she buried her face in his chest and let her emotions consume her.

When she was spent, Richard helped her to the kitchen where he pulled out a chair for her. Once she was seated, he poured her a glass of water and set it in front of her. He retrieved his drink and joined her at the table. They sat in silence, looking past one another for a time.

"She would have hated this." Ashlyn broke the silence.

"What?"

"Steph would have hated this," she repeated. "She couldn't stay quiet longer than ten seconds. She couldn't stand the quiet."

"She told me that your parents used to fight and then not talk to one another for days." Richard grinned. "She said because of that, silence made her anxious. If it was quiet, someone might be angry. It really scared her."

"I never knew that." Ashlyn looked at her brother-in-law. "I mean, I knew about mom and dad. But not that she felt that way. God, I used to give her the silent treatment."

"Believe me, I know," Richard said. "We would talk for hours working through those times. I had to convince her you still loved her."

"Seriously?" Tears came to Ashlyn's eyes. "Why didn't she ever tell me?"

"I don't know," Richard admitted. "What I never understood was why she was so worried. This came from your parents, but they stayed together."

"Stayed together, yes." Ashlyn sighed. "But they weren't happy. I don't think they really loved each other. They were just comfortable together."

"But your mother was devastated by your dad's passing." Richard remembered the aftermath of that time.

"Maybe she realized too late that she loved him after all." Ashlyn took a long drink of water. "Wouldn't that be ironic?"

"How so?"

"I don't think Steph knew," Ashlyn said. "But those fights between mom and dad were because she cheated on him. And not just once."

"You're kidding?"

"When Steph was away at college," Ashlyn grabbed Richard's drink and sipped from it. "She actually left him. Me too, I suppose. I was a senior. I came home from school to a note telling me how to fix dinner."

"That's awful."

"Dad never said a word." She took another draw on the Scotch. "Acted like she never lived there at all. Then after about three days, she showed up with her suitcase. We were eating dinner. In she walked. Passed us. Went to their room. Unpacked her things. A few minutes later she grabbed a plate from the kitchen and sat with us. Weird thing was, they never fought that time. Just silence. It was like it never happened."

"And you never told Steph?"

"I was seventeen and confused," Ashlyn said. "Dad acted like nothing was wrong. When she came back they both pretended everything was okay. What was I going to tell Stephanie? Besides, I was afraid it would mess her up. Why do you think I never married? I never had a good role model for a relationship until you two got together. But by then, I just found it easy being alone."

They sat in silence again. After five or ten minutes, Ashlyn said, "Steph would hate this."

They both laughed a good long time. It was therapeutic. Richard filled his drink and poured one for his sister-in-law. He set the drink in front of her and sat.

"She never told you about having problems with anyone?" he asked. "At work maybe? Or the gym? Anywhere?"

"Not that she ever told me." She cradled her drink with both hands like it was a warm cup of hot chocolate. She sipped and closed her eyes as the alcohol traveled down her throat. It was what she needed at that moment.

"With me?"

"What?" Ashlyn opened her eyes and looked at Richard.

"She never said anything," Richard said. "But did she tell you she was having problems or issues with me?"

"No." Ashlyn was sincere. "Of course not."

"You thought I did something to her," he pointed out. "Why would you think that if she never said anything?"

"I thought that because I had the impression she was with you last night." She sipped again. "Last night. When she was killed."

Richard lowered his eyes to his drink. "It just doesn't seem real. Like I expect her to walk in the door any minute and ask what I want to do for dinner. I would say I want to eat it, and she would give me that look she gets."

"I know that look," Ashlyn grinned, then let the corners of her mouth droop again. "Can't believe I'll never see that look again."

The two of them fell silent, continuing to drink and remember their wife and sister.

16

After Nettie, Jack wandered out of the office in search of a cup of coffee. He was directed to a small break room with the promise of a recently brewed pot. A buzz of conversations was taking place in the room as he entered, however, everyone became deathly quiet when he stepped through the doorway. He scanned their faces, seeing Paul McIntosh sitting at one of the two tables. Jack nodded to the man before turning his attention to the coffee maker on his left.

"You going to be here much longer, detective?" Paul asked, feeling a little brave sitting among his coworkers.

"Are you ready to confess?" Jack poured dark liquid into a white styrofoam cup.

"No." He looked at his coworkers nervously.

"Then I'll be here a bit longer." He scanned the faces in the room. All staring at him, but one. The holdout was a man in his late twenties who was focused on the microwave meal in front of him. Jack was about to say something when he noticed the earbuds. He held up his cup. "Thanks for the coffee."

Jack heard a grunt as he turned to leave and assumed it was Paul. The detective found his way back to Stephanie's office, asking the first person he saw to have his next interview sent in. About five minutes later the twenty-something from the break room, complete with earbuds dangling from his shirt pocket, walked in. He sat clumsily in the chair directly across from Jack.

"State your name, position, and what you do here." Jack jumped right in.

"Chad Booker, Accountant, bookkeeping," the young man said in a dry monotone.

"You worked with Stephanie Ellison?"

"She hired me," he nodded.

"Did you ever have problems with her?"

"No."

"Do you know of anyone else who had problems with her?"

"Nettie," Chad said. "But she has problems with everybody."

"How would you describe your relationship with Stephanie?" Jack asked.

"My relationship?" Chad's eyes widened. "She was my boss. We didn't have a relationship. Why would you ask that?"

"I mean how well did you get along?" Jack clarified. "Cordial? Standoffish?"

"We got along, I guess." Chad seemed to think about his answer. "I liked her. She was nice, friendly. I wasn't fond of her husband though."

"You met her husband?" Jack was surprised. "Did he come here often?"

"No," the young man said. "I had to drop some papers off at her place. He answered the door. Was not very, how did you put it, cordial?"

"Was Stephanie aware of how he was towards you?"

"She was standing right there."

"How did she respond?"

"She apologized for him," Chad said. "Told me he was stressed or something."

"Can you think of any reason someone would want to harm Mrs. Ellison?" Jack wrote in his pad as he spoke.

"Not that I know of." Chad closed his eyes a moment. "No. No one comes to mind."

"Can I ask where you were last night?"

"Me?" Chad was taken aback.

"Yes." Jack stopped writing and made eye contact. "Where were you last night?"

"I was on a date."

"I need more than that." Jack pressed. "When did it start? When did it end?"

"Picked her up at eight," he said.

"And when did you take her home?" Jack felt the man was trying to hide something from him.

"Ten."

"Short date," Jack commented. "Doesn't give you an alibi for the murder."

"Alibi?" Chad lowered his eyes to the table. "I stayed."

"You what?"

"I took her home," Chad said. "And I stayed there."

"For how long?"

Chad gave Jack an agonizing look. "Until this morning."

"Okay." Jack wasn't sure why he was so embarrassed. "I will have to have her name to verify."

"Do you have to?"

"Yes." Jack almost laughed. "I can't just take your word for it. I need a name."

"Kyra," Chad said sheepishly.

"Kyra what?"

"Strickland."

"Kyra Strickland?" Jack suddenly knew. "As in the receptionist?"

Chad's eyes closed again. "She's going to kill me."

"I doubt that," Jack said.

"She was very clear." He rubbed his temples. "She doesn't want anyone knowing about us."

"Why is that?"

"Company policy."

"There's a policy on dating coworkers?" Jack grinned.

"Well not an actual policy," Chad said. "But we're encouraged not to date or anything."

"And if you're found out?"

"Then one of us would be encouraged to quit." He didn't sound sure of his answer.

"And I'm guessing you both need the job," Jack said.

"We do."

"And did Stephanie find out?"

"What?"

"Did Stephanie Ellison find out that you and Ms. Strickland were dating?" Jack repeated.

"I don't think so." Chad frowned.

"Because if she did," Jack said. "That would mean both you and Ms. Strickland had motive."

"Motive?" He looked mortified. "No. No motive. I wouldn't do that."

"One of you could be forced out of a job you both need," Jack suggested. "Sounds like motive to me."

"It's not," Chad insisted. "First, Stephanie didn't know. And second, I wouldn't kill her over a job."

"Why would you kill her?"

"I wouldn't." Chad clenched his fists. "I didn't kill her. I wouldn't kill her, or anyone else for that matter."

"Did Kyra talk you into it?" Jack leaned closer and spoke sincerely. "It would be best to come clean now. If she turns on you first, you'll be the one going to prison while she gets a light sentence for cooperating."

"She won't turn on me." Chad gritted his teeth. "Because I didn't do anything."

"So Kyra did it?"

"No." Chad threw his hands up. "She didn't kill Stephanie. I didn't kill Stephanie. Neither of us had anything to do with it."

Jack sat silent, observing Chad's movements. "Okay. That's all I have for now."

He gave his 'don't leave town' speech, stood, and walked the young accountant out. Chad turned toward his desk and Jack turned to the front lobby. He poked his head around the corner.

"Ms. Strickland." He gave a half-hearted smile. "You're next. Stephanie's office."

"I can't leave." Kyra pointed to the empty lobby and entry door.

"Someone will cover you." He turned and walked away. Kyra rose to her feet, looking around nervously before falling in step behind the detective. As they passed by Beverly Wallis' office, Kyra turned to her boss's assistant and shrugged.

In Stephanie's office, Jack settled in behind the desk and directed the receptionist to sit in one of the chairs opposite him where Chad had been moments before. Kyra sat and looked around the office, her eyes stopping on one of the motivational posters.

"You okay, Ms. Strickland?" Jack asked.

"Just never been in here before." She stared at one of the posters.

"You didn't know Mrs. Ellison very well?"

"No." Kyra shook her head. "Saw her come and go, that was it. She sometimes said 'good morning' or 'hi'. But that was about all."

"So, you wouldn't know anyone who might want to harm her?" Jack asked. "Or get her out of the way?"

"No."

"What about Chad?"

"What about him?"

"Do you think Chad would have harmed her?" Jack watched her eyes for a reaction.

"No." Kyra looked panicked. "Why would you think that?"

"Because office romances are forbidden."

Her eyes went wide.

"And he told me that when Stephanie found out about the two of you," Jack lied. "That you asked him to kill her to protect your jobs."

"He what!?" she shrieked.

She was much louder than Jack anticipated, loud enough that most of the faces in the office space were turned their direction. She was fast, too. She came out of her chair and spun on her heels to the door.

"Where is he?" she yelled.

Jack leaped to his feet and pursued her.

"Chad?" She stormed through the desks. "Where are you, you lying son-of-a-bitch?"

Jack caught her by the arm and redirected her back toward Stephanie's office. "We're not done yet."

She struggled, but he held her firm and spoke in a soothing voice. "Give me your story. Then you can track down your boyfriend."

"He's not my boyfriend," she snapped. "Not anymore." She wrenched her neck, looking back over her shoulder. "Do you hear me Chad?"

Jack guided her back to the office and convinced her to sit, remaining standing between her and the doorway. She continued to look past him to the main room beyond, presumably searching for Chad.

"Why don't you tell me your version of what happened last night?" Jack probed.

"Last night?" She looked up at Jack.

"Yes." Jack nodded. "Chad says he picked you up at eight o'clock."

"That's right."

"And what happened after that?" Jack asked.

"We went to dinner." Kyra crossed her arms.

"Was it a nice place?" Jack asked. "Someplace special?"

"Jacques' Bistro," she said. "On Elwood drive."

"Sounds nice."

"It is." Her face lit up. "They have the best croissants. And their pastries are to die for. And have you ever had escargot?"

"Can't say I have," Jack replied.

"You should try it." She smiled. "It's life-changing."

"I'm sure it is," Jack agreed. "When did you leave the bistro?"

"I don't know." She thought. "Nine-thirty? Maybe a little later."

"And what did you do then?"

"He took me home." Her expression soured again.

"And?"

"And what?"

"Did he leave?" Jack pressed. "Did he stay? What happened after he took you home?"

"You know."

"I don't know," Jack said. "That's why I'm asking."

"We drank some more wine," she grinned. "And you know."

"What?"

"We had sex." She blurted. "How did you not get that? Don't men your age have sex?"

"Just needed to hear it from you," Jack wrote in his notes. "What time did he leave?"

"He didn't," she said. "Not until this morning anyway."

He finished his note. "Can you think of anyone who might have wanted to harm Mrs. Ellison?"

"No."

"Okay." Jack stepped away from the door. "You're free to go."

She stood and smoothed out her skirt. At the door, she turned back. "He didn't say what you said he did, did he?"

"No."

"Why would you do that?"

"Just trying to get to the truth."

"By turning us against each other?"

"If that's what it takes, Ms. Strickland." Jack sat behind the desk. "The two of you were hiding your relationship. I had to find out if perhaps you were hiding something more. A woman is dead. My concern is with catching her killer. "

Kyra exhaled audibly then stormed out of the room for a second time in search of Chad. This time to salvage their relationship.

17

Lacey Novak was the woman that everyone agreed was Stephanie's closest friend at the office. They took numerous lunches together. They spent time together on their days off and were always quite chummy. There were comments about the possibility that Stephanie was showing favoritism to her friend. Others understood that the relationship between them had begun long before Stephanie's promotion and gave it little thought.

Jack chose to speak to her last.

Lacey walked into the office tentatively. Her dark eyes were puffy from crying, and she carried tissues in a clenched fist. She was an attractive woman with European facial features and light brown skin suggesting a mixed race background.

She hesitated before sitting across from the detective. Her small frame shook with each breath she took. When she looked up, she did not look at Jack. Her eyes locked on a small figurine depicting a dog sitting with a newspaper in its mouth. The tears began to flow freely from her dark eyes.

Jack observed for a moment. "The figurine means something to you?"

"She wanted a dog." Lacey sniffed and used a tissue to dry her face. "I gave her that on her last birthday."

Jack glanced about the office. "This was a bit insensitive of me. Would you be more comfortable if we went elsewhere for the interview?"

She lowered her eyes and nodded.

"I've been sitting here all day," Jack stood. "Let's take a walk."

For a moment, Lacey did not move, her expression a blend of surprise and confusion. Jack rounded the desk and held out a hand. She absently took it and let him help her to her feet.

"There's a park nearby." Jack opened the office door. "Let's go there."

All eyes were on them as they walked through the office. Whispers began even before they were out of sight, speculating whether she was under arrest. They walked through the front lobby and Jack held the door open for her.

The detective glanced back at an embarrassed Kyra. "We'll be back."

Lacey barely spoke as they made the short trek to the park. True to his word, Jack started to follow the path, taking her arm to get her started. They covered about a hundred feet before he began.

"Tell me about your relationship with Mrs. Ellison."

"Mrs. Ellison." She gave him a sad smile. "I never called her that."

"What did you call her?" Jack wanted to get her talking.

"Stephy." She smiled again. "Her husband called her Steph. Everyone else used Stephanie. So Stephy was my special nickname for her."

"Well then," Jack said. "Tell me about your relationship with Stephy."

"She's the best," Lacey beamed. "Best friend. Best boss. I love her." Her face fell. "Loved her, I guess."

"So the two of you were close?" Jack asked.

"We got along great," she confirmed. "Used to do a lot together. She invited me to their house. Especially when there was a party of something."

"You know her husband? What's his name?"

"Richard?" Lacey gave Jack a look. "He's great. Nice guy. Treated Stephanie like a princess. Which she was."

"What about other people in her life?"

"You mean Brent and Wendy?" She turned to him.

"Brent Meadows?" Jack referenced his notes.

"That's him," Lacey scowled. "He works at Havencroft. Thinks very highly of himself and isn't afraid to tell you how wonderful he is. I guess he and Richard go way back."

"But you didn't like him?"

"It's not that I disliked him." She leaned in. "I'm just not crazy about conceited people. Now his wife, Wendy, she's a doll."

"Anyone else come to mind?" Jack asked.

"I don't remember anyone's names." She shrugged. "I only know Brent's name because of work. And Wendy has come to enough company gatherings that I learned hers. I'm an accountant for a reason. I know numbers. I love numbers and math. Socially, I can be a bit awkward."

"Knowing her as well as you did," Jack directed her to a park bench where they sat. "Can you think of anyone who might want to harm her?"

"Harm Stephy?" Lacey shook her head and her shoulder-length hair flowed like a wave from side to side. "No one. It just doesn't make sense."

"I noticed in her office several unanswered messages from an Andy G." Jack was looking through his notes again. "Any idea who he is?"

"Not really." She shook her head again. "I knew she was avoiding his calls but I never asked why."

"Do you happen to know his last name?"

She thought for a moment then raised a finger. "Green. Andy Green."

"Thank you." Jack wrote the name down. "Yesterday, Stephanie told her husband she had to work late. In actuality, she left work early. Do you have any idea what she did when she left? Was she seeing someone?"

"Stephy wouldn't cheat on Richard." Lacey almost scolded him. "There's no way."

"You have to admit it's a little suspicious that she lied to him." Jack sat back. "Why would she do that if she wasn't cheating on him?"

"I don't know," Lacey said. "But she wasn't. If he told you otherwise then he's lying. Maybe he is lying. Maybe she called to say she was coming home early. Maybe he said the opposite to cover his butt."

"I thought you said he was great," Jack pointed out.

"Not if he killed Stephy." She crossed her arms in defiance. "Then he's not great at all."

"So, you don't have any idea where she went when she left work yesterday?"

"No."

"She had an appointment on her calendar that was just an initial B," Jack said. "Any idea who B is?"

"I would assume Beverly."

"The CFO?"

"She had a lot of meetings with Beverly." Lacey scrunched her nose.

"What?" Jack pressed. "What's wrong with her having meetings with her boss?"

"Nothing." She rolled her eyes. "Beverly just isn't my favorite person. And I'm pretty sure I'm not hers. So, without Stephy, I will probably be out of a job soon."

"You think she'll fire you?"

"I think she might." Lacey seemed to drift away. "I don't think she likes me."

"You think now that Stephanie is gone, it clears the way for her to get rid of you?" Jack was making sure he had heard correctly.

"Yes. Oh, my God." Lacey's hand raised to cover her mouth. "You don't think Beverly killed Stephy so she could fire me? Do you?"

"I doubt that," Jack assured her. "If she was willing to kill someone just to get rid of you, she would have probably just killed you."

Lacey let that sink in. She nodded. "That makes sense. I guess you're right."

"You can't think of anyone who may have wanted to harm her?"

"No." She grimaced. "I'm sorry."

"Okay," Jack said. "I do have to ask. Where were you last night?"

"Me?"

"I have to ask," Jack repeated.

"Well." Lacey put a finger on the side of her jaw. "I left work around five. From there I went to the grocery store. Then I went home, made dinner, ate, then watched TV until I went to bed."

"What did you watch?"

"Pardon me?"

"When you watched TV," Jack clarified. "What were you watching?"

"I . . . uh."

"You don't remember what you were watching last night?" Jack asked.

"No." Lacey blushed. "I remember."

"And?"

"I was watching Hallmark movies." She diverted her eyes.

Jack grinned.

"Yes," she said. "I'm a closet romantic."

18

Jack questioned a few more employees at Havencroft Financial Group, learning nothing new. He checked his notes and found only one name to which he could not put a face. He rose from Stephanie's desk and stretched. Sitting for long periods of time seemed to get more difficult every year.

He stepped out of the office and searched for someone brave enough to look his way. When no one obliged him, he wandered toward the lobby where he found Kyra talking rapidly on her cell phone. Jack's shadow crossed her desk and she looked up stopping suddenly mid-sentence. "I'll call you back."

Jack gave her an insincere smile. "Where would I find Brent Meadow's office?"

"Left side," she pointed. "Fourth door."

"Thanks." He nodded and turned to follow her finger.

"He's not there," she added.

He turned back to the receptionist. "Where is he?"

She shrugged. "He and Stephanie's husband are tight. I imagine he's wherever the best friend of a grieving widower would be."

"Do you have a home address for him?"

"Don't you need a warrant or something?"

"Not for an address." Jack looked down at her.

"Fine," she huffed. "You want it text or email."

The idea of this woman having his phone number gave Jack an unsettling premonition of her calling him at three in the morning looking for help getting out of jail. Giving her his email was no less daunting. "Just read it to me."

He scribbled the address below Brent Meadow's name then read it back to Kyra who assured him it was correct. He turned to another page in his notepad. "What about Camden?"

"Who is Camden?"

"Camden," he repeated. "Stephanie Ellison has been meeting with him weekly for the past several months."

"Wait." The receptionist leaned forward. "On Thursdays?"

"Yes." Jack nodded. "So, you know him?

"Nope."

"Then how did you know about Thursdays?"

"Stephanie left every Thursday at two-forty-five," Kyra spoke smugly. "Easy guess."

"Where did she go?"

"How would I know?" Remembering who she was talking to, she followed with, "I mean, she didn't say."

Jack stared down at the woman. From the expression on her face, he could tell that she thought he was angry. In reality, he was making a mental list of the people he would need to ask about Camden. But it had already been a long day, and he wasn't going to round them up for more questions now.

He gave Kyra a half grin and asked her to pass on his appreciation to Beverly Wallis for the use of the office and access to the staff. The receptionist assured him she would do so and as Jack left the lobby, she pulled out her cell phone. He could hear her talking even before the door closed.

In the parking lot, the detective leaned against the front fender of his car and used his phone to search for Andy Green. He was quickly reminded of the magnitude of the task. Andy could be short for Andrew or not. The last name could be spelled Green or Greene. Because it was a phone call, he could be local, or literally live anywhere. There were easily thousands of results.

He was settling into the driver's seat when his phone rang. He pulled it out to answer, glancing at the screen. Seeing the caller's name, Jack realized he was about to receive an invitation to an autopsy.

"Mallory," he answered.

"Jack? This is Valerie O'Conner," the familiar voice of the coroner greeted Jack's ear. "If you want to stop by, I have some things to share about your victim."

"With an offer like that," Jack replied, "how could I refuse?"

He started the car and pulled out of Havencroft's parking lot into the flow of traffic that would take him toward the morgue. It was about a fifteen-minute drive, so he took the opportunity to call the chief to request that Shaun Travis be assigned to the case as his partner.

"What makes you think he would want to work with you?" Chief Sharon Hutchins asked. "Last time you got him shot."

"He got shot," Jack clarified. "I did not get him shot."

There was a long pause. "He was only released back to active duty two weeks ago."

"So, what's the problem?"

"I don't want him back in rehab because you overextended him."

"He was released," Jack argued. "Besides, he can sit at a desk for this. I need him to track someone down for me."

"At a desk?"

"Yes, ma'am."

Another long pause. "Okay, then, I'll let him know he's been assigned."

As soon as they hung up, Jack dialed Shaun's number. The young detective answered on the second ring.

"The chief assigned you to me," Jack informed him. "Meet me at the morgue in ten."

"You convinced her to let me off the desk?" There was excitement in his voice. "I could hug you. I should thank her."

"Don't."

"What?"

"Don't thank her," Jack said. "Just trust me. Don't speak to her. And get to the morgue."

"I'm still on the desk, aren't I?"

"Just get to the morgue." Jack snapped. "Or I'll request someone else."

"On my way."

While pursuing a killer who was abducting women while they walked their dogs, Shaun had found himself in the right place at the wrong time. He had been shot twice, once in the vest and once in the exposed tissue under his arm. The second bullet collapsed his lung. He had a long struggle getting back to his old self. Since then, he had been sitting in a small room with no windows reviewing cases that a disgraced detective had closed. It was discovered the detective had framed at least two men for crimes they did not commit which brought his other arrests into question. Ready to get back in the field, he would do anything to make it happen.

Jack parked and was opening the door to the morgue when he saw Shaun's car racing into the parking lot. The detective waited for his young partner to park and join him before entering.

"I can't thank you enough," Shaun greeted Jack with a firm handshake. "One more day on the desk and I would have started pulling my hair out. What's the case?"

"Murdered woman. An accountant." Jack opened the door so they could enter. "Lots of suspects. No real standout though."

"Married?" Shaun entered, followed by Jack.

"Nine years. No kids."

"I assume he's on the suspect list."

"He is," Jack confirmed. "But he has an alibi that I haven't had a chance to verify."

"Boyfriend maybe?"

"Don't know yet." Jack started down the hall. "After this, I need you to track down a guy, find out who he is. She's been avoiding his calls at work. Could be nothing. Could be a jilted lover."

"Real detective work." Shaun smiled. "Can't wait."

Together they made their way to autopsy where they found Valerie O'Conner at work on the body of Stephanie Ellison. She looked up when she saw them enter and waved them to her.

"Detective Travis, so good to see you up and about." She nodded to the young detective while she worked to stitch the autopsy incisions closed. "Jack, always a pleasure."

"What've you got for us?" Jack asked.

"Time of death is between eleven and eleven-thirty last night." Valerie continued to stitch.

"Well, if we can verify the husband's alibi," Jack turned to Shaun. "That would clear him."

"Unless he hired someone," Shaun suggested.

"Unless that," Jack agreed.

"Cause of death was, as expected, blunt force trauma." Valerie pointed at the woman's head where wounds were evident. She then turned Stephanie's head to show the back. "She was struck a total of eight times. Some hard enough to crack the skull. She had bleeding on the brain after the third or fourth blow. At that point, she would likely have died from her wounds within a few hours. "

"But he struck her several more times." Jack thought aloud. "That's a long time on a public trail, even at night. He really wanted her dead."

"She was struck in the forehead and from the back." Shaun leaned in to get a closer look at the wounds. "Is there any way to know which was first? If she was facing her attacker, it's possible she knew them."

"She could have known him, realized what was about to happen, and turned away." Jack grimaced. "Or she may not have known him, but was struck before she knew it was coming."

"God, that's a lot of hits," Shaun observed.

"Maybe it was personal," Jack suggested. "Wanted her to suffer. Kept hitting her to inflict more pain. You know the type. Tells her what's wrong with her and hits her again. Wanted her to feel every last blow."

"It's unlikely that she felt much of anything. Valerie finished the last stitch and cut the thread. "I'm almost positive she would have been unconscious after the second blow, if not the first."

"Unconscious?" Jack looked into the victim's face. "Most people who hit someone, causing enough damage to knock them unconscious would think they had killed them. Yet this guy kept hitting her."

"Rules out a mugging gone bad," Shaun said. "Sounds more like rage?"

"According to the report, the first officers on scene, it didn't appear her pockets were searched." Jack circled the table to stand next to Valerie as he looked for more bruising. "And her wedding ring was still on her finger. Unless she said something to set him off, or ran him off the road on the way to the park, it seems unlikely this was a random attack. It was personal. She was targeted."

The detective moved around the table again, stopping at the head. He examined the wounds. "What do you think caused these?"

"The shape of the wound suggests the corner of something." Valerie started pushing her instrument table to the side of the room where they would be cleaned and sterilized. "I did find small shards of glass and gray plastic, from a cell phone or laptop maybe."

"Laptop?" Jack pulled some papers from his jacket pocket and scanned through them. "There was a laptop bag in her car. Maybe she had it with her."

"So it may have been a mugging after all," Shaun said.

"If he hit her with it hard enough to crack her skull and break the corner of the laptop, it wouldn't be worth much." Jack shook his head. "Leave a diamond wedding set and take a broken laptop? Maybe this was about the laptop. Or something on the laptop."

"You think she had something on her laptop worth killing for?" Shaun asked.

"Someone may have thought so." Jack made notes in his pad.

"I've got one more thing for you." Valerie had washed her hands and was toweling them dry while walking toward the detectives.

"What's that?" Jack raised an eyebrow.

"Stomach contents suggest she ate about an hour before she was killed." She tossed the towel into a hamper. "And you won't believe what she had."

"Okay." Jack crossed his arms. "What did she have?"

"Escargot."

"As in snails?"

"That's right." Valerie smiled. "Not your everyday meal."

"Have you ever had escargot?" Shaun asked.

"Nope." Valerie wrinkled her nose.

"I had it once," Jack said. "When I was in France. Tastes like fish."

"Where do you get it around here?" Shaun asked. "Not that I want any."

Jack thought for a minute. "This is the second time I've heard about someone eating escargot today."

"You're kidding?" Shaun's eyes enlarged. "Who have you been hanging out with?"

"No." Jack pulled out his notepad and flipped through it. "It was an interview. Yeah. Here it is. Kyra Strickland said that she and Chad Booker had escargot at a place called Jacques'' Bistro."

"Are they suspects?" Shaun asked.

"They are now." Jack made another note in his pad.

19

Jack couldn't get the idea of Stephanie Ellison having a problem at work out of his head. Sure, she may have been lying about it. She had lied about having to work late because of it. But the detective could not shake the feeling that some of the best lies were imbedded in truth.

As an accountant, the most likely problem she would have at work was with the books. It could just as easily have been a coworker or any number of other things. Without knowing which, Jack had to work with what knowledge he had. Having a problem with the books, combined with the three o'clock meeting with "B", who could have been Beverly Wallis, the CFO. Maybe Beverly wanted to meet out of the office to discuss such a sensitive subject. It could be motive and opportunity tied up in one neat package.

He filled out the paperwork to request a warrant for Havencroft's financials, along with a forensics accountant to examine them. With that done, and nothing to do but wait, he called the sergeant's desk to see when Officers Walters and Mendez would be in. As it happened, the two men had just reported for their shift and were in the locker room getting ready.

Jack jumped from his seat and raced to the elevators. He wanted to catch them before they left on patrol. When the elevator did not arrive promptly, Jack took the stairwell down to the second floor. He burst through the doors and all eyes turned toward him. He ignored them and moved toward the locker rooms, scanning the faces as he went looking for the partners. When that proved unsuccessful, he entered the locker room.

"Walters!" He called out the name. "Mendez!"

A man peeked around the corner of one of the rows of lockers. It was neither of the officers Jack was looking for. The man ducked out of sight again and Jack moved forward. A fully uniformed man stepped into the main aisle. It was Walters.

"What do you want, Jack?" Walters was direct, but not combative.

"Need to talk to you and Mendez about the woman you found in the park." Jack stepped up to the officer.

"We didn't find her." Mendez stepped into view. "We were called."

"You were first on scene?"

"We were," Walters confirmed. "How's she doing?"

"Didn't make it," Jack furrowed his brow.

"Damn," Walters shook his head. "Guess that makes sense with you being here. They don't send homicide for the live ones, do they?"

"No," Jack said. "They don't."

"What can we do for you?" Mendez asked.

"I want to go over what you saw when you arrived on scene." Jack steered them toward the exit. "When you got there, the victim was still alive."

"She was hanging on." Walters grimaced.

"Did she say anything?"

"She was hanging on," Walters repeated. "But she was unresponsive."

"Who found the body?"

"A 9-1-1 call," Mendez answered. "Reported a woman passed out in the park. He didn't stick around. But we got his information. We were going to go track him down. But I guess it's your case now. You want his info?"

Jack nodded. Both men pulled out notebooks. Mendez read from his and Jack copied everything down. "Ethan Bridges."

"Maybe he saw something." Mendez put his notebook away.

"Or took something." Jack put his away as well. "Murder weapon wasn't found."

"Only reason to take that is if he did it," Walters said. "Which is a possibility. Guess we should have tracked him down that morning."

"Maybe." Jack agreed.

"Sorry detective," Mendez offered. "We were busy trying to keep her alive."

"You weren't wrong," Jack assured the officers. "Priority was the victim. I'll talk to Mr. Bridges. Thanks."

20

The empty bottle of scotch lay sideways on the table and Richard was working the lid off a bottle of bourbon he didn't remember he had. His sister-in-law held out her glass in anticipation. He steadied himself and only spilled a little of the precious brown liquid as he poured.

Realizing the time, Richard ordered some Chinese food from a local restaurant that delivered. It was a tradition he and Stephanie had when drinking too much. The driver, the same man who had delivered their order every time they had placed one, was confused to see Ashlyn instead of Mrs. Ellison. He smiled and nodded several times, but diverted his eyes. Richard gave him an extra five dollars for his tip, only later realizing the poor man probably thought it was to keep him quiet about his guest.

He grabbed plates and forks from the kitchen and dumped them, along with the food, on the dining room table. Their drinking slowed as they ate and the talking increased. Sharing stories of Stephanie dominated their conversation. Telling edited versions of the times they spent with her made them laugh, and sometimes cry. Often, they did both at the same time.

As the day came to a close, Richard decided to leave the food and dishes for morning. After a brief argument, he convinced his sister-in-law to stay in the guest room rather than drive home. He got her settled, poured another glass of bourbon, and climbed the stairs to his and Stephanie's bedroom. Standing in the doorway, he sipped the alcohol and prepared himself to enter the room they had shared for years and never would again. His plan, which seemed to be working, was to drink himself into a stupor so that he would be asleep within minutes after his head hit the pillow.

He crossed to his side of the bed, set the glass down, and shed his clothing, kicking his shoes into the corner of the room. He lay down and prayed for sleep. It did not come immediately, but when it came, he slept hard.

He woke with a start, panicked that he had overslept. He reached for Stephanie and when he did not find her, the events of the previous day came flooding in. Overwhelming sadness consumed him, followed by a headache that was the beginning of the worst hangover he would ever have. He swore off alcohol as he had done so many times in the past, knowing full well he would probably be drinking again by evening if not sooner.

Avoiding any movements that would aggravate his condition, he rolled and let his legs dangle over the side of the bed. He sat in that position long enough to decide he was ready. Sliding forward, he let his feet drop to the floor and stood. The room shifted but did not spin. Calling that a win, he headed for the shower, his eyes closed more than not.

He emerged from his room refreshed, with a clean change of clothes. He found Ashlyn in the kitchen staring into the refrigerator.

"What do you guys eat?" She did not look his way.

"We usually grab something on the way to work."

"What about the weekend?"

"Coffee." He stepped up to the brewer, dropped in a filter, and started adding grounds. "Want some?"

"You bet." Ashlyn shut the refrigerator and leaned against its door.

"Damn." Richard scowled.

"What's wrong?"

"I added grounds for you." He stared at the machine, holding the carafe in his hand.

"I said I wanted some," she reminded him.

"I know," he shrugged. "But I had already put in the usual amount. You know. Enough for me and Stephanie."

Her confused expression shifted to understanding with a touch of sadness. Her sister was gone and every day going forward was going to be a string of reminders of that void.

"After our binge last night," she said, "we can probably both use a little extra this morning."

He gave a half-hearted smile and turned on the faucet, holding the carafe under the stream. A few minutes later they both watched as the brewing finished. Richard poured his sister-in-law a cup and then himself. He passed the dining table, opened the French doors, and made his way to his favorite seat on the deck. Ashlyn followed.

They sat, drinking their coffee, watching the sun creep over the horizon. It was a beautiful moment and both found themselves wishing Stephanie was there to share it with.

They talked a little, but without the alcohol to calm their nerves, it felt awkward at best.

"You want something for breakfast?" Richard asked.

"No, thank you." Ashlyn looked into her nearly empty coffee cup. "I should really be going."

"Really?" Richard looked a little panicked.

"What?" Ashlyn questioned. "You want me here?"

Richard sighed deeply and looked at her with concerned eyes. "I need to go through her desk. I'm kind of afraid what I might find."

"I don't think she had any big secrets," Ashlyn said.

"Except she told me she was working late and left early instead," Richard reminded her. "I'm scared that I might find something that suggests she wasn't as happy as I thought we were."

"Are you serious?" Ashlyn sat up straight. "She was crazy about you. She was thinking about you guys starting a family. There's nothing in that desk that will say otherwise."

"You think so?" Richard asked.

"I know so." She set her cup down and turned toward her brother-in-law. "If she was unhappy, she would have said something. If not to you, definitely to me."

"I was hoping you might go through it with me," he said. "Her desk. I don't know if I can do it alone."

She nodded. "I can do that."

"Okay then." Richard shifted forward in his seat and stood.

"What? Now?"

"If there's something in there that'll help explain why Steph was killed, I want to know." He walked into the house with both cups in hand.

Ashlyn took a moment before joining him. He was sitting at Stephanie's desk when she walked in. She stepped up and stood just behind him where she could watch what he did from over his shoulder.

He put his hand on the center drawer and they both held their breath and tensed up just before he pulled it open. Pens, paperclips, and staples dominated the contents. They exhaled at the same time and Richard let out a small chuckle. He wasn't sure what they were expecting.

The top drawer on the left was filled with receipts, ledgers, and a variety of financial documents. The lower drawer held file folders in a hanging accordion-style organizer. Richard thumbed through them, finding user manuals, recipes, home repair records. Everything you might expect to find in a home desk.

On the right side, the two drawers were locked. Richard's idea that Stephanie had more to hide was reinforced. He yanked on the drawer handles repeatedly to no avail. He felt Ashlyn's hand on his shoulder and he stopped.

"Let me try." Her voice was soothing.

He put his hands up and backed away. "Be my guest."

She walked to the kitchen and pulled a butter knife from the silverware drawer. Returning to the desk, she dropped to one knee and went to work on the single lock that served both drawers. Within a couple of minutes, she was inside.

"Should I be nervous?" Richard asked.

"Dad used to keep his liquor in a cabinet with a similar lock," she explained.

The bottom drawer, like the one on the left, had an accordion organizer filled with folders. He started thumbing through. Nothing was there to suggest she was living a secret life or gave a clue as to why someone might want her dead. The only thing of interest was the folder marked 'Havencroft'. Richard pulled it out and laid it on the desk.

Inside, he found a copy of her company contract. There was a thin booklet listing her benefits, as well as several certificates of recognition dating back to the beginning of her tenure. He read through them with pride, wondering why she never mentioned them to him.

In the back of the file were several pages of spreadsheets from different dates ranging over the past two years. None of them seemed to be connected to the others, just random pages. There was nothing to explain why someone would want to hurt her, or kill her. He closed the folder and slumped in the chair. He was no better off than before.

He looked at his sister-in-law sitting across from him. "No answers."

"That you didn't find anything suspicious is a good thing, Richard." Ashlyn did her best to reassure him. "It's a win."

"It doesn't feel like one."

"No." She leaned against the wall. "I guess it doesn't."

"And now I have to go to the funeral home and make arrangements to bury my wife." Richard rubbed his face with his hands. "We should be picking out a piece of furniture instead of me picking out a casket. How do you even do that? Pick out a box that your loved one will spend eternity in?"

"I can help with that," Ashlyn volunteered. "If you don't mind."

"I thought you had to go?"

"I just felt weird being here, alone, with you." She took a deep breath. "I'm sorry."

"No need to apologize." Richard stood. "Brent is supposed to go with me. If you don't mind him tagging along."

"Don't mind at all." She pushed off the wall. "Could I use your shower and clean up a bit?"

"You know where it is." Richard pointed. "Towels are in the hall linen closet. And if you need a change of clothes. Well, you know."

"I don't think I could wear her things." Ashlyn started down the hall. "Not yet."

"You swapped clothes all the time."

"Not the same right now." She pulled the closet door open and retrieved a towel, then crossed the hall to the bathroom. "Be out in a minute."

21

Detective Shaun Travis was sitting at his desk again. The only good thing was he was looking into a current case rather than reviewing old ones. The first thing he had done that morning was request and receive a warrant for Stephanie Ellison's bank records in an attempt to track her movements on her last day.

To occupy the nearly three hours it took for the documents to be emailed to him, he called a number of restaurants in the area that might serve escargot besides Jacques'' Bistro. He found two others, taking down their addresses.

The email finally arrived and Shaun examined her final purchases. After leaving work for the day, Stephanie stopped at a convenience store near her work and made two purchases. An hour after that she made another purchase at a place called Alexandria's Boutique, followed by a pricey purchase at a place called Briana's. The last purchase she made was food and drinks at none other than Jacques'' Bistro.

Shaun called Jack to let the detective know what he had learned. Jack asked him to download a photo of Stephanie and go to the restaurant. He was tasked with finding out if anyone remembered the woman, and more importantly, if they remembered who she had been with.

Shaun pulled his gun and badge from his desk, made sure he had his keys and headed out with a smile on his face. It was good being on a case, investigating, and now interviewing possible witnesses. He was beginning to feel like the detective he was.

It was a twenty-minute drive to the bistro, and he arrived just as the lunch rush was getting underway. He stepped up to the hostess desk and asked to see the manager. They asked him to wait and continued to seat the steady flow of guests entering the building.

After ten minutes, Shaun returned to the desk, insisting on seeing the manager. The young woman manning the station assured him the manager would be right out. Shaun returned to his spot and watched the dining area for anyone who looked like they were in charge No one he saw seemed to fit the bill. Waitstaff rushed through with plates of food and tickets. Bussers cleared tables as quickly as they could and hostesses filled them again just as fast.

Shaun was startled by a small woman suddenly appearing at his side. "You wanted to see me?"

"Are you the manager?"

"I am," she said. "How may I help you?"

Shaun pulled out his badge and introduced himself. The expression on her face shifted from fake-cheery customer service to confused and anxious. "What's this about?"

"Were you on duty two nights ago?"

"Yes." She nodded. "Why?"

He pulled out his phone and brought up the picture of Stephanie Ellison. He turned it to her. "Do you happen to remember this woman?"

The manager leaned close and squinted. "Maybe? Maybe not? We have so many people come and go. Even if I recognized her, I couldn't tell when I saw her. The waitstaff would remember. Especially if she left a good tip or was a difficult customer. I'll see who was on duty that night."

"Thanks." Shaun stepped back against the wall. "I'll wait."

The manager gave him an unsure grin, glanced at the customers waiting to be seated then spun on her heels, retreating to the back of house. When Shaun saw her again, she was carrying a piece of paper, but she made two stops to talk with guests before making her way back to him.

"This is the list of waitstaff that worked that night." She handed him the paper. "Three of them are here right now."

"Can I talk to them?"

"It's kind of busy," the manager protested. "Can't it wait?"

"Maybe I should have mentioned this is a homicide investigation." Shaun looked at the list of five names.

"Homicide?" The manager looked distressed. "My God."

"Have the three stop by and look at the picture." Shaun indicated his phone. "If they don't remember her, I'll arrange to speak to the other two."

"Okay." She reluctantly agreed before vanishing to the back once more.

Shaun remained standing against the wall. He noticed the hostess was staring at him, so he gave her a nod and half grin. She turned her head away, looking down at the table chart in front of her.

A waitress walked up to him and Shaun looked down at her. She said, "You the guy with the picture?"

"I am." Shaun pulled the picture up on his phone and turned it to the young woman. "Do you remember her from two nights ago?"

She stared at the image for a moment. "I don't know. Looks familiar. But then, who knows? You should talk to Liza. She remembers everybody."

"Is she here?" Her name was on the list.

"I'll send her over." The waitress's ponytail bounced as she moved away. She scanned the room, saw a customer waving her down, and moved to their table.

Shaun watched her until she disappeared through a door to the back. He never saw her speak to a coworker. Frustrated, he started checking his phone for messages.

"Listen," a voice to his left said. "I need to get back to my tables."

Shaun looked up at her. "Uh."

"You okay?"

"Me?" He pointed at his own chest and laughed nervously. "I'm fine."

"Then?"

He stood looking into her bright blue eyes. Her blond hair was pulled back into a ponytail like her coworker. Shaun could not help but stare at her features, high cheekbones, dimples, small pursed lips. He was mesmerized. "Uh, are you Liza?"

"Yes." She nodded. "Missy says you have a picture."

"Missy?"

"You showed her the picture." Liza hooked her thumb over her shoulder. "She thought I might know whoever it is."

"Oh, yeah." Shaun looked at his phone and in an attempt to switch screens back to the picture of Stephanie, accidentally erased an email. "Crap."

"You sure you're okay?"

"I'm good." He got the image and turned it to her. "She was here two nights ago."

Liza smiled and Shaun felt weak in the knees. "Sure. I remember her. Sweet lady. Tipped really well. Is everything okay?"

"Do you remember if she was here with anyone?"

"Her husband," she said.

"You're sure it was her husband?"

"Well, no." Liza shrugged. "It's just, they both wore rings, and they were very serious most of the time they were here. Seemed like a married couple to me. Plus, she paid for everything."

"Had you ever seen them before?" Shaun asked.

"No," she replied. "This was their first time."

"Tell me about him."

"I didn't care for him." She looked at the dining room to her tables. "Was full of himself. Just a general scum bag. Part of me was hoping she was giving him the boot. You know."

"Did you ever hear a name?"

"No." She shook her head causing her ponytail to bounce from side to side. "Listen, I really need to get back."

"If you think of anything call me." Shaun handed her a card. She snatched it out of his hand and walked quickly to her nearest customer, apologizing. Barely audible, Shaun said, "or if you just want to."

He glanced around to be sure no one heard him. The hostess was staring at him. He shrugged then slipped out of the restaurant. He stood next to his car, pulling up his emails and going into the appropriate folder to retrieve the one he had deleted.

"Hey!"

Shaun looked up to see Liza running toward him. He smiled broadly, watching her approach. She stopped a few feet away. Breathing heavily, she said, "You asked about names. I don't remember hearing his, but he called her Steph."

"Steph?" Shaun stopped smiling. "Are you sure?"

"Positive."

"Thanks," Shaun nodded to her.

"No problem." She looked him in the face and gave him a slight smile. Her hand came up between them, showing him that she was holding his card. "I'll call."

She turned sharply and ran back inside. Shaun didn't stop smiling until he pulled back into employee parking at the department.

22

The doorbell chimed when Richard pushed the button. He stood to the side, to avoid the swing of the screen door, and waited. Ashlyn was two steps lower looking down at her feet, kicking at a small stone.

The door opened and Brent smiled. "Richard. Come on in. Who's this?"

"You remember Ashlyn," Richard reminded him. "Steph's little sister."

"Not so little," Ashlyn protested as she followed them inside.

"That's right." Brent pretended to remember. "So good to see you."

"Ashlyn is going to go with us to pick out the casket."

"Oh, the casket." Brent slapped his forehead. "I totally forgot. Let me go change. It'll be just a minute."

Wendy emerged from their room upstairs. "Who was at the door, Brent?"

"Richard and Ashlyn," Richard called up to her.

"Richard and who?" Wendy looked down at them.

"Ashlyn," Richard answered. "Steph's sister."

"I remember you." Wendy was gliding down the stairs. "From the wedding."

"That's right," Ashlyn smiled. "Wendy, isn't it?"

"Yes." Wendy reached the bottom of the stairs and gave Ashlyn a quick hug. "So sorry for your loss."

"Thank you." Ashlyn patted the other woman's back.

"What brings you here?"

"I'm going with Richard to pick out a casket." Ashlyn grimaced. "Can't let him mess up her final resting place."

Wendy grinned. "She'd never forgive him."

"Like I said," Brent said. "I'll change and we can go."

As if on cue, Brent's phone rang. He pulled it out and answered. "Hello?"

"Is this Brent Meadows?"

"Yes." He shrugged at the others. "Who is this?"

"I'm Detective Jack Mallory," Jack announced. "I've been trying to get a hold of you."

"What can I do for you, detective?" Brent made eye contact with Richard.

"I need to talk to you," Jack said. "Ask some questions."

"I understand." Brent made a show of being bored for the others' benefit. "When do you want to do this?"

"Right now." Jack insisted. "You can come here, or I can meet you where you're at."

"We're about to head out," Brent informed the detective. "Can we do this later?"

"This is a homicide investigation, Mr. Meadows." Jack's voice became sharper. "I can send a squad car to pick you up if needed."

"No," Brent said. "That won't be necessary. I'll come there."

"I'll be waiting." Jack hung up.

Brent held his phone out in front of him.

"What was that about?" Wendy asked.

"I have to go in for questioning." Brent put the phone away, making eye contact with Richard "I won't be able to go with you. He wants me now."

"I'll go," Wendy volunteered.

"You don't have to," Richard said.

"It'll be good to feel useful." She shrugged him off. "Let me get my purse."

Brent moved away from the others. "Hey, Richard. Can I show you something really fast?"

Richard turned and followed his friend into the next room.

"Before I go," Brent wrapped an arm around the other's shoulders and spoke in a hushed voice. "The alibi thing. We were in your basement watching a game and drinking beer. Right?"

"That's what I said." Richard sighed. "It still bothers me."

"You can't change it now." Brent patted his shoulder. "If you do, they'll think you're guilty for sure."

"Richard?" Ashlyn called out. "You ready?"

"Coming." Richard looked at his friend. "See you when we get back."

They returned to the main room together. Brent went upstairs to change. The others piled into Richard's truck and pulled away.

The funeral home was about twenty minutes away and Richard pulled into an open space not far from the entrance. There was a large sign immediately in front of him informing passersby what they would find inside. Richard glared at the words, refusing to remove his hands from the steering wheel. After coaxing from both women, he finally relented, and they entered together.

"May I help you?" The man standing in the entry hall was tall. Freakishly tall. He wore a dark suit that must have been tailor-made for him, as it fit him perfectly, and Richard was pretty sure his size didn't come off the rack. His name tag introduced him as Farkas Burjan and Richard could only stare up at it, wondering what nationality it was.

"We're here to make funeral arrangements," Ashlyn answered. "For my sister. His wife."

Farkas bowed his head, looking sincerely saddened. Then he waved his massive hand toward a door behind him. "Shall we?"

They shuffled through the door. The room on the other side had two round tables, surrounded by seating and covered with brochures.

The rest of the room was a showroom of caskets. It was a lot to take in.

Pulling a chair away from the closest table Farkas waved the others to sit. He lowered himself into the chair, his knees clearly visible above the tabletop.

"We here at Schaefer and Hines would like to first emphasize how sorry we are for your loss." The man's voice was low, soothing, almost hypnotic. "That being said, we are here for you and your family during these difficult times. Specifically, once we have an agreement and a contract, we will take care of everything."

Richard looked from the man to the women, to the caskets, and back again.

"We have different levels for the family to celebrate the life of the loved one." He laid a brochure on the table in front of each of them. "As you can see we have a variety of choices to accommodate your financial situation."

The women picked up the brochures and thumbed through them. Richard stared down at the one in front of him.

"Do you want to look at the calendar and select a time for the viewing and ceremony?" Farkas pulled a small tablet from somewhere and began tapping the screen. "Do you have a date in mind?"

All eyes turned to Richard. He sat for a minute before he realized he was the center of attention.

"Murder case," he said. "I don't know when she'll be released."

"Oh my," Farkas seemed shaken. "I'm so sorry. Of course, we can leave the date as pending."

"Have you ever had to deal with a murder case before?" Ashlyn asked.

"Unfortunately," Frakas held his hands open and nodded. "Far too often, I'm afraid."

"How long does it usually take?" she asked. "You know, before you can have the funeral?"

Farkas grimaced. "It depends. Open and shut case and we could have her in two or three days. If the investigation drags on," he shrugged. "Could be a while."

Richard threw his head back and squeezed his eyes shut. "This is never going to end." He stood and moved into the showroom amongst the coffins.

Ashlyn started to stand but Wendy's hand on her shoulder stopped her. Wendy said, "I've got him. You deal with . . ." She gestured at Farkas and followed Richard.

Ashlyn turned to the large man who looked to be sitting at the kid's table during holiday dinner and shrugged before leaning back in her seat and crossing her arms.

Wendy caught up to Richard and put a hand on his arm just as she had done to Ashlyn. "I know this is hard. I can't imagine having to pick out Brent's coffin."

"Pick out a coffin." His voice was flat as he stared at the one directly in front of him. "Burial or cremation? Should I be picking out an urn? Should we hold the funeral on a Tuesday or a Thursday? Do we hold the services here or at a church? Should I get a single plot or a family? What about a crypt? I don't know what Stephanie would want."

"Then go with what you want, Richard." Wendy pleaded with him. "What do you want?"

"I want my wife to not be dead!" He shouted and stormed out.

23

An officer led Brent Meadows through the department and ultimately into an interrogation room. He sat in the chair the uniformed policeman pointed to and looked around the small room. There were three chairs and a small table. There was no mirror on the wall as he expected from watching a million cop shows and movies. But there was a camera mounted in one corner of the room just below the ceiling. He found he couldn't look away from it.

He shifted uncomfortably in the chair several times while he waited for what seemed like hours though in reality was only about thirty minutes. The door opened and a man in a suit stepped in, made sure the door was closed, repositioned one of the remaining two chairs, and sat, squarely facing Brent.

"I'm Detective Jack Mallory." He held out a hand. Brent took it and they shook. "Sorry to keep you waiting. Thanks for coming in on such short notice."

"It didn't sound like I had a choice." Brent kept his emotions in check but wanted his point known.

"Sure you had a choice," Jack smiled. "We would have been glad to pick you up."

"Not really a choice."

"Listen," Jack leaned back, in a more casual position. "Let's not get into a huffing match. I needed to talk to you and you were being a bit hard to find. But you're here now. And I'm sure you want to help us in the investigation of Stephanie Ellison's murder since you and she were . . . What were the two of you again?"

"Friends."

"And coworkers." Jack pulled his notebook out. "You and Stephanie both work for Havencroft Financial Group."

"That's correct." Brent inhaled sharply.

"Anything romantic between you?" Jack asked. "When you met?"

"No." Brent seemed offended. "I was with Wendy."

"Come on." Jack pretended to look through his notes. "You wouldn't be the first man to stray. A pretty new girl at work?"

"Never happened," Brent insisted. "And that's not how we met."

"You were friends before you became coworkers?"

"She and Wendy were roommates in college," Brent explained. "There was no way I was going to mess up what we had by trying to get with Stephanie. In fact, we introduced her to Richard, my best friend."

"Your best friend?" Jack wrote in his notebook. "The victim's husband? Richard Ellison?"

"That's right." Brent nodded. "Richard and I, we go way back. And they were best man and maid of honor at our wedding."

"And you're his alibi." It was not a question.

"That's right." Brent sat forward a little. "I was at his place watching a game we had recorded."

"Do you do that often?" Jack asked.

"As often as we can," Brent replied.

"How often?" Jack scribbled in his pad.

"I dunno," Brent shrugged. "Two, three times a month."

"On this particular night, you did," Jack wrote while he talked. "Was it planned or spur of the moment?"

"Stephanie had to work late," Brent explained. "We took advantage."

"But you work in the same office." Jack tapped the table. "You had to know she left early that day."

"Left early? Jack told me she was working late."

"That's what he told us," Jack said. "You didn't know?"

"I had a meeting with a client." Brent wagged a finger. "I left before she did."

"You left before her?" Jack thought aloud. "So you don't know why she lied?"

"Lied?" Brent defended. "That's a little strong."

"She told her husband she was working late." Jack challenged. "Then told her employer she had to go home early. She did neither. Any idea where she might have gone?"

"Me?" Brent a hand on his chest. "How would I know?"

"You were friends. Colleagues." Jack sat back. "She didn't say anything to you?"

"We work for the same company, sure," Brent explained. "But not in the same department. And she was friends with Wendy, my wife. I was friends with her husband, Richard. We had almost no interaction without our spouses around."

"But didn't you . . ." Jack thumbed through his notepad. "Here it is. You introduced Richard to Stephanie. But you're saying you didn't really know her? What made you think she'd be a good match for your friend?"

"I didn't say I didn't know her," Brent argued. "I said we didn't have a lot of contact at work. I introduced her to Richard because she seemed nice. And she was good-looking. I thought he'd like her and he did."

"Do you think Richard could have hurt her?" the detective asked.

"No."

"You don't think he killed her?"

"I know he didn't." Brent was adamant.

"Because you're his alibi."

"That's right."

"Oh, yeah." Jack pointed his pen at the man. "Kind of late to be watching a game wasn't it?"

"Richard records them all." Brent shrugged. "We watch when we can."

"I understand that. I really do." It was Jack's turn to place a hand on his chest. "I love a good game. My problem is, you both had to work the next morning. If you left at midnight, drove home, and got ready for bed. What? Twelve-thirty? What time do you have to be up to get to work by eight?"

Brent looked at him.

"No." Jack shook his head. "I'm really asking. What time?"

"Seven."

"Seven?" Jack was shocked. "That's cutting it pretty close."

"I do fine," Brent said.

"You do fine on six hours of sleep?"

"Not every night," Brent admitted. "But sometimes it works out that way."

"Okay." Jack nodded. "I can see that. Get in a game. Deal with a short night and all."

"Right."

"What about Mrs. Ellison?"

"What about her?" Brent sighed.

"You were there until midnight," Jack repeated. "You and Richard are watching the game. Even working late, midnight seems excessive. Neither of you questioned why she wasn't home yet?"

"I didn't really think about it, honestly." Brent sat up a bit straighter. "She wasn't my wife."

"And Richard never voiced a concern?"

"I'm sure he did," Brent said. "But I can get pretty tunnel-visioned watching a game. He may have said something and I just didn't hear him."

"Your best friend may have said he was worried about his wife and you didn't hear it?"

"Maybe."

"You don't think he would have repeated it? Gotten your attention?"

"I don't know?" Brent huffed. "I'm just telling you what I know."

"But you don't know if the man next to you watching the game was concerned about his wife who wasn't home at midnight?"

"Of course he was concerned," Brent snapped. "I just don't know if he mentioned it to me."

"How was their relationship?" Jack lowered his voice to calm things down. "Richard and Stephanie? How were they?"

"They were perfect." Brent seemed to go someplace else. "The perfect couple."

"And you and your wife?"

"What? Me and Wendy?" Brent came back from where he went. "What does that have to do with anything?"

"Sounds like Richard and Stephanie had something special," Jack pointed out. "Do you and Wendy have that?"

"Sure, we have something special," Brent crossed his arms. "Not the same as them, but just as good."

"So no jealousy?"

"Me jealous of Richard?" Brent laughed. "God no."

"What about Wendy?"

"Wendy?" Brent frowned. "What about Wendy? Why do you keep mentioning her?"

"You and Richard were together," Jack said. "That left Wendy home alone. Maybe she was jealous of what they had. Maybe she met with Stephanie, got into an argument, killed her. Home and in bed before you get there."

"No." Brent shook his head. "Wendy isn't like that. She loved Stephanie. She wasn't jealous. Didn't have any reason to be. She had me. So, you just stop that right now."

"Mr. Meadows," Jack sat forward. "Right now I have two options. Either Stephanie was out there alone at night for no reason and was killed by a random stranger or she went there to meet someone she trusted, or at least knew, and they killed her. So, no. I won't stop. Not until I figure out who the killer is."

"Well," Brent inhaled sharply. "It wasn't Wendy. Don't waste your time looking at her."

"Who should we look at?"

"What? How should I know?"

"You're telling me who not to look at." Jack positioned his pen over his notepad. "So, tell me who I should be looking at? Who had it in for Mrs. Ellison? Give me names."

"I don't have names," Brent said. "I told you. We didn't have much contact at work. And outside work was me and Wendy with Richard and Stephanie. I hung with Richard. Wendy with Steph."

"And Richard never shared anything?"

"No." Brent tightened his arms around his chest. "Besides, Richard would have told you about anyone he might have told me about."

"No one comes to mind?"

"There's that old coot next door," Brent snapped a finger. "Don't know his name. But that guy's nuts."

"What about Camden?" Jack asked.

"Who is Camden?" Brent wrinkled his brow.

"The man Stephanie was meeting every Thursday." Jack checked his notes. "You don't know him?"

"Never heard of him," Brent said. "Who is he?"

Jack sat silently for a moment. "Okay. We're done for now. Don't leave town. Be available when we need you again. And if you think of anything, you call me."

Jack showed him out.

24

Finding Andy Green proved to be a much greater challenge than Shaun thought it would be. When Jack asked him to locate and question the man who had been leaving Stephanie dozens of unanswered messages, the young detective thought he would be on his way in a matter of minutes. But that was nowhere near the case.

First was the challenge of what his first name actually was. Andy could be short for Andrew, but also Anderson. In addition, it may not be short for anything. Andy could be the man's legal name. While searching for the three names in connection to Green or Greene, more than sixty possibilities popped up.

With a heavy sigh, Shaun started the daunting task of working through the list to single out the man he needed to question. He was encouraged when two of the first few he checked were easily eliminated. The two men were unable to have made the calls. One was in an assisted living facility, unable to make calls without help. The other was a current resident of the state prison. From there, things went downhill in a hurry.

Thinking a man trying to reach Stephanie would try every avenue, Shaun cross-referenced the list of possible matches with the numbers in her phone records. It quickly became evident that this person must not have had her cell phone number.

The fact that none of the messages had a return phone number suggested that Stephanie knew the man, or at least knew how to reach him. Shaun wondered if it wasn't an individual he was looking for, but rather a business; a salesman trying to sell her something she looked at once six months ago. The thought of that weighed heavily on the detective.

With another heavy sigh, Shaun began cold calling the numbers associated with the many names on the list. It was tedious and time-consuming. The majority did not even answer, forcing Shaun to make a second list to try again later or to physically visit the address.

A few answered but, when asked if they knew a Stephanie Ellison, were quick to proclaim he had called a wrong number and hung up. One simply hung up without a word. One offered to help look for her; Shaun wasn't sure how the man was going to do that. One invited the detective to dinner because he had a nice voice and the man had a niece who was single.

With more than twenty names left on the list. Shaun dialed the next number and listened to it ring while his mind wandered to what he was going to do for food. He could always stop by Jacques' Bistro. Maybe Liza remembered something else. He wondered if he could afford it.

"Hello?" A woman answered the phone.

"Hello?" Shaun was caught unprepared.

"Who is this?" the woman asked.

"So sorry to bother you." Shaun sat up and searched for the pen he had been using all morning but suddenly couldn't find. "I'm looking for an Andy Green."

"He isn't here," the woman responded. "Can I take a message?"

"Actually, you might be able to help me," Shaun said. "Have you ever heard of a Stephanie Ellison?"

"Stephanie Ellison?" The woman tried the name. "I don't think so."

"Okay," Shaun sighed. "Can you have Mr. Green call me at . . ."

"Wait," the woman interrupted. "Do you mean Stephanie Rollins? I think her name may be Ellison now."

"Rollins?" Shaun realized the name sounded familiar. He shuffled sticky notes until he found the one he was looking for, right next to his elusive pen. "That's her maiden name. Yes. So, you know her?"

"We went to high school together," the woman said. "But why are you trying to reach her through my husband? He hasn't seen her for years."

"Could you have your husband call Detective Shaun Travis?" Shaun gave her the number.

"Detective?" The woman was flummoxed. "What is this about?"

"Just have him call." Shaun hung up and added the information for that Andy Green to the case file.

He was finishing up and felt someone watching him. Raising his eyes from his desk, he saw Jack standing in front of him.

"You had anything to eat?" Jack asked.

"I was just thinking about it," Shaun admitted.

"Let's go." Jack waved an arm toward the elevators. "I'll treat."

"Well, I can't turn that down." Shaun picked up his desk phone and forwarded his calls to his cell. That done, he jogged to catch up to Jack who was holding the elevator for him.

Shaun stepped inside and the senior detective let the doors close. In one hand Jack clutched a manila folder, thick with papers.

"Working lunch?" Shaun pressed the button for the garage.

"Is there any other kind?" Jack smiled. "I thought we could compare notes while we eat."

Jack drove, taking them to a diner a couple of miles from the department. They chose a corner booth and sat across from one another. A waitress appeared and dropped menus in front of them, quickly taking their drink orders before moving on.

Jack spread some photos over the table. A woman passing by the table on her way to the restroom gave him a horrified look. He gave her an insincere smile.

"This bench isn't somewhere you go to meet someone casually." Jack put a photo of the crime scene in front of Shaun. "This is a place you meet someone when you don't want any chance of being seen."

"You don't think she was walking?"

"At that hour?" Jack pulled a picture of the victim and set it on top of the other. The woman, returning from the restroom, had her hand raised to block her eyes as she rushed by. "Look how she was dressed. She wasn't exercising."

"Okay. I'll agree to that." Shaun studied the image. "So who was she meeting?"

"She was at the bistro with a married man, maybe Richard, maybe not." Jack pointed at a headshot of the husband. "If it was Richard, he lied about his alibi and his friend lied for him. If it wasn't, we need to figure out who he was. He may be the one that took her to the park."

"Maybe the husband caught her out with this other man," Shaun suggested. "Took her to walk and talk it out. Things escalated and she ended up dead."

"Which would bring us back to Richard and his friend lying about his alibi." Jack let his mind wrap itself around Shaun's idea. "What bothers me is that even if they weren't lying, Richard made no attempt to locate his wife even after she didn't return home by midnight."

"That doesn't sound like a close couple to me," Shaun noted.

"That's right." Jack planted a finger on the table. "Everyone says these two were the perfect couple, but his actions suggest otherwise. It doesn't add up. One of Stephanie's coworkers, Chad Booker, said he delivered something to her at home and Richard was rude. Maybe he has a dark side, a temper."

The waitress stepped up to the table with their drinks. Her eyes were transfixed on the photos trying to find a place on the table to put the glasses. Jack cleared a space. Shaun pulled his menu across to cover some of the more harsh images.

"Ready to order?" The words caught in her throat.

"I'll take a cheeseburger and fries," Jack muttered. "Medium."

"Same." Shaun looked up at the woman who nodded and moved away.

"I don't think Richard was home." Jack took a drink.

"The man at the restaurant called her Steph."

"The nickname only her family and friends used." Jack followed Shaun's train of thought. "I think it was Richard."

"So he's our main suspect?" Shaun asked.

"He's at the top," Jack confirmed. "Despite his alibi. But let's run through the other possibilities. Don't want to be accused of only focusing on one suspect."

"Who else do we have?"

"There's Benjamin Johnson."

"Isn't he the neighbor?" Shaun asked.

"Yeah." Jack thumbed through his notes. "He and the victim had an ongoing disagreement about their property line. He was definitely not upset to hear she had died. We should look into whether he left his home that night."

"She told Richard there was a problem at work, didn't she?" Shaun asked.

"That's what he said."

"We should look into that," Shaun suggested. "Maybe she discovered someone at the firm was doing something shady. She could have been killed for that."

"I think if that were the case, she would have been shot," Jack grimaced. "Not beaten."

"Sure, if money was being laundered for a drug cartel and they found out she was going to report it, they would shoot her and be done with it." Shaun agreed. "But what if Stephanie confided in someone? She found evidence of whatever was going on and she decided to talk to someone she thought she could trust. Only they were the guilty party and killed her in a panic?"

"That would fit the narrative." Jack wrote in his notebook. "Can you arrange a warrant and get a forensic accountant to look at Havencroft Financial's books?"

"Sure thing." Shaun took out his phone and typed a note to himself.

"Next we have Paul McIntosh." Jack tapped his notepad. "He is one of the accountants that worked for the victim. He may have been resentful of the relationship Stephanie had with Lacey Novak. Doesn't have an alibi. He seemed nervous during the interview, maybe worried he was caught. But after, he seemed more emboldened. Like he felt he had gotten away with it since I hadn't slapped cuffs on him."

Shaun typed the man's name into his notes. "Paul McIntosh. I'll look into him."

"Nettie Huber didn't like Stephanie." Jack moved on. "Wanted her job. Always at odds with her, according to their coworkers, and her own admission. Her alibi is her cats, so none."

"She wanted Stephanie's job." Shaun picked up on the obvious. "That gives her motive."

"Yes and no." Jack checked his notes. "She says they would never give her the promotion. If she truly believes that, she wouldn't have motive."

"She could be saying that to make it look like she didn't have motive." Shaun offered.

"After talking to her," Jack shook his head. "I think she's probably right."

"That bad?"

Jack nodded. "But I'll ask who is in line to take Stephanie's place."

"Whether it's Nettie Huber or someone else," Shaun said, "they are going to be a top suspect."

"Yep," Jack agreed. "Then there's the couple, Chad Booker and Kyra Strickland. He's another accountant. She's the company receptionist. Breaking the rules by dating coworkers."

"How do they enforce that?" Shaun raised an eyebrow.

"Apparently they encourage one or both to resign," Jack said. "If Stephanie found out and tried to settle the matter quietly, they may have taken the opportunity to silence her. Money is always a motivator in these situations."

"Kill your boss to keep your job?" Shaun tossed the idea around. "That's a new one."

"Not really." Jack took a drink. "About four or five years ago, a woman was fired. She killed her boss that night, then reported to work the next day like nothing happened. Problem was, everyone in the office knew she was fired."

"I take it that didn't go well for her."

"If I recall," Jack tried to think back. "She got twenty to life."

"Do they have alibis?" Shaun asked. "The couple?"

"Each other." Jack flipped to that part of his notes just to be sure.

"So if you suspect they acted together," Shaun said, "they don't have one."

"Right," Jack agreed.

The waitress came by with refills and promised their food would arrive shortly. The two men watched her make her way through the dining area.

"That brings us to Lacey Novak." Jack turned back to Shaun. "The woman that everyone at Havencroft named as Stephanie's closest friend."

"Does she have a motive?"

"Not one I'm aware of, but you never know," Jack answered. "She seemed to take the news of Stephanie's death worse than anyone else. Or she could be a good actor. She claims that she is fond of Richard, but when I hinted that he may have killed her, she turned on him rather quickly."

"Alibi?"

"Hallmark movies," Jack read. "At home, alone."

Shaun laughed. "So, no."

"Another one with no alibi is Wendy Meadows." Jack stretched his back. "She was supposedly at home asleep while her husband was at Richard's place watching sports. No motive that I've found. Could have been jealousy or something. I haven't questioned her yet."

"This list is getting pretty long," Shaun observed.

"And besides the Meadows," Jack pointed out, "we've only looked at her work."

"Anyone else?"

"There's someone named Camden that has been on her calendar every Thursday afternoon for the past two months or more." Jack closed his notepad. "The receptionist said she left work at that time each week, so it was an out-of-office meeting. We need to track him down and see what the story is there."

The waitress delivered their meals as promised, asking if they needed anything more. They both shook their heads. She smiled, glancing down at the photos before stepping away.

"Did you find Andy Green?"

"I did," Shaun confirmed. "Had to leave a message for him to call me. But according to his wife, yes, he's married, and she says the three of them went to high school together."

"Old flame rekindled?" Jack lifted the bun on his burger to examine the toppings. Satisfied he smashed it back down.

"Could be." Shaun raised his burger. "Hopefully I'll hear from him and we can find out."

They fell into silence as they ate.

25

Leaving the funeral home, Richard took the highway north. He drove straight out of town, contemplating continuing out of state and even out of the country. With Stephanie gone, there was nothing to bind him. But, he didn't have his passport, so the latter wasn't really an option. And there were too many things to deal with to run away. Not to mention, disappearing would all but guarantee becoming suspect number one.

He eventually turned around in a small town he had never paid any attention to before. It was the kind of place Stephanie would have enjoyed going to, just to look around. A place where you would find small shops selling things you didn't know people sold; things made by hand with pride and care.

More than an hour had passed since leaving the funeral home when Richard suddenly remembered he had driven Wendy and Ashlyn there. He had left them. He pulled out his phone, selected the name he was looking for, and called. It was answered on the first ring.

"Jesus, are you okay?" Ashlyn asked.

"I left you there." He said it like she might not be aware.

"You did," his sister-in-law said. "But don't worry. It isn't the first time a guy left me high and dry. I know how to get myself home."

"I'm so sorry." Richard's voice cracked.

"Like I said, I'm fine," Ashlyn assured him. "I'm more concerned with you. I've never seen you like that."

"I've never been like that," Richard said. "But you got home okay?"

"Wendy and I shared a ride," Ashlyn explained. "We both made it home safe and sound."

"Okay." Richard nodded to his phone. "I'm glad. Listen, I'll call you again. Right now I have to get my head straight."

"I understand." Ashlyn's voice softened. "Richard. Take care of yourself."

Richard disconnected without saying more. Scrolling to Wendy's name next, he stopped himself, deciding to be more direct with her. Pulling hard on the steering wheel, he changed course for the Meadows' house, expecting to arrive there in about fifteen minutes.

Although Ashlyn was family, Richard had known Wendy since she started dating Brent during their freshman year of college. He owed her more than an apology over the phone.

Traffic was heavier than usual and Richard found himself behind a slow driver who he yelled at through the windshield. The pointless ranting released some of his stress. But he was more than happy to finally reach Brent's neighborhood. When he turned onto the Meadows' street, he could see his long-time friend pulling into his driveway from the opposite direction. Parking on the street, he gave Brent a quick wave before joining him in the yard.

"Richard," Brent greeted him with an arm across the shoulders. "How are you holding up?"

"Wendy didn't tell you?"

"I'm just getting home from my interrogation." Brent started for the door, guiding Richard along. "She hasn't told me anything."

"That was a long time." Richard considered how long ago they had left. "Did it go okay?"

"It was fine." He retrieved his keys from his pocket, dropped them, scooped them up, and unlocked the front door. "What was Wendy supposed to have told me?"

"I had a meltdown at the funeral home." Richard lowered his head.

"Right," Brent grinned. "How bad was it?"

"Pretty bad."

"It wasn't that bad." Wendy was standing a few feet from the door. She gave Brent a welcome home kiss.

"I left you there." Richard reminded her.

"I know." Wendy stepped forward and hugged him. "But Ashlyn and I managed to get home just fine."

"You left them there?" Brent tilted his head. "I don't understand."

"I . . ."

"He got upset." Wendy interrupted. "Needed some space. So he left. Ashlyn and I called a car service and came home."

"I told you it was bad."

"Aside from the yelling and the door slamming, everything was fine." Wendy smiled. "And the ogre said to call him when you're ready to reschedule."

"The ogre?" Brent turned to his wife.

"He was huge." Wendy looked to Richard. "Wasn't he huge?"

"He was very large." Richard agreed.

"Sorry I missed that," Brent smiled. "Not every day you get to see an ogre."

They moved deeper into the house to the living room and sat.

"Where have you been?" Wendy asked her husband.

"Police interrogation," Brent frowned. "You know that."

"For that long?"

"Well, I had to pull off the road to take a client call after," Brent said. "Not sure how long that took."

"Wendy?" Richard shifted uncomfortably in his seat. "Steph didn't tell you why she was leaving work early did she?"

"No, Richard," Wendy assured her. "She didn't. I would have told you if she had."

"I just," Richard lowered his eyes. "I just don't understand why she lied to me."

"Don't beat yourself up over this," Brent said. "It doesn't matter anymore. I'm sure she would have told you when she got home. Maybe she was going to surprise you."

"It's just another secret," Richard pursed his lips.

"Stop it." Wendy snapped. "She wasn't keeping things from you."

"She was." Richard shot back. "She lied about having to work late. How many times has she done that?"

"Maybe she didn't want to worry you," Wendy suggested. "Maybe the reason she left is the same reason she was killed."

"You think she knew she was in danger?"

"I don't know." Wendy shrugged.

"No," Brent assured him. "I don't think she knew."

"How can you be sure?" Richard asked.

"Because," Wendy responded. "If she knew she was in danger, she would have told us, and gone to the police. She didn't do either."

"The only other option is that she was into something shady," Brent added. "And we know she wasn't the type to do that kind of thing."

"I'm not sure what I know anymore." Richard ran his hand across his face.

They sat in awkward silence for a few minutes before Richard spoke again.

"I was convinced the police couldn't find a reason for me to want to kill Stephanie." He stared at the floor. "Then I was reminded that we took out life insurance policies on ourselves a few years back."

"A lot of people have insurance policies," Wendy said. "It's not a big deal."

"It's a motive," Richard countered. "Money is a big motive for killing your spouse. At least that's why they tell me."

"How much?" Brent asked.

"How much what?"

"The insurance policy," Brent said. "How much is it?"

"What does that matter?"

"Brent," Wendy scolded. "Why would you ask that?"

"I'm just curious." Brent raised his hands defensively.

"A million." Richard sighed.

"Damn," Brent drew the word out. "You could pay off your mortgage, and any other debt you have with that kind of money."

"Yet, I'm going to use it to pay for a funeral." Richard frowned. "Stephanie's dead, Brent. I didn't win the lottery. She's dead."

"I know." The hands raised again. "I'm sorry. I just. I'm not thinking straight. I do think when this is all over you should use some to get away for a while."

"Brent!" Wendy snapped.

"You know," Richard stood. "I think I'm going to go."

"What did I say?" Brent came out of his chair. "Richard?"

Wendy rose and followed after him, but he was out the door before she could catch him. She turned back to her husband with a scowl.

"What?" Brent asked. "What's wrong with him getting away? It's a good idea."

"You're still talking like the money is a reward," she explained. "If something happened to me, are you just going to think about going on vacation?"

Brent stared at her. "Nothing is going to happen to you."

"A week ago, we would have said the same thing about Stephanie." She walked past him toward their bedroom.

Brent watched her go. She went inside and slammed the door behind her. When he heard the lock click, he dropped back into his chair.

26

The two detectives finished their lunch and talked more about the case until they finally settled their check. Jack drove them back to the department, parking in the same space he had that morning.

For the ride up the elevator, they were joined by a young uniformed officer who stood stiffly the entire way.

Jack nudged Shaun's arm and gestured his chin toward the third man. "Remind you of anyone?"

"Pardon me?" The officer turned.

"Talking to my partner," Jack said.

The officer turned back to the door.

"Are you talking about me?" Shaun asked.

"I was," Jack confirmed.

"I was never like that." Shaun purposely relaxed his stance.

"You were exactly like that." Jack smiled. "Still are, sometimes."

"Are you referring to me?" The uniform turned again.

"You okay, officer?" Jack scowled. "You seem a little paranoid."

"Don't mind him," Shaun said. "He can be an ass sometimes."

"I wasn't being an ass," Jack defended. "He's the one who butted into our conversation."

"So I'm the ass?"

"Check yourself, officer." Jack snapped. "I outrank you."

The officer looked Jack in the eyes for a moment. "Yes, sir."

"You're still being an ass," Shaun said.

"You should be glad it's him and not you." Jack grinned and patted Shaun's shoulder. He turned to the officer. "Relax. I'm just kidding."

The officer gave him a half nod then turned back to the doors as they approached his floor.

"Check into the neighbor." Jack turned his attention back to Shaun. "Find video around the neighborhood and the park. See if you can spot his car anywhere other than his home that night. And whatever you can get on Paul McIntosh."

"I can do that."

The elevator doors opened and the officer stepped off.

"Have a good day," Jack said as the doors closed again.

"Why do you do that?" Shaun asked.

"Because I can."

"You may need his help someday."

"I need yours now." Jack pressed the button for their floor again. "I also want you looking for the mysterious Camden. Talk to anyone who knew the victim. See if any of them know who he is. And check her credit card transactions for Thursday afternoons over the past month or so. Maybe that'll point us in the right direction."

"I'll work on it."

The elevator doors opened, and they stepped out and crossed the room. Jack's phone rang, and he slowed to answer as Shaun moved on toward his desk.

"Mallory."

"Detective?" The voice was unfamiliar to him. "This is Tony in the forensics lab."

"Tony," Jack repeated. "What can I do for you?"

"It's what I can do for you, detective," Tony said. "I had a notation to call you after we processed the victim's car in the Ellison case."

"What did you find?"

"We dusted for prints," Tony started. "We'll run them against the victim and see what's left. We will need to get the husband's prints to eliminate them as well."

"I'll work on that."

"There was nothing significant about the car itself." Tony continued. "The victim's purse was on the passenger side floorboard. It contained her identification, credit cards, cash, and all the usual contents. Nothing out of the ordinary. Nothing appeared to be missing."

"Doesn't tell us much does it?"

"Not much." Tony agreed. "But we also found a satchel. There was a charging cable for a laptop but no laptop. Several notebooks and several dozen pens."

"We suspected there wouldn't be a laptop," Jack said. "Any indication if this was a personal or business computer?"

"The notebooks seem to cover both possibilities," Tony said. "So no way to know."

"Okay." Jack was suddenly impatient. "Anything else?"

"The trunk had a bag from an Alexandria's Boutique," Tony answered quickly. "There were some tags in the bottom of the bag, but the blouse in the bag wasn't new."

"I think Shaun is looking into that." Jack spoke more to himself than to the tech. "I'll get you those prints as soon as I can."

Jack disconnected the call before anything more could be said. He dropped the phone into his pocket and started for his desk when he saw Chief Hutchins standing in the doorway of her office glaring at him. He slowed again and turned to look at her. With a quick nod toward the interior of her office, she disappeared inside.

Jack gave a quick glance over his shoulder in case he wasn't the intended recipient of the invitation. No such luck. He changed course to her office, stopping in the doorway where she had been standing when he saw her.

"What's up?"

"Come in and shut the door." She pointed at one of the chairs across from her.

He didn't like the sound of her request. Usually, when he was told to close the door, it was something above his pay grade, or he was in trouble. He couldn't think of anything he might have done to warrant a conversation, but he hated being brought in on things he should not know and could do nothing about. It usually just served to piss him off to no end.

He pulled the door shut and took a seat in the chair she had pointed at. "What's this about?"

"What did I tell you about Detective Travis?" She sat, elbows on the arms of her chair, hands clasped together in front of her.

This was about Shaun. Again he couldn't come up with anything. "That I could use him on this case."

"At his desk." Chief Hutchins clarified. "You could use him as long as he was at his desk. He hasn't been at his desk, detective."

"I took him to lunch." Jack shrugged. "The man can't eat?"

"You know as well as I do that he has been gone longer than a lunch break." The chief tapped her fingers together. "He was gone for more than an hour earlier in the day."

"Are you watching him?" Jack shifted in his seat. "No. Don't tell me. Yes, he was gone earlier. He was with me at the morgue. I thought he might want to get out for a bit. And I thought it would be good to have a different perspective on the autopsy. We weren't chasing suspects down the street."

"And that's it?" she challenged.

Jack knew Shaun had gone to Jacques' Bistro. "That's it."

"Keep it that way."

"I'll remind him." The detective sighed. "Anything else?"

"Are you making any headway?" She lowered her hands. "Do you have a suspect?"

"I have an abundance of suspects," Jack admitted. "Hope to narrow it down soon."

"No chance the husband did it?"

"There's always a chance," Jack said. "He has an alibi, but it's his best friend. They may have done it together."

"Are you looking into that possibility?"

"I'm looking at all possibilities until I have a definite reason not to."

"Good." The chief stood, her hands subconsciously brushing her pant legs straight. "Detective, I need you to close this without turning it into something huge."

"You're referring to the dog walking case." Jack rose to his feet. "I don't determine what a case becomes. I follow clues where they lead me. The case is what it is. If there's more to it, then it might become big. That said, I hope to close the case quickly."

"Do that." Sharon circled her desk. "Keep me in the loop. And leave Detective Travis at his desk."

"Will do." Jack retreated to his own desk.

Shaun was sitting at the desk next to Jack's. It belonged to a detective who had retired a few weeks before. He had been a good detective back in the day, about the time Jack joined the team. More recently he had been less detective and more chair warmer. There had been days when Jack would forget the man was even there.

"Saw you being summoned to the chief's office." Shaun waited until Jack was seated. "Everything okay?"

"You got me in trouble."

"Me?" Shaun tapped his chest. "What did I do?"

"You didn't stay at your desk." Jack rolled his eyes. "This is kindergarten. You have to ask permission to move."

"How am I supposed to help you without ever leaving the desk?"

"Just make yourself seen from time to time," Jack suggested. "If you go somewhere keep it short and make a point to pass her office before you leave, walking toward your desk, and again after you return."

"You sound like you've done this kind of thing before." Shaun smiled like he had just gotten some blackmail information.

"I was grounded a lot when I was a kid." Jack gave a tilt to his head. "I learned how to work the system."

"You're saying that being on desk duty is like being grounded?" Shaun asked.

"Exact same thing," Jack confirmed. He looked at the expression on Shaun's face. "What?"

"I'm trying to picture you as a trouble-making teen." Shaun grinned. "Not much of a stretch."

"You need to watch yourself," Jack grumbled. "Or I'll tell the chief I don't need you anymore."

27

Shaun sat at his desk with a large cup of coffee, pulling up traffic cameras from the possible routes from Stephanie's neighborhood to the park. The closest camera to the Ellison's home was two miles away at a busy intersection. He watched the video recording from just before sunset to midnight the day of the murder, fast forwarding to scan the images as quickly as he could. He was looking for any vehicle that matched Richard's truck or the neighbor's car. If he saw one, he slowed the image to compare.

He repeated the process for every camera in a five-block width for the entire distance. It was a grueling process, taking hours. He stood to walk around numerous times, refilling his coffee once. He made a point of passing the chief's office each time.

He was relieved when his cell phone rang. The number on the screen was unknown to him, but at least it was a break from staring at the monitor.

"Detective Travis," he answered.

"Detective Shaun Travis?" a woman's voice asked him.

"Yes, ma'am." Shaun tried to place the voice, wondering if he knew them. "How may I help you?"

"I, uh . . ." Her voice drifted off leaving only silence on the line.

"Are you okay?" Shaun sat up. "Are you in danger?"

"Oh. No. I'm fine," she stammered. "I'm sorry. I shouldn't have called."

"Wait," Shaun said. "Who is this? How did you get this number?"

"I'm sorry," she repeated. "I shouldn't bother you."

"You're not bothering me." A half-truth. "Who is this?"

"It's Liza Perry," she responded.

"Do I know you?"

"Oh. God." She panicked. "I'm sorry. I thought . . ."

"Wait. Liza?" Shaun said. "From Jacques'?"

There was silence on the phone and Shaun was convinced she had hung up until she said, "Yes."

"Did you remember something?"

"No," she said. "Nothing like that."

It was Shaun's turn to be silent.

"I'm sorry." She apologized for the fourth time. "I thought when we were talking earlier, I thought . . ." She sighed heavily. "Did I misread you? God, I'm so embarrassed."

"Don't be," Shaun assured her. "You didn't misread me."

"Really?"

"Really."

There was an awkward silence for a moment.

"I guess we should get some coffee sometime," Shaun suggested. "Or dinner?"

"Dinner would be good." Shaun smiled.

"It would be." Liza agreed.

The phone on Shaun's desk rang and the light indicating line one lit up. "Listen. I have to get this call. Can I call you back? We can work out when and where."

"Okay," she said. "I'm free tonight."

"Tonight then." Shaun glanced at the light on the phone. "I'll call."

He disconnected the call and lay his cell phone on the desk, reaching for the other. He lifted the receiver and pressed the line one button. "Detective Travis."

"Uh, detective?" A man's voice greeted his ears.

"Yes." Shaun shifted in his chair and rested his elbows on the desk. "Can I help you?"

"This is . . ." The man started but drifted.

"Sir?" Shaun tried to place the voice but couldn't. "Are you there? Do you need help?"

"Yes," he answered quickly. "I mean, no. I mean, I'm here and I'm okay. I just. I'm returning your call. I'm Andy Green."

"Mr. Green." Shaun pulled a notepad and pen to him. "Thank you for calling."

"I didn't think I had a choice." The man sounded distant and distracted. "My wife said this was about Stephanie. I know I've been persistent. I can't believe she called the cops. If she didn't want to talk to me, she could have just said so."

"Why have you been calling her so much?" Shaun asked.

"Really?" Andy's voice sounded stronger. "Didn't she tell you anything?"

"Let's say she didn't," Shaun said. "Why were you calling?"

"The reunion," Andy answered. "Why else?"

"Reunion?"

"Our fifteen-year class reunion." Andy sighed. "I was class president. She was vice. We're supposed to plan the reunion, just like we did five years ago. What is her problem? Everything was fine last time."

"Mr. Green, where were you two nights ago?"

"Two nights ago?" Andy sounded confused. "Why?"

"Just answer the question."

"I was in Chicago on business," he answered. "I got back this morning. What's this all about?"

Shaun wrote what he heard on the notepad, then marked through Andy Green's name. "You should probably plan your reunion alone. Mrs. Ellison has been killed."

"She what?" Andy was shocked. "She's dead?"

"Yes, sir." Shaun rubbed his hand across his eyes. "Sorry you had to learn this way."

"I was a suspect?"

"Your calls came across as a possible stalker," Shaun explained. "But now they make sense. I'll check your alibi, but assuming it pans out, you are in the clear. Thank you for calling."

Shaun hung up the phone and sat back. One less suspect. Which meant he had to get back to the video search. He squeezed his eyes closed, then opened them. Pressing the play button, followed by the fast-forward, Shaun concentrated on the images racing across his screen. It was a painstaking process made easier by knowing who he would be having dinner with.

28

Richard sat in his favorite chair on the back porch staring out into the trees behind his house. In one hand, he held a half-empty glass. In the other, he gripped the neck of a bottle of scotch he had picked up on the way home. It, too, was half empty. His thoughts were swimming in the fog the alcohol created in his mind. Just as he was convinced he had succeeded at what he was trying to do, his thoughts came together again. He brought his hands together and topped off the glass.

Brent had never been one for tact. As kids, his ability to say the absolute worst thing at exactly the best time was one of the things that bonded the two friends. In their teen years, the comments became more crude, the laughs that much stronger, their bond that much tighter. Sometime in their college years, it became less about the humor and more about expression, until it reached a point where Brent simply didn't seem to know how to say the right thing. He no longer had a filter. If it came to his mind, he said it.

With some notable exceptions, Richard had always appreciated his friend's candor. Today, however, gave him pause. For the first time, Richard wondered about his friend. The man was in sales. He must use a filter when he was with clients. Why couldn't he offer the same courtesy to Richard? And if he couldn't, why couldn't he just shut up?

He took a long drink of scotch and his head started to spin. It was a feeling he hated, yet he welcomed it. He took another drink to be sure he didn't lose it. In this state, he couldn't think. He couldn't dwell on his wife's death. He couldn't be angry with his friend for saying the wrong thing. He couldn't hate himself for not being there to save Stephanie.

Yet he did. Each of those things and more were still prominent in his thoughts. Even as the space around him spun like he was on a bad amusement park ride, he could not stop his thoughts from coming through. He wanted to scream but knew it would end with him throwing up the alcohol that he needed so desperately to do the job he intended.

Brent's comment came back to the front of Richard's thoughts, and he was suddenly struck by the fact that his friend had been correct. When this was over, he did need to get away. But not on a vacation. He needed a change. He needed to go somewhere he wasn't known, somewhere he wouldn't be reminded of the life he no longer had. He needed to start over.

His phone rang. Richard set his glass on the small table next to his chair, the bottle on the ground on the other side. He patted his pockets then looked around, trying to remember where he had left it. The ringing should guide him, but the fog in his brain prevented him from concentrating.

Richard pulled himself to his feet, but his head spun one way and the floor the other, forcing him to sit again. He noticed his phone then, setting on the table next to his glass. He stared at it, not remembering putting it there. Picking it up, he answered.

"...lo?" Richard's head pounded. His face felt numb. "Whozzzz thisss?"

"Richard?"

"Richard who?"

"Richard, are you okay?"

The woman's voice sounded familiar. But anyone who knew Richard would know that he wasn't okay. They would know that Stephanie was dead and that he was far from okay. He pulled the phone away from his ear and disconnected the call.

With a grin, he put the phone back down and picked up his scotch. As he sipped from the glass, the phone rang again. Moving the glass to his left hand he answered the call, inhaling deeply before saying, "What you want?"

"Richard Douglas Ellison," the woman said. "Don't you hang up on me again."

The fog cleared slightly. The voice. The tone. "Mom?"

"When your mother asks if you're okay," she said. "You don't hang up on her."

"I didn't know it was you." Richard sat up straight. "I'm just tired of people asking me how I am. Stephanie is dead. I'm not okay."

"I know." She sympathized. "But when you answered, it sounded like you were having trouble speaking. I thought there was something wrong with you."

"I'm drunk, mom," Richard said. "That's all."

She was silent a moment. "I'm flying in tomorrow morning."

"You don't have to do that."

"I've already got the ticket," she said. "I'll be there at ten. Can you get me? Or should I get a car?"

"I'll get you." Richard put his glass back on the table. "Text me the details. I don't trust me to write them down."

"Have you eaten?"

"No."

"Eat something," she ordered. "Then sober up and get some sleep."

"I will."

"You promise?"

"Sure, mom." Richard rubbed his eyes. "I promise."

"See you tomorrow," she said. "Love you."

"Love you, too, mom." Richard disconnected the call, put down his phone, and picked up his glass. He would sober up. Just not yet.

29

Jack stood on the front porch of a ranch-style home located near the park where Stephanie Ellison's body was found. It was owned by Ethan Bridges, the man who found her and called 911. He had been jogging when he passed the unconscious woman on the park path. He did not have a cell phone on him and walked home before calling it in. Officers were focused on the victim and never followed up with the witness.

Jack could have called and taken a statement over the phone but wanted to have a face-to-face with the man. Just because someone reports a crime, doesn't rule them out as being a suspect. Sometimes criminals report their crimes to explain why their DNA might be found there, or to throw suspicion away from them. Jack wanted to observe the witness's mannerisms when he answered his questions.

The detective pressed the doorbell, one of the types with a camera, and waited. It wasn't much of a wait. The door opened and a thirty-something man greeted him with a smile, which faded as soon as he made eye contact.

"You're not Jill." The man sidestepped and leaned to look around Jack and to the street. "Where's Jill?"

"Are you Ethan Bridges?" Jack made no attempt to move out of the way.

The man looked back at him. "Who's asking?"

"Detective Jack Mallory." He held up his badge. "I'm investigating the murder of Stephanie Ellison."

"Who . . . ?" The color drained from the man's face. "Oh. The woman from the park. I didn't know her name. She was dead? I thought she was just passed out drunk. You say she was murdered?"

"She was," Jack confirmed. "And you are Mr. Bridges?"

"Yes."

"And the victim?" Jack watched Ethan's face. "You didn't know her?"

"Never seen her before."

"Not even around the park?" Jack asked. "Maybe in passing?"

"I suppose it's possible." Ethan's face scrunched. "I see hundreds of people in passing every week. But I don't know them. And I wouldn't be able to identify them."

"Tell me how you came to discover her body." Jack put his badge away and pulled out his notepad.

"She was beside the trail." Ethan waved a hand like he was showing the detective. "You couldn't miss her."

"And why were you there?"

"Why was I there?" His hand went to his chest. "It's a walking trail. I was jogging."

"You were jogging?" Jack looked back through his notes. "It was three o'clock in the morning."

"It was." Ethan nodded.

"You always jog that early?"

"I do."

"Why?"

"I have to be at work at five," the man explained. "I jog, go home to shower, and change. Then I eat breakfast. That leaves me about thirty minutes to get to work."

"What is it you do?"

"I'm in radio."

"You have a morning show?"

"Do I sound like I'm on the radio?" Ethan chuckled. "No. I'm a producer."

Jack nodded. "So you were jogging by and saw the victim?"

"That's right."

"And then what?"

"What?" Ethan thought back. "I saw her lying there. I called out to see if she was okay. She moaned. I decided she was drunk and continued home where I called 9-1-1."

"You didn't stop to check on her?" Jack said.

"I just told you I called out to her."

"Did you touch her?" Jack asked. "Roll her? Check for a pulse?"

"No." Ethan looked disgusted. "I just told you she moaned. I didn't see the need to check for a pulse."

"Did you see anything around the body?" Jack asked. "A laptop perhaps?"

"Nothing like that," Ethan shook his head.

"Something else then?"

"No." Ethan shook his head. "I didn't see anything around her. But I wasn't looking either."

"What about on the trail?" Jack frowned. "Before coming across the body, did you see anyone else on the trail?"

"You think I may have seen the killer?"

"I don't know," Jack said. "Did you pass anyone on the trail?"

Ethan stood silently for a moment. "I don't think so. I honestly don't remember. Sorry I can't help."

A car door shut behind Jack, and he turned to see an attractive woman rounding her car. He turned back to Ethan who was looking past him to the woman.

"You did fine," Jack said. "You can't tell me what you don't know."

The woman ascended the steps behind him and Jack stepped to the side. She stepped up and gave Ethan a brief hug.

"Ethan." She half turned. "Who's your friend?"

"Not a friend," Ethan corrected. "He's a detective."

"A detective?" The woman turned to face Jack. She was similar in age to Ethan, but out of his league. "Are you in trouble, Ethan?"

"Do you have reason to think he might be?" Jack asked.

"Not that I can think of." She grinned. "Detective . . . ?"

"Mallory," he introduced himself. "Jack Mallory."

"Well, Detective Mallory, Jack Mallory," she locked her eyes on his. "What brings you here?"

"And you are?"

"Jill." She held out her hand. "Jill Donahue. Nice to meet you."

Jack shook her hand. "Who are you to Ethan?"

Jill turned to Ethan and smiled. "Ethan and I. Ethan and I have been friends since . . . How long has it been, Ethan?"

Ethan stammered. "Twenty-three years."

"That long?" She seemed surprised. She turned back to Jack. "Twenty-three years."

"And you would vouch for his character?"

She got a devious grin. "That depends on what this is about."

"Mr. Bridges discovered a body in the park." Jack put his notepad away.

"My God," she gasped. "Ethan? You didn't tell me about that?"

"I was going to tell you at dinner," Ethan shrugged.

"And you're a detective." She looked at Jack again. "And detectives don't investigate heart attacks."

"No, ma'am, we don't." Jack agreed. "This was a homicide."

"And you think Ethan was involved?" She stifled a laugh. "That's impossible."

"What do you mean impossible?" Ethan asked.

"I mean," she stopped laughing. "I mean, you're Ethan. You're too nice to hurt someone. You wouldn't kill anybody."

"Well, that's true." He blushed. "But I wouldn't say impossible."

Jack pulled out a business card and held it out. "If you remember anything, give me a call."

Ethan took the card. "I doubt I'll remember anything. But if I do, I'll let you know."

"I'll leave you to your dinner," Jack excused himself. "Ms. Donahue."

"Nice to meet you, detective." Jill smiled. "Other than the whole murder thing."

"And the thinking I'm a suspect," Ethan added.

"And that," Jill acknowledged. "Maybe next time will be more pleasant."

"Next time?" Ethan turned to her.

Jack, halfway down the steps, stopped. "You think there'll be a next time?"

"You know," Jill shrugged. "If there is a next time."

Jack smiled. "Until then. If there is a then."

A few seconds later he was driving into traffic.

"You like him," Ethan accused her.

"He's handsome," Jill said.

"It would never work."

"Because he's a detective?"

"Because of his name," Ethan declared.

"His name?"

"Seriously?" Ethan put his hands on his hips. "Jack and Jill? It would never work."

Jill laughed. "You may be right. Let's go eat."

30

Shaun pulled up to the curb in front of the Riverview Apartments. Ironically the building did not have a view of a river. Apparently, the original project was to be built at another location, but the land sale fell through. The owners already had signage and documents ordered with the intended name. Rather than losing the money, they went ahead with what they had. Besides, The No View At All Apartments didn't have the same ring to it.

Shaun stepped out of his car and straightened his jacket. Glancing up at the eight-story building, he entered the lobby and took the elevator to the fifth floor. Walking down the hall, he knocked gently on apartment 535. He stood awkwardly, shifting from side to side, trying to appear casual. When the door didn't open, he knocked again, more loudly.

"Just a minute," a voice called from within.

Shaun stepped back and waited again. The door opened and a short brunette girl, dressed in sweatpants and a clashing sweatshirt, stood in the doorway. "You must be the detective."

He missed a beat before responding. "Is Liza here?"

"She's getting ready," the girl moved out of the way. "Come on in."

Shaun thanked her and stepped into the sparsely furnished living room.

"I'm Gayle." She shut the door, crossed the room and fell onto the worn couch, pulled a blanket over her legs, and turned the volume up on the television. "You can have a seat. She might be a while."

"I'm okay." Shaun glanced at the screen and saw one of those shows where the girl has to choose between several suitors. He looked back to Gayle who was engrossed.

"Sorry, I'm running late," Liza said behind him.

Shaun spun. "That's okay. I just . . ."

He froze.

"What?" She looked down to see what was wrong.

"You're beautiful," Shaun said. The waitress he had met had transformed. Her hair was loose around her bare shoulders. She had changed from her slacks and dress shirt into a form-fitting black dress that took his breath away. "I mean. I knew you were pretty. But . . . wow."

She smiled shyly. "You think so?"

"Of course he does," Gayle said from the couch without looking away from her show. "I keep telling her she's gorgeous. Maybe she'll believe me now."

"Believe her," Shaun said. "You are stunning. Are you ready to go?"

"I am."

They moved to the door.

"Have fun!" Gayle called after them. "I won't wait up."

"Yes, you will," Liza pulled a light jacket out of the coat closet and Shaun helped her put it on.

"Yes. I will," Gayle confirmed. "But if he's a cop, who do I call if you don't come home?"

"I'll get her home safe," Shaun assured her.

"Wouldn't you say that even if you planned to kidnap her?" Gayle turned to him. "I mean, who says, I'm going to take her to a secluded cabin and kill her?"

"Gayle," Liza chastised. "He's not going to kill me. I apologize for her, detective."

"Call me Shaun," he said. "And don't worry. She's worried about you. That's a good thing."

"I'll be fine," Liza said to Gayle.

"Here." Shaun handed Gayle a card. "If you can't reach her, you can call me."

"What?" Gayle looked at the card. "So you can tell me she's in the restroom when she's actually in your trunk?"

"Something like that." Shaun smiled.

Gayle flicked the card with her finger. "Okay."

Liza's roommate turned back to her show and lost interest in the couple. The two of them slipped out of the apartment and took the elevator back to the lobby. When they reached Shaun's car, he opened the door for her, then rounded the vehicle to get in the driver's seat.

"So, where are we going?" Liza asked. "And please don't say Jacques'."

"I didn't think you'd want to go there." Shaun started the car. "I was thinking about The Red Brick."

"Nice." Liza approved.

They shared small talk on the way to the restaurant. Shaun tried to keep his eyes on the road but couldn't help stealing glances of his companion from time to time. Each time she gave him a smile that warmed him.

The Red Brick was an upscale pizzeria that was known for unique flavor combinations prepared in a red brick oven. The restaurant was moderately busy but not so much that there was a wait. The hostess greeted them and led them to a table in a quiet corner. She handed each of them a menu before retreating to the front desk.

Shaun gave the menu a quick once over. "Have you ever eaten here before?"

"No." Liza studied her menu. "What about you?"

"Me either." Shaun grinned. "I was going to ask for your recommendation. None of these are what you would call traditional pizzas."

"I'm not sure what some of these toppings are." Liza looked up. "Everything sounds so interesting. I can't decide."

"If you want we could each order one and share," Shaun suggested. "That way we get to try a couple of things."

"That would be nice. But we still have to decide."

The waitress stepped up to the table. "Hi, guys. Can I get your drink orders?"

"Water for me." Liza was quick to answer.

"Two waters." Shaun followed her lead.

"Okay." The waitress jotted on her order pad. "Have you had a chance to look over the menu? Or do you need more time?"

"What would you recommend?" Shaun asked.

"My favorite is the Thai Chili Chicken," she said. "But everything is good."

"Let's try that," Liza said to Shaun.

"Okay," Shaun nodded. "One of those. And a Spicy Reuben. If that's okay."

"Sounds good." Liza smiled.

The waitress wrote the orders down, took the menus, and spun away. "I'll be back with your waters."

Shaun watched her walk away, stopping at another table briefly before moving on. "Do you ever find yourself judging other waitresses based on your experience?"

"All the time," Liza admitted. "Of course, I understand what they are going through. So, I'm pretty forgiving in my judgment."

"I can imagine you have to deal with a lot of nonsense."

"It's amazing how rude some people can be," Liza confirmed. "But the nice ones outweigh the bad. I look forward to seeing most of my regulars."

"What's the worse customer you've ever dealt with?"

"That's easy." Liza leaned forward. "There was this one guy. He was relentless. Complained about the food, the atmosphere, me. But he was also handsy. Kept trying to touch me. My hands and arms at first. But then he started grabbing at my butt. I was furious."

"What'd you do?" Shaun was concerned.

"I went to the owner and told him what was going on," Liza said. "I'm lucky to have a boss who cares about his staff. He went out and spoke to the man. I didn't have any more trouble with him after that. Didn't get a tip, but at that point, I wasn't expecting one."

"Sorry you had to go through that," Shaun said.

"It's okay. It's all temporary anyway."

"You have other plans?"

"I'm taking classes," Liza explained. "Trying to finish my degree."

"What are you studying?"

"I'm working on my Bachelor of Science in Nursing," Liza answered.

"A nurse?"

"Yes."

"The heart of the medical industry," Shaun said. Liza tilted her head. "My mother is a nurse."

"She is?" Liza's eyes brightened. "I'd love to talk to her."

"Uh," Shaun stammered.

"Oh my gosh." Liza blushed. "Tell me I didn't just ask to meet your mother on our first date."

"You did." Shaun grimaced. "I think that's more of a second date conversation."

"Second?" Liza chuckled. "Are you sure?"

"Okay," he smiled. "Maybe third."

"What would she say if you brought a girl home to meet her after one date?"

"First of all, I don't live with my mother, so it wouldn't be bringing her home." Shaun clarified. "Second, if I was introducing you to her, she'd probably start planning a wedding."

"A wedding?"

"She really wants grandkids," Shaun explained. "But I would never tell her it was just a first date."

"How many weddings has she planned?"

"What?"

"You said, if you introduced me to her she'd plan a wedding," Liza reminded him. "Sounds like she plans a wedding for every girl you introduce her to. I was just wondering how many that was? You know, what's my competition?"

It was Shaun's turn to blush. "No competition. I haven't introduced her to anyone since high school. And she wasn't in the wedding planning stage at that point."

"Well that's good." Liza laughed. "Seriously, you haven't introduced a single date to your mom in all those years?"

"Not one."

"Why?" Liza asked. "Does she live in another state?"

"She and dad actually live about three miles from me," Shaun said. "We have dinner about once a week."

"You're a good son. Yet you don't introduce her to your girlfriends?"

"I haven't really dated," Shaun sighed. "And after I got shot . . ."

"You what?" Liza looked concerned.

"I was shot by a suspect," Shaun tightened his lips. "I'm still on restricted duty. Well, that's not true. I was released, but my captain wants me to ease back into the job."

"So your boss cares about you too?" Liza reached out and put her hand on his. "That's good."

The waitress appeared and set their waters down. "Food should be right out."

"So tell me." Liza waited for the waitress to leave. "Why did you decide to become a detective?"

"That's an interesting story," Shaun said. "I became a cop because I wanted to help people. I never even thought about being a detective. But then I helped a detective on a case. Working with him, learning from him, it changed everything. He made me want to be like him. Instead of helping people, it became about helping get justice for the victims."

"Sounds like he was quite an influence," Liza said.

"He was, or rather, he is," Shaun said. "He mentored me. We're partners now."

"He wasn't at the restaurant when you were there."

"No. He was following another lead." Shaun looked down at Liza's hand on his. "Technically, I'm supposed to stay at my desk."

"Shame on you," Liza teased.

"I'm glad I went." Shaun smiled and squeezed her hand gently.

"Me too."

The pizza came and they shared pizza and stories about their lives. The conversation was easy and relaxed, like old friends catching up after a long absence. There was a lot of laughter mixed in and the evening seemed to fly by.

The waitress stopped by. "Can I get you anything else? A to-go box?"

"Do you want a box?" Shaun asked Liza.

"I'm good."

"I'll take the check then," Shaun held out his hand.

She handed him the check and promised to return.

The expression on Liza's face became serious.

"What's wrong?"

"I just remembered something," she said.

"Did you leave the water on or something?"

"About your case."

Shaun shifted. "What about it?"

"I told you the woman paid for everything."

"Right."

"When I came to their table with the check, he insisted I give it to him," Liza recalled. "I remember because I was going to give it to him anyway because he was dressed in an expensive suit. But he snatched it right out of my hand. It wasn't until I returned for the payment that she handed me her card. He looked a little embarrassed, like he couldn't pay. So they couldn't have been married."

"Because if they were, it wouldn't matter which of them paid." Shaun finished her thought.

31

Detective Shaun Travis arrived at the department early the next morning only to find Jack already at his desk, his head bent over a steaming cup of coffee. The senior detective looked up as his protégé sat at the desk across from him.

"Morning boss," Shaun greeted.

"Shaun. You're early this morning." Jack looked at his watch. "And don't call me boss."

"So are you, sir."

"Jack or detective will do."

"Okay, Jack."

"You have anything new?"

"Andy Green called me back yesterday," Shaun reported.

"Andy Green?"

"The guy calling Stephanie at work all the time."

"Oh, okay," Jack remembered. "And?"

"They went to high school together," Shaun explained. "He was class president. She was V.P. Turns out he was trying to reach her so they could plan their fifteen-year reunion."

"Doesn't rule him out," Jack said.

"He was out of town at the time of the murder," Shaun said. "I already checked and confirmed. He's not the killer."

"Well, I spoke to Ethan Bridges, the guy who found her," Jack shared. "It doesn't look like he's good for it either. Won't rule him out yet, but he doesn't seem likely."

"I did learn one thing that might be helpful," Shaun said.

"What's that?"

"The waitress from the restaurant remembered that the man Stephanie was with insisted on taking the check. But when she came back to get payment, it was Stephanie who paid." Shaun repeated what Liza had said. "Said the guy seemed embarrassed."

"Embarrassed?"

"If it was her husband, he wouldn't have a reason to be embarrassed," Shaun said.

"So who was she with?"

"I'm going to dig into her other charges to see if I can figure that out."

"Good idea." Jack took a drink of his coffee. "The warrant came through. I'm going to go back to Havencroft with a forensic accountant. There's something off about that place."

"Sounds like we'll both be busy," Shaun said.

"Listen," Jack said. "Stay at your desk and keep your head down. You'll be back on the streets before you know it."

"I know." Shaun sighed. "I'm ready now, though."

"I know you are," Jack nodded. "We just have to convince Chief Hutchins."

"Seems impossible," Shaun grumbled.

"It'll happen," Jack assured him. "She can't keep you on the desk forever."

Shaun rolled his eyes and turned to his computer. He found the email he had accidentally deleted at the restaurant. He was glad he was able to recover it. It was the email that contained the bank records for Stephanie Ellison. After receiving the information, he had gone straight to the restaurant and had not followed up with anything else.

He opened the document to examine her purchases again. The last charge, as he knew, had been Jacques' for the dinner she had with her mystery date. Shaun scrolled down until he found the first purchase of the day, just after she left work for the day. That charge had been at a convenience store not far from Havencroft Financial Group.

"She must have driven straight there," Shaun told Jack. "The time stamp on the charge was made shortly after she left the office."

"Out of gas or planning for a long drive," Jack pondered. "Nothing unusual there."

Shaun brought up a map and marked the Havencroft building and then the gas station's locations.

"The next charge was at Alexandria's Boutique." Shaun read the information from the list.

"That's the name on the bag we found in her car." Jack sat up.

"Which we already know is a women's clothing store." Shaun nodded.

"When did that one take place?"

"Nearly an hour after the convenience store," Shaun answered.

"We know the blouse in the bag was worn," Jack said. "It had a stain on it."

There had been tags from a new top in the bag with the soiled blouse. It made sense that she wouldn't want to run around with a dirty top.

"So she stopped for a replacement," Shaun said. "Nothing unusual about that."

"She took nearly an hour looking for a new top," Jack thought aloud. "Why not drive home and change? She had plenty of time."

"Didn't want to run into her husband," Shaun suggested. "She told him she had to work late. Why worry about a stained top if she's working after hours."

"Maybe she just wanted to look good for her date," Jack added.

Shaun marked the address of the boutique on the map and turned back to the phone records.

"Next charge was to a Briana's," Shaun read from the list.

"Which is?"

"Just a second." Shaun opened a new window and did a quick search of the name. Of the five top results, two were from other cities. Only one of the remaining three was within a five-mile radius of Alexandria's. Shaun clicked on the link. "It's a hair salon. She had her hair done."

"New top. New hair." Jack contemplated. "It sounds more and more like she was going on a date."

"Which would explain why the man was embarrassed at her having to pay." Shaun nodded. "Not the best first impression."

"Gives him motive," Jack said. "If she said something that embarrassed him further. Or simply set him off."

"Gives the husband motive too," Shaun reminded. "If he found out his wife was cheating on him."

"Follow up with the clothing store and the salon," Jack said. "Maybe they'll remember her. She could have confided in someone what she was doing that night." Jack looked at his watch. "I have to get to Havencroft. It's almost time to issue that warrant."

32

Jack pulled into the parking lot of Havencroft Financial Group and saw the forensic accountant standing beside his car. He had worked with the man once before, but he was at a loss as to what his name was. Trying several names out loud as he parked, none of them sounded right. He stepped out of his car and held out a hand to the man.

"Detective." The man shook his hand with a firm pumping action. "It's been a while."

"It has," Jack agreed. The accountant was tall and lean and reminded Jack of an actor from the fifties or sixties. Ironically, Jack couldn't remember the actor's name either.

"Shall we get started?" The man was looking up at the office building. "Financial companies take forever. Especially if they are trying to hide something."

A short time later they stepped into the lobby where Kyra Strickland sat behind her desk.

"Detective." She looked up. "We weren't expecting you today."

"Is Ms. Wallis available?" Jack asked.

"I'm afraid not," Kyra smiled slyly. "She had to take her car to the shop. An almost new Mercedes and already needing repairs. Can you imagine? Do you want to make an appointment?"

"That won't be necessary." Jack held up a folded piece of paper. "We have a warrant. Who would be in charge?"

"Just a minute." The smile faded from Kyra's face as she picked up her phone and punched in an extension. She spoke in a hushed voice to whoever answered the other end. A moment later she hung up and turned back to Jack. "He'll be right out."

"I'm sure he will," Jack smirked.

As promised, a man stepped into the lobby from the back offices. He had one of those looks, the kind that suggested he didn't like to be bothered with the little things; like the day-to-day operations, employees, or anything unpleasant. He examined the two men dirtying up his lobby and struggled to hide the distaste in his expression. Jack stepped forward with an extended hand.

"Detective Jack Mallory." He shook his hand in much the same way the forensic accountant had shaken his. "And you are?"

To his credit, the man held his ground to Jack's approach. "Victor. Victor Havencroft. Kyra said you have a warrant. What's this about?"

"Havencroft?" Jack released the man's hand. He pointed to the logo on the wall above Kyra's head. "As in . . ."

"Yes," Victor acknowledged. "This is my company. Now please explain why you're here."

"Of course." Jack took a step back. He shifted to one side and held out a hand toward the accountant. "This is . . ."

"Um, Daniel Fisher." The lean man looked at Jack. "You can call me Dan."

Jack snapped his fingers. "That's right. Dan." He turned back to Victor. "Dan, here, is a forensic accountant. He is here to look through your books."

"Our books?" Victor looked up at Dan. "Looking for what?"

"Motive, of course." Jack handed the warrant to Victor. "What else?"

"Motive for what?" Victor looked confused.

"For murder." It was Jack's turn to be confused. "You are aware one of your employees was killed."

"Stephanie. Yes." The man's expression hinted at sorrow. "Terrible business. But what does that have to do with my company?"

"The laptop she was carrying is missing," Jack explained. "But nothing else of value was taken. We think the killer did not want whatever was on that computer to come out. So, now we want to see if the information came from here. And if so, what was it. And who gained from it being kept secret."

"You think one of my people killed her?" Victor challenged. "We are a family."

"And like any family," Jack looked Victor in the eyes. "There's always that one, the bad egg, the one not invited to the family gatherings. The one capable of doing whatever it takes to get ahead."

"Not my people."

"Maybe you, then," Jack suggested.

Taken aback, Victor said, "I would never."

"Forgive me for not taking your word for it." Jack held Victor's gaze. "My colleague will need a place to work. Stephanie's office would work fine. And access to your records. All of your records. The more cooperative you are, the faster the process will go. The faster he'll be out of here."

Victor looked at the warrant. "Can I call my lawyer?"

"You can call whoever you want," Jack answered. "But you can't stop this. Since Beverly isn't available, I would like Lacey Novak to help Dan with what he needs. Unless you have someone else in mind."

"No, Lacey will do fine," Victor waved a hand. "Kyra, let Ms. Novak know we need her please."

"Yes, sir." Kyra called the accountant.

Lacey appeared a few moments later and, after a brief explanation, led Dan to Stephanie's office.

"I'll check in on him later." Jack nodded to Victor and exited the building.

33

Alexandria's Boutique was not what Shaun was expecting. When he was young, his mother had dragged him along when she would shop for new outfits. The stores she took him to were all the same; over-stuffed racks of clothes spread throughout with large signs declaring sales and low prices. Multitudes of women would be rummaging through the offerings, lining up at the dressing rooms, and again at the checkout lanes. It was what Shaun associated with women's clothing stores.

Walking into Alexandria's, Shaun was instantly uncomfortable. Instead of racks of dresses, slacks, skirts, and tops, there were only mannequins lining the walls with complete outfits, separated by doorways leading to dressing rooms. In the center of the boutique were sofas and chairs with small tables where women sat; chatting, drinking, and waiting. There were no lines, no checkout stations.

"Good morning," a nicely dressed woman greeted him with a warm smile. "Welcome to Alexandria's. May we help you? A gift for that special someone perhaps?"

Shaun instinctively checked his watch. It was shy of noon. But it did not feel like morning to him. "I need to speak with someone in charge."

The woman's smile faltered slightly, though she recovered just as fast. "Would you want the manager or the owner?"

"Either would do," Shaun responded. "As long as they can answer questions."

"I'll see which one is available." The woman swung an arm toward the nearest chair. "Would you care to have a seat?"

"I'm good." Shaun did not move.

Her smile faltered a second time, and she turned away before it returned. Shaun watched as she crossed the store to speak with a sharply dressed woman who glanced his way. She was middle-aged, maybe older, and wore too much makeup. She nodded to the employee and approached Shaun with a certain amount of hesitation.

"Tammy said you wanted to speak to me," the woman said. "How may I help you?"

Shaun showed her his badge. "I'm Detective Travis. And you are?"

"Melinda Cunningham," she said. "I'm the owner. What's this about?"

"I need to talk to you about one of your customers." Shaun pulled out his phone to find a photo of Stephanie.

"One of my customers?"

"Yes. Her name is Stephanie Ellison." He turned his phone to Melinda. "This is her."

"Oh, I remember her," Melinda smiled. "Sweet lady. Spilled her lunch on her top. Needed a new one in a hurry. She was meeting someone."

"That's her." Shaun put his phone away. "I'm surprised you remember that much."

"I always remember the nice ones." Melinda smiled. "We talked while we shopped for her. She had something about her. Made you feel comfortable. You know?"

"When you were talking," Shaun said. "Did she happen to say whom she was meeting? Or what they were meeting about?"

"You know, I don't think she ever said." The woman looked off as if in thought. "I just assumed it was a date."

"But you don't know?"

"No." She shook her head. "I just remember she wanted to make a good impression. You never told me what this was about. Is she okay?"

"I'm afraid not," Shaun said. "I'm investigating her murder."

"She was murdered?"

"A few hours after leaving your store."

"Oh, my God." Melinda put a hand over her mouth. "That poor girl."

"So, if there is anything you can remember," Shaun prompted. "We could use any information you have."

"I don't think I know anything."

"She was wearing the blouse she bought from you when she was found," Shaun informed her. "Did she say where she was going next? Maybe a place to change?"

"She changed here," Melinda responded. "She wanted to get out of the dirty top."

"Thank you," Shaun wrote in his notes. "That helps. Anything else you can remember?"

"Well, now that you mention it," the woman sighed. "I didn't think anything of it at the time. But after she paid for the blouse, because we are rather expensive, she said her husband was going to kill her when he found out how much she spent."

34

Richard drove to the airport wearing the darkest sunglasses he owned. They did little to protect his very sore eyes from the harsh light of the sun as he drove directly toward it.

He spent ten minutes looking for a space close to the doors so he and his mother would not have to walk too far with her luggage. By the time he reached her gate, the plane had already landed and the passengers were beginning to disembark.

The sunglasses had been moved to his head like a dark tiara, as he stood waiting. Richard shifted from foot to foot with his eyes glazing over to the point that he totally missed her coming through the doorway. He was startled to alertness by her hand on his arm.

He frantically looked around him until he was able to focus on her. "Mom?"

"Hello, Richard." The woman wrapped her arms around him and pulled him in close for a hug. Richard hugged her back.

"How was your flight?"

"You don't want to get me started on that," she warned. "First, I asked to not be seated by any children. You know how I am with children."

"I do." Richard remembered exactly what it was like to grow up in a household that did not favor kids.

"And can you believe," she looked around as if to be sure the wrong people didn't overhear. "They sat me by not one, but two of the sniveling little brats."

"They didn't," Richard mocked.

"They did." She took a deep breath. "Then, when I asked to be moved, they said they couldn't move me. Can you believe it?"

"I can't," Richard held his hands out. "I have no words."

"When I told her the least she could do is give me some free drinks, she laughed at me," his mother pouted.

"She laughed?"

"Well not laughed," she admitted. "But she may as well have. Let's go get my cases."

They started toward the luggage carousel.

"I swear," she announced. "If they have lost my luggage, I will sue them for all they're worth."

"All they're worth, huh?" Richard said. "I'm pretty sure the most you would be awarded would be all your luggage is worth."

35

Shaun stopped by the department and made a show of passing by the captain's office. First circling around to appear to be coming from his desk and a few minutes later on the way back. He nodded to her as he walked by the second time. Her gaze made him uneasy and left him wondering if she knew he had been out.

He fired up his computer and began a search of the name Paul McIntosh, one of the accountants from Havencroft who did not have an alibi. He did a quick check of his criminal record, his DMV records, and his credit history.

The first was limited to parking and speeding tickets, all paid off in a timely manner. There were no DUIs or drug possession that would suggest a problem with substances. No physical altercations or restraining orders that would suggest violent tendencies. Shaun knew that no record did not exclude the possibility of these issues. It just meant he had never been caught.

The other records were a little more interesting. Shaun picked up his phone and dialed Jack.

"Mallory," Jack answered.

"Jack. It's Shaun," the younger detective announced.

"You have something?"

"I was looking into Paul McIntosh like you asked."

"And?"

"He doesn't have a criminal record," Shaun said. "But the man has three vehicles registered in his name. Not old clunkers either.

I'm talking mostly new. A pickup truck. A sports car. And a luxury sedan."

"That's a lot of money in wheels," Jack whistled. "He must be up to his eyeballs in debt."

"That's just it," Shaun continued. "According to his credit history, he has no debt. Not even a mortgage. And his home isn't cheap either."

"No debt?"

"None."

"Sounds like someone living beyond their means," Jack processed. "We may need to have another talk with Mr. McIntosh."

36

Leaving Havencroft, Jack decided it was time to interview the one person on his list that he hadn't spoken to one on one. Wendy Meadows was the victim's close friend and the wife of Richard's alibi. Jack was hoping that by talking to Wendy he might gain a better understanding of Stephanie's life and possibly answers to some questions that refused to stop nagging at his detective's brain.

He stood on the porch and rang the doorbell. He had not been to the Meadows' home before. When he interviewed Brent, he had done so at the station. Jack thought it might be better to question the wife at her home, where she would be more relaxed and hopefully more apt to speak freely.

The door opened and a blond woman stared back at him. "May I help you?"

"Wendy Mcadows?" Jack askcd.

She was small in stature, but not frail. There was a sadness in her eyes. Jack couldn't help but wonder if that look was from the loss of her friend or from her marriage. It was a look he remembered well from his own marriage. His wife had been very sad toward the end of their years together.

"Yes." Wendy looked the detective up and down, trying to assess the danger level of the stranger in front of her.

"Detective Jack Mallory." Jack handed her a card. "I'm investigating your friend's death. Would you mind answering some questions?"

"Will it help you catch the bastard who killed Stephanie?" There was a strength to her voice that defied both her size and her grief.

"I hope it will," Jack confessed. "Although I can't guarantee anything."

"Well if you think it might help," Stephanie said. "Ask away."

"Would you mind if we went inside?" Jack asked.

Wendy stepped aside to let him in and gave him directions to the living room, where they sat.

"I want to say I am sorry for your loss," Jack started. "I understand that the two of you were close."

"She was my best friend." Wendy's eyes watered. "She was such a wonderful person."

"When did you meet?" Jack wanted to get her talking, something that was easier to do when discussing the happy times rather than the bad.

"College," Wendy smiled. "We were roommates. I arrived on my first day to move into my dorm and there she was. Already unpacked and reading a textbook of all things. But that was Stephanie for you. She was so smart. She didn't throw it in your face, but she was always the smartest person in the room."

"The two of you hit it off?" Jack asked.

"Not at first," Wendy chuckled. "She was there to study. I was there to party. Almost lost my scholarship my first year. Me coming back to the room in the middle of the night wasted was not the best way to get on Stephanie's good side."

"How did you turn it around?"

"My dad did." She looked down at her hands. "He got my grades just after Christmas break. Told me if I lost my scholarship he would not be paying for college and I would not be moving back home. I could straighten up or become homeless."

"That's harsh."

"I don't know if he would have followed through with it." Wendy looked up at Jack. "My mom probably would have fixed everything.

It was something she did. But the sound of disappointment in his voice was more than I could take."

"What did you do?"

"I cried." Wendy forced a smile. "I cried while Stephanie held me and promised she would help me if I wanted her to. After that, I studied more. Partied less. But when I went, I took Stephanie to keep me in check. She opened up more and we became the best of friends. And now someone has taken her away from me and I want them to pay."

"I want them to pay as well," Jack assured her. "That's why I'm here. Being so close, I assume she confided in you a lot."

"We shared everything," Wendy confirmed.

"Tell me about her relationship with Richard."

"When I met Brent, it put a strain on my relationship with Stephanie," Wendy remembered. "I was spending more time with him and she was feeling like a third wheel. When it was just the two of us, it was fine. But if Brent came over, it was stressful."

"She didn't like Brent?" Jack interrupted.

"It wasn't that she didn't like him," Wendy said. "But their personalities clashed. She was reserved. He was over the top. I found it charming. She found it abrasive. I spent a lot of time getting him to back off and keeping her from bolting."

"How long did that go on?"

"Until Richard," Wendy stated. "Richard was a childhood friend of Brent's. They went to separate universities, which is why I didn't meet Richard until fall break of our second year. Brent told me his friend was going to visit and that he thought we should go on a double date with him and Stephanie. I thought it was an awful idea. Setting Stephanie up on a blind date with a friend of Brent's? That could only lead to disaster."

"But obviously it didn't," Jack pointed out.

"Brent convinced me to ask Stephanie." She looked at her hands again. "And I don't know why, unless it was to please me, she agreed to go on one date with him. So the four of us met at a café we liked. Stephanie and I arrived first. We were nervous. She was nervous about spending the evening with another Brent. I was nervous that if it went poorly it would only deepen the rift between the man I loved and my best friend."

"And again, that didn't happen."

"Richard was the polar opposite of Brent." Wendy laughed. "I mean, it was like meeting a male version of Stephanie. He was quiet, charming, funny. Not that Brent isn't charming and funny. He is. But it was two different types of funny. Brent was physical and crass. Richard was intellectual and tactful. His humor snuck up on you and made you laugh unexpectedly. Stephanie adored him, and he adored her. They were made for one another."

"How did that work?" Jack asked. "Him being at a different university?"

"He came to see her almost every weekend." Her smile broadened. "And over the Christmas break, he transferred to be closer to her. After that, they were inseparable."

"And they lived happily ever after," Jack said. "But I know from experience that happiness isn't always that easy."

"It was for them," Wendy declared.

"Yet relationships change over time," Jack lectured. "Some evolve into something stronger. Some disintegrate."

"Are you speaking from experience, detective?"

"I am," Jack offered. "But I want to know about Richard and Stephanie. How was their relationship over the years? Did it get stronger? Or did they struggle?"

"Stronger," she said. "For sure."

"Come on," Jack countered. "You're telling me they never had problems?"

"They fought sometimes," Wendy said. "What couple hasn't. What are you getting at?"

"What about affairs?" Jack asked.

"No way." Wendy was adamant. "Richard would never. He's not . . ."

"Not what?"

"Nothing."

"You were going to say something." Jack pushed. "What was it?"

"It was one time," Wendy clarified. "I was going to say he wasn't Brent. He cheated on me a few years ago. But we worked through it. Richard was harder on him than I was. He would never do that to Stephanie."

"What about Stephanie doing it to him?" Jack asked.

"What?" Wendy gasped. "Are you serious? No way."

"The evening she was murdered," Jack explained, "Stephanie met someone for dinner. A man. Do you know who he was?"

"What?" Wendy was taken aback. "What are you talking about? Stephanie wasn't cheating on Richard."

"Do you know who she was with?" Jack asked. "Why she was meeting a man, not Richard, at a restaurant that evening?"

"I don't know," Wendy admitted. "But she wasn't having an affair."

"How do you know?"

"Because we told each other everything."

"She didn't tell you she was meeting this man for dinner," Jack pointed out.

"She would have," Wendy insisted. "The next time we spoke she would have told me all about it."

"How do you know it wasn't an affair?"

"It wasn't," Wendy argued. "I know it wasn't."

Jack paused for a moment, letting Wendy cool down.

"That night," he finally started again. "Your husband says he was Richard's alibi. Do you know when Brent left for the Ellison's house? When he returned?"

"Honestly," Wendy sighed. "I went to bed early that night. Had a meeting in the morning. I don't know when Brent left. I didn't even know he had. But he came to bed around one in the morning, maybe a little after. Listen, if he said he was with Richard, he was. Richard would never hurt Stephanie, so he doesn't even really need an alibi."

"Did she keep a journal or diary?"

"No."

"In the past few weeks," Jack said. "Did she seem off in any way? Did she express any concerns?"

"She was stressed." Wendy looked off into the distance. "Not that that was unusual. But she was stressed more than normal."

"Did she tell you why she was so stressed?"

"She said it was something about work," she looked back at the detective. "But she didn't tell me any more than that."

"I imagine her job was stressful." Jack thought about the coworkers he had interviewed.

"It was," Wendy balled her hands into tight fists then relaxed them. "But this was different. She was acting different."

"She didn't mention a name?" Jack pressed. "Someone who might be responsible?"

She shook her head. "She didn't tell me anything. Just that work was getting to her."

"What about your husband?"

"What about him?"

"He works for the same company, doesn't he?" Jack asked.

"Yes."

"Is he stressed?"

"Of course," Wendy said. "Part of the job."

"Would he know what had Stephanie so stressed?" Jack watched her face.

"I doubt it." Wendy looked away. "They aren't in the same department. I don't think they saw each other very much."

"What does he do?" Jack asked. "Your husband?"

"Sales." Wendy closed her eyes. Jack was wondering if he should attempt to wake her when she opened them and spoke. "He sold money. Trying to get people to take out loans. And he's good at it. He was the company's top earner the past two years."

"Impressive," Jack stated, though he didn't really care. "But the top earner didn't see the woman in charge of the money?"

"Brent isn't at the office as much as you may think," Wendy explained. "He's out making cold calls, trying to remind people they need his help to buy that new car, or to remodel that kitchen. He can't sell to his coworkers."

"I see the problem there." Jack smiled. He stopped for a moment and flipped back through his notes. "What about the name Camden?"

"Camden?"

"Does the name Camden ring any bells?"

"No." Wendy shook her head. "I don't know any Camden."

"Alright." Jack flipped back another couple of pages. "Do you have any idea where Stephanie was going on Thursday afternoons? She had a weekly appointment with a Camden. You two told each other everything but you don't know who he is?"

"Thursdays?"

"Every Thursday."

"She had massage therapy on Thursdays." Wendy pointed at Jack in triumph.

"Massage therapy?"

"Yes."

"Every Thursday?"

"I told you she was stressed"

"I guess she was." Jack made a note. "Can you think of anything else?"

"Not really," Wendy answered.

"And the night of the murder," Jack looked her in the eyes. "Your husband was with Richard. So, you were alone?"

"I guess so," she shrugged. "Like I said. I didn't even know he had left."

"So you don't have an alibi." Jack watched for her reaction.

"What?" She sat up straight. "What do you mean by that?"

"I know the two of you were best friends," Jack said. "At least in the beginning. But how was your relationship more recently? Any animosity between you?"

"Animosity?" Wendy repeated the word. "No. Why would there be?"

"Well, she had the perfect marriage," Jack pointed out. "And you had a husband who cheated on you. Weren't you a little jealous of her?"

"Jealous?" Wendy huffed. "No. I wasn't jealous. I loved Stephanie. I was happy that she was happy. We were best friends to the end. Nothing could change that."

37

Richard stood in his kitchen staring out at the living room and the patio beyond. There were empty bottles and glasses on nearly every surface. He had stopped drinking. Not because he felt he should, or because his mother had told him to, but rather because there was nothing left in the house that could numb him.

His mother stood next to him with her hands on her hips looking at the carnage. "It looks like you had a wild party in here."

"Nope. Just me," he said, wondering to himself why he hadn't made some attempt to clean up before leaving for the airport. "Well, me and Ashlyn."

"Ashlyn?" His mother turned on him. "Ashlyn who?"

"Ashlyn," Richard repeated. "Stephanie's sister. We sat up drinking and talking about her."

"Take your sunglasses off," his mother ordered.

Richard pulled them up to his head.

"You're hungover right now, aren't you?"

"Yes," Richard admitted. "I'm hungover from trying to drink enough to forget my wife was murdered."

"Sit down." She pointed at a bar stool next to the kitchen island. "I'll fix you something to eat. You haven't eaten, have you? I didn't think so. I'll fix you something to eat and then we can clean this place up."

"You don't have to do that, mom," Richard protested.

"Are you going to do it?"

"Eventually."

"I'll do it." She opened the refrigerator to take inventory of what she had to work with. There wasn't much. She opened some cabinets and the pantry. "What did you two eat?"

"We didn't, mom," Richard said. "We starved ourselves."

She looked at him with a frown. "There's no need for that."

"You know what there's no need for?" Richard asked. "Criticism. I just lost my wife. I need support, not scrutiny."

She stood silent for a moment. "I'm going to take my bags to my room. Give us a minute to reset."

"You do that." Richard watched her walk away with her suitcase and overnight bag.

He fell to his knees before rolling into a sitting position with his back against the stove. With his face buried in his hands, he cried for longer than he thought he would. When he felt spent, nothing left to come out, he sat back and unmoving for another half hour before he pulled his phone out of his pocket, scrolled through his contact list, and hit the call button.

"Jack?" Ashlyn answered on the first ring.

"Could you have lunch?" he asked. "I don't want to be alone with my mom."

"What about Brent?"

"He's not what I need right now," Richard said. "I need someone willing to slap some sense into me if needed."

"I can do that," she responded.

"I know you can."

"Sure," Ashlyn said. "I'll go."

"We'll pick you up in ten." He looked down at his clothes. "Better make it thirty."

"I'll be waiting."

Richard ran upstairs and knocked on the guest room door. "Mom? Get ready. We're going out for lunch."

"I said I would fix you something," she responded through the door.

"There's nothing here to fix," he reminded her. "Just be ready in twenty minutes."

He did not wait for an answer. He went to his room and took a quick hot shower, changing into jeans and a t-shirt that didn't reek of liquor. After he shaved for the first time in days, he stood and stared at the man in the mirror, barely recognizing him. There was a sadness behind his eyes he had not had before. That he understood. But there was something about his face that seemed different. Maybe the lack of sleep, lack of food, and excess of alcohol caused a change. He looked thinner than he had since he was a kid. But it was a hardness in his features that made the most difference, like he had aged ten years in just days. He realized then that the face was his father's. A face he hadn't seen in twenty years.

Without thought, he punched the mirror. The glass shattered in a spider web of cracks spreading from the point of impact. Pain shot through his hand and arm causing him to scream in a mixture of pain, anger, and agony. He looked down at his hand, holding his wrist with the other. The knuckles were cut, blood running down his fingers, covering his wedding band. Oddly he did not feel the open wounds, only from within. He wondered if he had fractured something.

Turning the warm water on, he rinsed the blood away, cleaning the cuts before wrapping them in gauze. While he was taping the bandage in place, he remembered when they had bought the roll of gauze. Years earlier, Stephanie had tripped on the corner of an area rug. She reached out to break her fall and her arm slammed down on a glass that splintered, shards flew everywhere, except for those that had been thrust into her forearm.

Two hours later they had left the emergency room and gone straight to the pharmacy to fill her prescription and to pick up what would be needed to change the dressing. Richard also remembered that for weeks after that, they would go out and people would stare at him like he had done something to hurt her. She laughed it off. He always felt hurt that anyone thought him capable of such a thing.

"What happened?" His mother was waiting in the hall for him. "I heard you yelling."

"It was nothing." He brushed it off.

"Your hand." She pointed at the bandages. "What did you do?"

"I cut myself shaving, mom." He walked past her. "Let's go."

They arrived at Ashlyn's house a few minutes later than he had said. She was watching for him and came out of the house, checking that the door was locked, and climbed into Richard's truck behind his mother.

"Sorry I'm late." He put the truck in gear and backed out of the driveway.

"No worries." She leaned forward. "Hey, Mrs. Ellison."

"Mom, this is Ashlyn," Richard introduced.

"We met at the wedding," Ashlyn smiled. "Deborah, isn't it?"

"It is," Deborah smiled. "I'm surprised you remembered."

"I'm good with names," Ashlyn sat back. "But don't ask me to remember anything else."

"I can't even remember names," Deborah said.

"I can vouch for that." Richard glanced over his shoulder.

"What'd you do to your hand?" She pointed at the bandages.

"Didn't like the way some guy was looking at me," Richard said. "So I smashed his face."

"Are you serious?" Ashlyn looked at Deborah. "Is he serious? Was the guy okay? You shouldn't do things like that. You could have been hurt. More, I mean."

"Relax." He put his bandaged hand up between them. "Don't worry. It was just a mirror."

"A mirror?" Deborah spoke up. "Is that what I heard?"

"Jesus, Richard." Ashlyn sighed and settled back in her seat. She pulled the seatbelt across her and snapped the buckle into place. "You shouldn't scare me like that."

"Sorry."

"Why are you punching mirrors?" Deborah asked.

"Mirror." Richard corrected. "Just one. And I don't know. One minute I'm brushing my teeth, the next I'm cleaning up the blood. Nothing makes sense right now."

"You miss her don't you?" Ashlyn's voice softened.

"You have no idea."

They drove in silence leaving Richard to process the idea of having lunch with his mother and his dead wife's sister only days after her death. There was something surreal about it. The idea of doing normal, everyday things without Stephanie seemed wrong. Carrying on without her seemed wrong.

"Where are we going?" Ashlyn asked.

"I thought we would go to Dakota's."

"Dakota's Steak House?" She squirmed. "I'm not really dressed for that."

"You're dressed better than me," Richard pointed out. "Honestly, I feel like killing something, and eating a big slab of meat is my compromise."

"Understood." She gave him a sad smile.

"Don't do that." He pointed at her in the rearview mirror.

"What?"

"Don't start treating me like a little orphan boy." Richard pulled into the parking lot of the restaurant. "I chose you so I wouldn't have to put up with that. Just be you."

"Sorry." Ashlyn nodded. "Won't happen again. Now, why don't you shut up and park."

He turned to her, shocked. Then, when he processed the conversation, he smiled. "Thanks."

"No problem."

Inside, Richard put his name on the wait list which the hostess promised would be no more than fifteen minutes. Ashlyn suggested they wait at the bar, but Richard declined after a quick glance at his mother. They stood in awkward silence until ten minutes later when his name was called earlier than expected.

The hostess led them through the dining room to a corner booth and laid menus on the table in front of each of them after they took their seats. They were still reading through the offerings when their waitress appeared.

"Hi, my name is Kendra," she said brightly. "I'll be your waitress this afternoon. Are you here for a special occasion?"

"No." Richard closed his eyes.

"Can I get you anything to drink?" She smiled.

"Water for me," Richard was quick to answer.

Ashlyn looked up at her brother-in-law. "Water for me, too."

"Make it three," Deborah added.

"Okay." The waitress wrote on her order pad. "Are you ready to order or do you need a minute?"

"A minute." Ashlyn was first to answer.

The waitress retreated and Richard returned his attention to the menu.

"What was that?" Ashlyn asked.

"What was what?" Richard looked up again.

"Water?" she questioned. "Since when do you drink water?"

"What does that mean?" Deborah asked.

"I drink water." Richard defended. "Besides, I've had more to drink in the past two days than I have in the past two years. I need a break. You can have a drink if you want."

The waitress returned with their waters, a basket of rolls, and a plate of butter. They ordered their meals and she was gone again.

"I was a waitress once," Ashlyn offered.

"Really?" Richard looked toward their waitress. "I just can't picture that."

"It didn't last long," Ashlyn elaborated. "I really hated that job."

Richard chuckled. "That I can picture."

"I was waiting tables when I met your father," Deborah said. "Meeting him was the only good thing about that job. All these years later, I can still remember how much my feet hurt at the end of a shift."

"How about you?" Ashlyn turned to Richard. "You ever have a job you couldn't stand?"

"When I was sixteen years old," Richard thought back. "My father told me to get a job to build character. So, I found one on a road crew. I thought I was going to die that summer. It was so hot and tar smells so bad. I went home every evening covered with that stuff and smelling like God knows what. It took me an hour or more to get that shit off me."

"Language," Deborah said.

Ashlyn laughed.

"Sorry, mom."

"I have to say," Ashlyn smiled. "I bet you looked sexy in your reflective vest."

"I remember that summer," Deborah thought aloud. "I couldn't get the tar out of your clothes. I think replacing your wardrobe cost more than you made."

Richard shook his head, took a roll from the basket, tore it in half, and spread butter on one of the pieces. "We need to talk."

"We are talking," Ashlyn said.

"About the funeral home," Richard clarified. "I would like the two of you to go back with me later if you can."

"Of course," Deborah said.

"I can," Ashlyn assured him. "Are you sure?"

"I'm sure." Richard bit into the roll and savored the flavor. "I'll be fine this time. I just need you there for support and maybe to help pick things out."

"This time?" Deborah looked from one of them to the other. "What happened last time?"

"Didn't go well," Ashlyn smiled.

"Call it a meltdown," Richard said. "That's what it was."

"I'll be there," Ashlyn said. "We'll get through it together."

"Whatever you need, son," Deborah added.

"Thank you."

"It's what family does." Ashlyn patted Richard's arm.

The waitress appeared again, placing plates of food in front of them. She asked if they needed anything else and when they did not, she left them alone again.

"Still can't picture you as a waitress," Richard smirked.

"Just eat, or I'll spit on your food," Ashlyn said.

"Oh," Richard nodded. "Now I can picture it."

38

Detective Travis slipped into Briana's Hair Salon and fell in line behind the one customer that was at the counter. Unlike Alexandria's, Briana's was an affordable option. The atmosphere was warm and filled with light conversation.

"Do you have an appointment?" The receptionist waved him forward after finishing with the customer.

"No. I . . . "

"Well, we can probably work you in." The receptionist scanned the appointment book. "If you don't mind a little wait."

"No," Shaun said. "I don't need a haircut."

The receptionist looked up at him over the top of her glasses. "Are you sure?"

Subconsciously, he ran a hand across the back of his head. "I'm sure."

"Then how can I help you?"

"I need to speak to someone about a customer." He showed her his badge. "She had her hair done here a few days ago. I need to know who cut it."

"Strange. But okay." She sat back a little. "When was the appointment?"

He gave her the date and time that coincided with the 'B' in Stephanie's calendar along with her name. The receptionist looked through the entries until she came to the right one. "Okay. That would have been Beatriz. She's with a customer. You'll need to wait a few minutes."

Shaun was about to protest but thought better of it. He took a seat and waited. He studied each of the hairdressers in turn as they worked on the women seated before them. Each had different styles of interacting with their customers, some quietly worked hard while others were having full-blown conversations, stopping what they were doing from time to time if the story became particularly juicy or if something needed a more detailed explanation.

Shaun's phone rang and Jack's name showed on the screen. He answered as fast as he could. "Hey boss."

"Just call me Jack," the senior detective replied. "I need you to do me a favor."

"Sure thing."

"Check Stephanie Ellison's charges for Thursday afternoons," Jack said. "Should be a repeating charge. If it's a business, get me an address."

"I'll get on it." Shaun looked around the salon. "Let me call you back."

"I can wait," Jack said.

"I'll call you back," Shaun repeated.

"You're not there are you?"

Shaun was silent.

"Just don't get caught," Jack ordered.

"I'm almost done," Shaun said. "I'll get back right after."

"Call me when you do."

Shaun promised that he would, put his phone away, and returned to looking at the people in the salon.

Two women walked to the front counter, deep in a conversation they had begun while one cut the other's hair. The two continued talking while the transaction was rung up and payment was made.

"Same time next week?" The hairdresser was tall, thick, but not overweight. Her close-cropped hair was blond with streaks of pink. Her skin was pale and blotchy. She was the complete opposite of her petite, oriental customer.

"I'll be out of town next week." The woman searched her purse for what Shaun assumed were her keys. "I'll be back the week after."

"Okay," the hairdresser responded. "I'll pencil you in."

Triumphantly the customer pulled her hand out of the purse with her keys clutched tight. "Thank you."

The woman walked out and when the door closed the hairdresser turned to the receptionist. "Who do I have next?"

"This policeman wants to talk to you." The receptionist pointed at Shaun.

He took the cue and stood. The hairdresser turned to him with a quizzical look.

"Is something wrong, officer?" she asked as he approached.

"Detective," Shaun corrected. "Detective Shaun Travis. You're not in any trouble. I just have some questions about one of your customers."

"One of my customers?" She smiled. "Are you sure? They're a pretty mild bunch."

"Can I get your name?" he asked. "For my notes."

"Beatriz," she said. "Beatriz Bauer."

"Thank you." Shaun wrote the name down. "You had a customer named Stephanie Ellison."

"Stephy?" The woman was suddenly defensive. "What about her?"

"You knew her?"

"I've been doing her hair for ten years." Beatriz narrowed her eyes. "Maybe twelve. Why did you say 'knew her'? Did something happen?"

"Stephanie was murdered," Shaun said. "The same night you did her hair."

"Oh my God." Beatriz was a little louder than she meant to be and everyone in the salon turned to stare. She lowered her voice again. "What happened?"

"That's what we're trying to determine." Shaun made eye contact with a few of the gawkers, and they turned away. "I need to ask some questions about that day. And about Stephanie."

"What do you want to know?"

"Did Stephanie have regular appointments?"

"No." Beverly shook her head. "She usually just called when she felt she needed a trim, or more."

"What about this last appointment?" Shaun asked. "How far in advance did she schedule it?"

"A couple of days maybe," Beatriz answered.

"Was that the norm?"

"No." The hairdresser shook her head. "She usually called a week or so in advance."

"Did she say why she was in such a hurry?"

"Don't think so." Beatriz thought. "Wait. She said she was meeting someone or going somewhere."

"She didn't mention a name or location?"

"No." Beatriz frowned. "Just said it was important."

"Ten to twelve years?" Shaun contemplated. "That's a long time. I'm guessing the two of you talked a lot?"

"I guess so." Beatriz shrugged. "I mean, I usually do most of the talking. But Stephy could hold her own."

"So she probably told you things," Shaun glanced over his shoulder. "Things she might not tell anyone else."

"I don't know what she told anyone else," Beatriz said. "But she told me plenty."

"Did she ever mention having problems with anyone?"

"All the time," she confirmed.

"Really?" Shaun flipped the page in his notepad. "Work? Home?"

"Both."

"Did she give any details?" The detective shifted his stance.

"I think someone at work was eating her yogurts," Beatriz recalled. "And one of them cracked a joke at her expense that she did not find funny at all."

"What about home?"

"Her husband got on her nerves sometimes," she said.

"How?"

"If I remember correctly," Beatriz looked up at the ceiling. "I think he had problems with putting his dishes in the dishwasher. Oh, and he never took out the trash without being asked."

"You sure remember a lot, for not having regular appointments." Shaun pointed out.

"You think so?" She looked him in the eyes. "In my job, you have to remember things to keep the clients happy. But you're right. What I'm remembering may not have been her at all."

"You're kidding, right?"

"I know she said she was getting her hair done for something important," Beatriz insisted. "But the rest may have been one of my other customers."

"I need you to be sure."

"I don't think I can be."

Shaun sighed audibly. "Do you remember anything else that you're positive she said?"

"Sorry." Beatriz pursed her lips. "I just don't know."

Shaun pulled out one of his cards and handed it to her. "Well if you think of something give me a call."

"Okay." Beatriz stared at his card. "Wish I was more help."

"That's okay." He walked to the exit.

"Wait." She called after him. "I do remember something."

"What's that?"

"She asked me for the best way to break bad news to someone."

"Did she say what the news was? Or who she had to break it to?"

"She didn't say what it was," Beatriz ran a hand through her pink hair. "But I got the distinct impression she had something to tell her husband."

39

Jack sat in his car under the shade of a tree at a park. He silently watched ducks floating on the surface of the small body of water enclosed by the park grounds. A steady stream of walkers, runners, and cyclists passed by on the walking path. None of them seemed to notice him sitting there, or at least no one cared enough to look his way.

A call had come in, prompting him to pull into the parking lot so he could take notes. The information he received made him question the husband's innocence once more.

He opened his notepad and began skimming the pages for Richard's phone number. When he found it, he laid the pad on his lap where he could read the number while he dialed. It rang twice before Richard's voice greeted him.

"Mr. Ellison?" Jack knew it was him.

"Yes?"

"This is detective Mallory," Jack clarified. "Investigating your wife's murder."

"I know who you are," Richard said. "Do you have news?"

"Afraid not." Jack shifted in his seat and the notepad slid off his leg to the floorboard. "Shit."

"Pardon me?"

"Sorry." Jack switched the phone to his other hand and reached down to retrieve the pad. "No answers. But I have questions."

He grunted as he felt around until he finally found what he was searching for and pulled it back up.

"Are you okay?"

"I'm fine." Jack settled back again. "Can you answer a couple questions?"

"Whatever," Richard muttered. "What do you want to know?"

"You didn't tell me that your wife had an insurance policy," Jack said. "In fact, when I asked, you said the only policy she might have was through work. Why is that?"

"I didn't remember," Richard answered. "We took them out a few years back. Our lawyer reminded me of it. After you and I talked."

"You didn't remember she had an insurance policy?" Jack wasn't convinced. "How does that work?"

"How does what work?"

"She was paying premiums on insurance policies and you never noticed the charges?" Jack accused. "You never noticed the letters from the insurance company? How did you not remember?"

"I didn't know!" Richard barked. "I didn't handle the bank reports. My wife was an accountant. She balanced the checkbook. She paid the bills, so she handled the mail. I didn't notice. I wasn't attentive. I . . . I didn't know she was lying to me about staying at work late. I didn't know where she was. I wasn't a good husband. Is that what you want to hear?"

"I hear what you're saying, Richard." Jack watched a group of young women power walk past the car. "But it's hard for me to believe. And it does give you another motive."

"I had no motive to kill my wife."

"Money is always a motive," Jack disagreed. "How much was the policy for?"

Richard was silent on the other end.

"How much, Richard?"

"I swear I didn't remember it."

"How much?"

"A million." Richard's voice was so low it was almost inaudible.

"That's a lot of motive."

"Not to me," Richard countered. "I don't want the money. I want my wife back."

There was silence, and Jack realized the man had hung up on him. Not the brightest move, but the detective had seen worse. He was preparing to call Richard back when his phone rang. He answered without looking.

"You didn't really think that was a good idea did you?"

"Sir?"

Jack pulled the phone down to look at the screen to see who he was talking to. "Shaun?"

"Yes, sir."

"What do you need?" Jack tried to not sound dismissive. He wasn't sure he was successful.

"Is everything okay?" Shaun asked.

"Richard Ellison hung up on me."

"Are you serious? Doesn't sound very rational. What prompted that?"

"He was failing to convince me that he didn't remember his wife's million-dollar insurance policy." Jack relayed. "And hanging up didn't help his argument. Now, why don't you tell me why you called?"

"I did what you asked," Shaun said. "I looked at the credit card records. There was a weekly charge to a place called Tranquility. It's a massage and acupuncture parlor."

"Send me the address." Jack started his car and backed out. He glanced back at the gently rocking waters. The irony of leaving a tranquil place to go to a place called Tranquility was not lost on him. "Do me a favor. Go to Havencroft. Ask Beverly Wallis who Stephanie's successor will be. And talk to Paul McIntosh about his expensive tastes and how he pays for them."

"Will do," Shaun said. Jack could feel his grin through the phone.

It took him fifteen minutes to get to the mini-mall that housed the massage parlor. It was sandwiched between a discount shoe store and a dying department store. Jack easily found a parking space and pulled himself from the car. He stood and stretched his back and legs before heading into the business.

The waiting room was dark and poorly decorated. There were two men sitting on opposite sides of the room, their faces buried in their phones. Jack stepped up to the young woman sitting behind the cheaply made receptionist counter. She was reading and made no attempt to close the book when she looked up at the detective.

"Do you have an appointment?" she asked.

"No."

"We are booked," she announced. "I can make an appointment for you next week if you like."

"No."

The woman stared at him, confused.

"Is there a Camden working here?"

"You need an appointment," she said, sternly.

Jack held his badge in front of her face and repeated, "Is there a Camden working here?"

"Hey, mister," the man nearest him said. "She said you needed an appointment."

Jack turned his face to the man with an intense scowl.

"Or not." The man held his hands up in submission.

Jack turned back to the woman. She sat hugging her book. He gave her the same look he had given the man, and she shrank down into her chair.

"Camden," he said between gritted teeth.

"He works here," she nodded.

"Where?" He looked down the hallway leading to the back room.

"He's not available right now," she insisted.

"Where!?" Jack had lost any patience he may have had.

"Room three," she answered. "But he's with a client."

Jack ignored her and started down the hall.

"Sir!" The receptionist called after him. "Sir! You can't go back there."

Jack walked to room three and opened the door.

"Occupied," a man's voice said.

"Is your name Camden?" Jack stepped into the room. The man, dressed in white, stood behind a massage table. The woman lying on her stomach had a strategically placed towel draped across her. She raised her head when he entered. The sound of ocean waves breaking on rocks filled the room, along with the scent of candles that burned along shelving on the walls.

"Yes." The man circled the table. "But I am with a client. You'll have to wait your turn."

"I don't have the time or patience to wait." Jack pointed at the woman. "She looks relaxed. She can wait."

"What? It doesn't work that way," the woman said.

Jack showed his badge.

"You're a cop?" Camden stared at the badge. "What do you want with me?"

"Answers." Jack put the badge away. "Come into the hall and I'll get you back to this as fast as I can."

"I still don't understand." Camden followed Jack out of the room.

The detective pulled the door closed.

"What's your last name, Camden?"

"Pittman." He tilted his head in confusion. "Shouldn't you already know that?"

"Why would I ask if I already knew?" Jack looked him in the eyes. "I need you to tell me about a client of yours."

"Are you really a cop?" Camden protested. "I'm not telling you anything about my clients."

"First of all, you're not a doctor or a lawyer," Jack put a finger in the man's face. "You don't have doctor-patient or client confidentiality. Second, it's one client. A Stephanie Ellison. A regular on Thursday afternoons."

"I know her." Camden shrank from the finger. "Why are you asking?"

"She's been coming to see you for some time now." Jack lowered his hand. "Have you developed any kind of rapport with her?"

"What do you mean?"

"Have you talked to her about what makes her so tense she needs your services?"

Camden looked up and down the hall. Looking for anyone who might overhear, or just for backup, Jack didn't know.

"Work," Camden finally said. "At least that was it at first. But something changed."

"Changed how?"

"Shouldn't you just ask her?"

"I'm asking you."

"Well," Camden hesitated. "She was making a lot of progress. Seemed less and less tight, you know. She was doing well. Then about three or four weeks ago she came in tighter than I had ever seen her. And nothing I did really helped her. Something was going on with her."

"She never said what it was?"

"No."

"Did she ever mention any names?"

"No."

Jack handed him a card. "If you think of anything let me know."

Camden took the card. "I'm going to call her and tell her about you."

"Yea, well that isn't going to work," Jack started down the hall. "And you might want to cancel her appointments."

"What is this about?" Camden called after him.

"Her murder, Camden," Jack called over his shoulder. "It's about her murder."

The massage therapist stood slack-jawed while Jack left the building.

The detective walked across the parking lot and settled back into his car. As he did, his phone rang. He looked and saw Shaun's name on his screen. "Mallory."

"Jack?" Shaun said. "We've got the phone records for Stephanie's phone."

"And?"

"I thought you might want to hear the last text sent to her phone."

"What is it?" Jack asked.

"'Going to bed. Drive safe. See you in the morning.'" Shaun read.

"Okay." Jack was unfazed. "Who sent it?"

"Richard Ellison."

Jack sat up straighter. "When?"

"Nine p.m," Shaun said.

"Tell me, Shaun," Jack said. "Why would you tell your wife you're going to bed if your friend is at your house watching a game?"

"I wouldn't."

"He lied to us," Jack thought aloud. "Again."

40

Richard sat on the back patio of his home staring at the phone in his hand. He had just hung up on the detective investigating Stephanie's murder, the same detective who probably suspected him of being involved. If Detective Mallory had any doubts before, he more than likely had lost them. Richard couldn't believe how stupid he had been.

He waited a few minutes, expecting a callback. His mind raced for a good explanation for disconnecting the call, other than the detective had simply pissed him off. That would only serve to reinforce the idea that he may have lost control and killed his wife.

When the call back did not come, he wondered if he should call the detective and convince him that his service dropped the call. Was it believable? Maybe. Would Mallory buy it? Richard doubted it. He concluded the best thing for him to do was go on with his day and hope the police didn't show up to arrest him.

Going about his day meant taking his mother and meeting Ashlyn at the funeral home in half an hour. They were going to make a second attempt to make arrangements for Stephanie. It wasn't something he wanted to do, not that he was supposed to be looking forward to it.

Richard stood and stretched, realizing he had not moved in some time. His legs were stiff and a pain in his calf threatened to cause him to limp. He worked the muscle until it was loosened up then headed inside. His mother was in the kitchen cleaning the counters.

He glanced around and saw that all the bottles were gone. He hadn't even noticed what she was doing.

"Mom, you shouldn't have done this."

"I wanted to." She scrubbed the countertop directly in front of her. "It's one less thing for you to worry about."

"Thanks." He crossed the room and gave her a quick hug. "Are you ready to go? We need to get to the funeral home."

"Just need to freshen up." She pulled off the rubber gloves and laid them across the divider in the sink. "I'll only be a minute."

He watched her climb the stairs before turning his attention to the rest of the house. He wondered where she had put the mail he had on the island, the remote for the television, and the book that had been on one of the end tables; the one Stephanie had been reading. The disappearance of the book bothered him the most.

It was nearly a half hour before her 'only a minute' ended. She came down the stairs looking much the same as she had before. He didn't say anything, simply turned and led the way to the garage. She followed dutifully, and he opened the passenger door for her.

A few minutes later they arrived at the Schaefer and Hines Funeral Home where Ashlyn was already waiting for them. He parked his truck next to her much more practical economy class car. She stepped out of the vehicle and waved at him over the roof of her small car. He raised his hand just over the door frame and gave her a single wave in return before opening the door and stepping down to the ground.

"You made it." Ashlyn gave him a half smile.

"We did." Richard looked warily at the building before turning to his sister-in-law. "Sorry we're late."

He hooked a thumb toward the other side of his truck where his mother was shoving the door shut. She rounded the vehicle, smoothing out wrinkles from her clothing as she walked.

"Shall we get this over with?" With a somber expression, Richard pulled open the door and held it for the women as they entered. He glanced back to his truck before following.

Everything was as it had been the day before including the giant of a man, Farkas Burjan, who bowed slightly in greeting.

"Welcome back." There was caution in his voice.

"Well aren't you a big one," Deborah observed.

"We are here to try again." Ashlyn looked like a child talking up to the man.

"Not trying again," Richard dismissed. "We're here to get this done. So, lead the way."

With another slight bow, Farkas took them back to the room and the same table they had been sitting at the day before. They sat, Farkas repeated the same spiel, and the brochures came out.

Farkas opened one of the colored pamphlets. "As you can see, we have several options for . . ."

"Which one is the best?" Richard interrupted the large man.

"Pardon me?"

Richard tapped one of the brochures. "Which is the best?"

"Well, the platinum is our most expensive package."

"I'll take that one," Richard said. "The platinum."

"Richard," Deborah spoke up. "That's too much."

"I loved my sister, and she deserves the very best," Ashlyn said. "But your mother is right. Deborah wouldn't want you to spend so much on her."

"I want the best."

"That is the best, sir," Farkas assured him.

"It's too much," Ashlyn insisted.

Skimming through the descriptions, Deborah said, "The gold package is enough. Even the silver, for that matter."

"Well, the gold," Ashlyn challenged the other woman.

"The platinum," Richard demanded.

"Let me get the paperwork," Farkas struggled to stand, then left the room.

"Why are you doing this?" Ashlyn turned to Richard. "You don't have to prove to anyone that you loved Stephanie. We know you did."

"One million," Richard's response was unexpected and startled his sister-in-law.

"What?" Ashlyn was confused.

"What does that mean?" Deborah asked.

"Her insurance policy." He looked down at the ground.

"What insurance policy?" Deborah looked at him.

"A few years back we took out insurance policies," Richard explained. "One million dollars each. What am I supposed to do with that? I can't put it in a college fund for the kids we didn't have. I can't use it to buy her a better house or take her on vacations. What am I supposed to do with all that money other than spend it on her funeral?"

"Oh, Richard." His mother patted his arm.

"I, uh . . ." Ashlyn stammered.

"Exactly." Richard grabbed up a brochure and slapped it onto the table in front of the women. "So, she's getting the best casket. And she's going to have the best service. I'll just have to figure out what to do with the rest of it later. Maybe I'll give some of it to you, Ashlyn."

"This isn't what she would want," his sister-in-law looked down at the brochure.

"How do you know?" Richard asked. "This might be exactly what she would want. Do you know? Did you ever talk to her about it? I didn't. We always thought we had plenty of time to discuss those things. But we were wrong. Weren't we?"

"Consider the . . ."

"Ashlyn." Richard stopped her. "You aren't going to change my mind. Not on this. Just help me decide the details of the service. And pick out the best casket. That's what I need from you right now. Okay?"

"Okay." Ashlyn nodded. "I can do that."

"We can," Deborah agreed.

Farkas returned with a contract on a clipboard. The large man pulled a pen from his pocket and held it out. Richard took it and turned the clipboard toward him. Farkas guided Richard through each page.

The contract required dozens of decisions to be made, lines to be signed or initialed. As promised, Ashlyn and Deborah talked out the choices with him until they came to a conclusion for each. When they finished, Richard laid the pen on top of the papers.

"That just leaves the casket," Farkas pulled himself to his feet again. He gathered the pages of the contract and straightened the edges before snapping them securely into the clipboard. "Do you have an idea of what you want?"

Richard stared into the showroom, shaking his head. "No idea. Just point me to your top of the line."

41

"Thanks for coming back," Detective Mallory entered the interrogation room and sat directly across from Brent Meadows.

"You keep making it sound like I have a choice. But we both know I didn't have one." Brent leaned back in his seat. "You know, when the policemen showed up insisting I come with them and all."

"I can see where you might feel that way," Jack acknowledged. "But you are here, so let's talk."

Brent did not react, only stared at the detective.

"I want to go over some of your answers from our previous interview."

"Ask again," Brent said. "But I'm not going to change my answers."

"I would hope not." Jack raised an eyebrow. "I would hate to think you lied to me before. I just need some clarification."

"Okay." Brent shifted in his seat. "I'll do my best."

"I know you will." Jack tapped the table between them. "You know how I know?"

"How's that?"

"Because you want justice for Stephanie," Jack declared. "Just like Richard does. Just like I do. Right?"

Brent gave him another blank stare.

"I am right, aren't I?" Jack gave him a concerned look.

"Sure," Brent stumbled over his answer. "I mean, yes. I want justice for Stephanie. I just don't see how you asking me more questions is going to make that happen."

"Well let's go through them," Jack suggested. "Maybe it'll become clear to you."

"Alright," Brent shifted again. "Go ahead and ask."

"Okay." Jack looked at his notes. "You stated that you were Richard's alibi because you were at his home watching a game that he had recorded."

"That's right."

"That's where I get confused." Jack flipped back further through his notes. "According to phone logs. Mr. Ellison sent a text to his wife at nine o'clock that night."

"Why would that be odd?" Brent shook his head. "Haven't you ever texted your wife while doing something else?"

"Well, no." Jack grinned. "Because I'm not married. But that isn't what is at issue here."

"What then?" Brent asked. "What is at issue?"

"The context of the text." Jack pulled out a piece of paper and turned it to the man. "It says 'Going to bed. Drive safe. See you in the morning.' Kind of strange for someone who is watching a game with a friend. Don't you agree?"

Brent looked at the page, reading the text that was printed on it. His phone rang and out of habit he pulled it out and checked the screen.

"Do you need to get that?" Jack asked.

"No." Brent let the phone slip back into his pocket. "Where were we?"

"The text message." Jack pointed at the printed copy between them. "I mean, if you left at midnight, as you said." Jack found the entry in his notes to confirm. "Most games last about three hours. So the two of you would have just been starting."

"Well, we fast-forward through commercials," Brent said. "He probably sent the text before I got there. He may have forgotten I was coming."

"Seems forgetting is a habit of his," Jack muttered.

"What?"

"You two get together two or three times a month," Jack reminded him. "You made plans for that night. You really think he would have forgotten?"

"I don't know." Brent shrugged. "He has a lot on his mind sometimes."

"Okay." Jack leaned back. "Let's say all of that is true. You show up sometime after nine, after he sent the text."

"Sounds right."

"You say he was worried about Stephanie not being home," Jack said. "It's getting late and his wife, the love of his life, is still not home."

"Right." Brent nodded. "He was worried."

"But he never sent her another text." Jack picked up a copy of the phone records. "Never tried to call and check on her, even after you left. He just went to bed. The woman you and your wife told me Richard loved so much, and he didn't try to make sure she was okay even though she wasn't home at midnight. Don't you find that strange? Their relationship being so good, like you said."

"I suppose you could call that strange," Brent lowered his head.

"It was almost like he didn't expect her to come home," Jack suggested. "Why wouldn't he expect her to come home? You know. If he didn't kill her?"

"That's probably something you would have to ask him." Brent looked up at the detective. "But I know he wouldn't hurt her. He just isn't capable."

"That's what I keep hearing," Jack confessed. "But the facts are telling me a different story."

"Well, the facts are wrong."

"The facts are wrong?"

"You know what I mean," Brent huffed. "You aren't reading the facts right."

Jack remained silent for a minute, staring at his witness. Brent squirmed under his gaze.

"Did Richard ask you to be his alibi?" Jack sat forward. "It would be a lot better for you if you admitted it now. If we find out you've been lying to us further in the investigation, we're going to have to charge you with obstruction. And whatever else we can think of. Are you willing to go to prison for him?"

"I'm not going to go to prison for him." Brett was defiant. "You know why? Because Richard did not kill Stephanie."

"You're sure about that?"

"Yes!"

"What about you?" Jack asked.

"What about me?"

"Did you kill her?"

"My God," Brent exclaimed. "Are you even a detective? Stephanie's killer is out there somewhere. You need to stop harassing her friends and family and get out there and find them."

42

Shaun walked into Haven Financial Group and looked around the lobby. He quickly stepped up to the receptionist, while she was trying to tuck her book away.

"You must be Kyra." Shaun greeted her.

"Do I know you?" She tilted her head to one side and smiled at him.

"No." He pulled out his badge and her smile faded. "You know my partner, Detective Mallory. I'm Detective Shaun Travis. I need to see Beverly Wallis and Paul McIntosh, but not at the same time."

Kyra let out her breath with a silent sigh. She had been worried the detective might be there for her or Chad. She picked up the phone and pressed a button. She spoke softly into the receiver, glancing up at the detective from time to time. When she hung up she smiled.

"She'll be right out."

Shaun nodded and took a step back, turning to the hallway leading to the back. A moment later a tall brunette walked up to him with hand extended.

"Beverly Wallis," she introduced.

Shaun took her hand and the two shook. "Detective Shaun Travis."

"You know that other detective already spoke to me?" She pulled her hand away nervously.

"He's my partner," Shaun clarified. "He asked me to follow up on a couple of things."

"Nothing serious, I hope." Beverly turned and led the way to her office.

"No, ma'am," Shaun said.

"That's good." She let out a nervous laugh. "Would hate to think I was a suspect. Are you getting close?"

"We're narrowing it down," Shaun assured her.

"That's good." She entered her office and shut the door after Shaun was inside. "Stephanie was a wonderful person. She deserves justice."

"We'll get it for her." Shaun looked around the office.

"What were you wanting to ask me?"

"Stephanie was the Accounting Manager, correct?" Shaun asked.

"Yes." Beverly nodded. "That's right."

"Now that she's gone," Shaun said. "Who will take her place? Will it be Nettie Huber?"

"Oh, God no." Beverly laughed again. "She's lucky to be working here. She was one of Victor's first hires. A friend of the family, or distant cousin, I don't remember. He won't fire her, but will never promote her."

Shaun typed what she said into his phone. "Is she aware? That she wouldn't get the promotion?"

"Fully," Beverly sat in her executive chair and became instantly more at ease. "Victor and I both sat down with her and suggested she find another job. We explained that she was welcome to stay on, but there would be no opportunities for advancement."

"And she stayed?"

"She gets paid well for what she does here." Beverly grimaced. "No one else would pay her like we do. And no one else would keep her. So, no. She won't leave. Not on her own."

"So who is in line for the Accounting Manager job?"

"Most likely, Lacey Novak," Beverly said. "Victor and I haven't talked yet. But she was the one who worked most closely with

Stephanie. She knows the ins and outs of the business and is fully qualified."

"Really?" Shaun raised his eyebrows.

"Why does that surprise you?"

"It's just that when my partner interviewed her," Shaun explained, "Lacey indicated that she was not liked and only had a job because Stephanie protected her."

"She said that?" Beverly was taken aback. "Whatever would have given her that idea?"

"She thinks you, in particular, don't like her." Shaun continued.

"Well, it's true I don't associate with the underlings," Beverly adjusted herself in her seat. "I talked to Stephanie. I expected her to pass the information on to the others. Maybe she thought that meant I didn't like her. But I assure you there is no ill will there. I can also assure you that if I wanted to get rid of her, there was nothing Stephanie could have done to stop me."

"Any chance Ms. Novak knew that?"

"Maybe," Beverly nodded. "I would think that Stephanie would have let her know. She was working with her to get her trained to cover Stephanie's vacations."

"Interesting." Shaun glanced at his notes. "I need to speak to Paul McIntosh now."

"Okay," Beverly stood. "I'll put you in Stephanie's office and have him sent to you."

43

B rent sat low in the backseat of the police car driven by the officer that Detective Mallory had asked to take him home. Keeping his head down and a hand up, trying to avoid the prying eyes of his neighbors, Brent muttered under his breath, his leg bouncing a mile a minute.

The officer turned into his driveway and parked. He had to exit the vehicle and circle around to open the door for his passenger since the doors could not be opened from inside. Brent slid out and stood at the edge of the concrete. The officer shut the door and returned to the driver's side. Just before climbing in behind the steering wheel, he said, "Have a nice day, sir."

The dumbfounded look on Brent's face did not fade until the squad car was out of view. Brent turned to the house without making a move toward it. He turned away, crossed the driveway, and entered his own car. Backing out of the driveway, he barely missed another vehicle that was coming down the street. The driver of the other car laid on his horn and slammed on the brakes. Brent glanced back, changed gears, and sped away.

The drive to Richard's house was only a few blocks and Brent arrived in a matter of minutes, pulling into the driveway and skidding to a stop behind his friend's truck. A moment later he stood on the front porch hammering his fist on the door.

The door swung open. "What the hell is the matter with you?"

It wasn't Richard, but Ashlyn standing in front of him.

"What are you doing here?" Brent did not hide his disappointment.

"Good to see you too." Ashlyn looked the disheveled man over. "Couldn't bring yourself to clean up?"

"Where's Richard?" Brent pushed his way past the woman and into the house.

"Come on in," Ashlyn said to his back. "He's out back."

Ashlyn returned to the kitchen where she was helping Deborah make sandwiches for dinner. Brent walked determinedly until he saw Richard's mother. He slowed. "Hey, Mrs. Ellison."

"Brent." Deborah acknowledged him. "Good to see you."

Brent nodded before rushing to the deck. Ashlyn only gave half of her attention to watching Brent collapse in the chair next to her brother-in-law.

"Hey, Brent," Richard greeted. He looked his friend over, noting the unkept attire. "What's up?"

"That detective brought me in for more questions." Brent glanced back to be sure Ashlyn hadn't followed. "He suspects I'm lying about your alibi."

"Jesus, Brent," Richard sighed. "I knew that was a bad idea. You should have left it alone. Now it looks like I'm covering something up."

"I told him I wasn't lying," Brent assured him. "But he says you sent a text to Stephanie at nine saying you were going to bed."

"I forgot about that," Richard closed his eyes. "No wonder he thinks we're lying. I should come clean before it gets any worse."

"No." Brent insisted. "I told him you forgot I was coming over. They can't prove otherwise. Your alibi is still good. You just have to stick to the story. If they ask, tell them you forgot we made plans."

"You know how weak that sounds?" Richard scoffed.

"It doesn't matter," Brent said. "What matters is what they can prove. They can't prove I wasn't there. It gives you the alibi you need. You can't go down for this. Promise me you'll stick to the story."

"Fine." Richard took a deep breath. "If only to keep you from getting in trouble for trying to help me."

Brent nodded. His body relaxed, and he sat back in the chair.

"What are you two boys talking about?" Deborah asked.

Brent tensed up again, wondering what she had overheard.

She handed Richard a plate and took the second plate to another nearby seat where she sat, holding the food in her lap. She looked from one to the other. "You don't want to tell me?"

"Guy stuff," Brent said.

Ashlyn laughed as she walked out to join them, carrying her own plate.

"What's so funny?" Brent frowned.

"You came storming in here like the world was coming to an end," Ashlyn explained. "And you expect us to believe you're talking about guy stuff?"

"What he meant was he's having issues at work and wanted some advice," Richard lied.

"Well, that makes more sense." Ashlyn took a bite of her sandwich.

"Why are you even here?" Brent asked.

"We went to the funeral home with Richard to arrange for Stephanie's funeral." Deborah picked at the sandwich on her plate. "We asked her to stay."

Brent turned to Richard. "Sorry I wasn't there for you, man."

"No problem," Richard responded. "We got it done."

"You got it done," Ashlyn said between bites. "We were just there for support."

"Well, you did that well." Richard had yet to touch his food.

Brent's phone rang. He pulled it from his pocket and checked the screen. "Sorry. I have to take this. Damn clients won't leave me alone."

"Go ahead," Richard gestured. "I understand."

Brent stood and went inside to find a quiet place to talk.

Ashlyn gave Richard a slight grin and nod, before returning to her food.

"Did I thank you for going with me?"

"You did," Ashlyn smiled again. "But it's nice to hear."

"My God." Brent rolled his eyes as he stepped out on the patio. "Do you two need a room?"

"Brent!" Deborah exclaimed.

"No!" Ashlyn threw her hands up. "Eew. Why would you say that?"

"Jesus, Brent." Richard turned to him. "Stephanie just died. And she's Stephanie's sister. Sometimes you should really think before you speak."

"Sorry." Brent put his hands up defensively. "With everything going on, I'm just rattled. I didn't mean anything by it."

"I know you didn't mean it, but that's not the point," Richard argued. "I could really use my friend right now, and you just aren't being that."

"What do you mean, I'm not being your friend?" Brent came out of his chair. "Are you serious? After what I've done for you? How can you say that?"

"What are you talking about?" Richard demanded.

"You know what I've done."

Richard stared at him a moment. "Yeah, well, I'm still not sure that was a help to me."

"What are you talking about?" Ashlyn interrupted. "Why so cryptic?"

"Not your business!" Brent yelled.

"Brent!" Richard yelled back.

"Richard?" Deborah said. "What's this about?"

He turned to the women and in a more civil tone said, "It's nothing. He just did me a favor that may not have been a favor at all. You know how it is."

"Not really." Ashlyn searched Richard's eyes for clarification. She then looked at Brent with disgust. "I think I should go."

"Good idea," Brent agreed.

"No." Richard stood. "I'd rather you stayed. Brent's the one out of line. He can go."

"What?" Brent was stunned. "You're kicking me out?"

"I need her here." Richard faced his friend. "She's helping me. You're agitating me. We'll get together later, when you've calmed down. You know I'm right."

Brent looked down at his hands that were balled into fists and nodded. "I know. I'm sorry. I'll call you when I'm not so tense. Ashlyn, I'm sorry for being such a jerk."

She did not respond, did not move. Brent turned away, stepped up to Richard, and wrapped his arms around the man in a bear hug, releasing quickly. Richard had just enough time to pat him on the back before they were separated again.

"You're my best friend, Brent." Richard squeezed his shoulder. "I just need calm right now."

"I know. Good to see you, Mrs. Ellison." Brent turned away and walked into the house. Richard watched him until he was out the front door. He stood silent until he heard Brent's car door and the engine start.

"I am so sorry." He faced Ashlyn. "We've been friends forever. But sometimes he just goes off the rails."

"I get it." Ashlyn relaxed. "I used to have friends like that."

"Oh really?" Richard raised an eyebrow. "What did you do?"

"Got new friends."

44

Shaun was reading the motivational posters that hung on the walls of Stephanie's office when Paul McIntosh arrived. The accountant took one look at the detective and frowned.

"Sorry." Paul glanced around. "They said the detective wanted to talk to me."

"I'm the detective." Shaun stood. "Detective Shaun Travis. Please, shut the door and have a seat."

"Uh? Yeah, okay." Paul stepped into the office and closed the door. He chose the seat closest to the exit, pulled it ever so slightly away from the detective, and sat at an angle for a quick getaway. He noticed that, unlike when the other detective had spoken to him, the shades on the windows facing the interior space were drawn. No one could see him squirm.

"I want to thank you for your time," Shaun started.

Paul turned to him as if only realizing he was there. "Yeah. Sure."

"You're Paul McIntosh?"

"Yes."

"You're an accountant here?"

"Yes."

"Wow," Shaun nodded. "You must have to deal with a lot of money in a business like this."

"I guess." Paul shrugged.

"Must be hard to keep track of everything," Shaun rested his elbows on the desk. "I mean I would probably lose half of it in the shuffle."

"The shuffle?" Paul shifted uncomfortably, his head cocked to one side.

"You know," Shaun pointed to a stack of ledgers on Stephanie's desk. "This money goes here. That money goes there. The shuffle."

"That's not exactly how it works." Paul sat straight. "I mean it is, but it isn't. We enter the data we're given. Money is moved, but only as instructed. We don't lose track of it."

"You don't?"

"No."

"Never?"

"Never."

"You ever tempted?" Shaun asked. "You know. Make an account. Make a few entries. No one would ever know."

"No." Paul seemed disgusted. "I would know. And eventually, someone else would know. You can't hide things like that forever."

"Is that what happened?"

"Is what what happened?

"Stephanie found your secret account?" Shaun said. "So you had to kill her?"

"Are you insane?" Paul's eyes widened. "I don't have a secret account. And I sure didn't kill Stephanie."

Shaun pulled some documents from a folder on the desk. He turned them toward Paul and laid them on the desk. "Can you explain how a low-level accountant can afford these cars? And your house. That must have been a small fortune. Yet you have no debts. How is that possible?"

Paul sat forward, looking at the documents the detective had presented. "Is that what this is about?"

"Can you explain?"

"I own a couple of cars," Paul threw his hands up and let them drop. "So I must have killed Stephanie."

"You own three very nice vehicles and a home," Shaun pointed at the papers. "Not exactly affordable on the salary you are pulling here. Not unless you're supplementing your income."

"Well then," Paul sat back. "There can only be one way to do that."

"Mr. McIntosh," Shaun's voice was stern and forceful. "Would you rather we have this conversation at the station?"

Paul froze for a brief moment. When he spoke, the meekness was the polar opposite of the detective's. "No."

"Then if you have an explanation for what I'm seeing here," Shaun indicated the documents. "Why don't you share what it is."

Paul nodded in resignation. "Have you ever heard those stories of rich uncles?"

Shaun nodded.

"Well, that is literally what happened to me."

"You're rich?"

"No." Paul shook his head as he adjusted himself in his chair. "My uncle was rich. On my mom's side. He had a ton of money. Never married. No kids. And one day he was driving to work, or back, I don't know. Anyway, he's driving along, minding his own business and some kid in a pickup truck runs a red light, and broadsides my uncle. He was killed on impact. The dumb ass was going eighty in a forty-five zone. My uncle never had a chance."

"So you are rich?"

"My uncle had a will." Paul shifted himself again. "Left most of his money to my mom. But he gave me a sizable chunk."

"And you were just too loyal to leave your job?" Shaun asked.

"Not exactly." Paul glanced at the documents on the desk. "See I went a little crazy. Bought a new truck. Then decided I wanted a sports car. Oh, and you always need a fancy car for dating. You see where I'm going? Then I needed a place to park them. Bought a house with a three-car garage, five bedrooms, four bathrooms, a deck, a pool. It's really nice."

"Okay."

"Well," Paul shrank into himself a bit. "That was all the money. I had all this stuff and no more money. Insurance. Property taxes. Maintenance. They all cost something. Not to mention my house has a bed, a couch, and a tv. That's it. So no, I don't continue to work here out of loyalty. I work here so I can pay the utilities and eat."

"And you have the documents to back up your story?"

"Sure do." Paul grinned. "One thing you learn in this business is: you document everything and throw away nothing."

45

Jack sat at his desk, the case file spread out before him. He was reading from beginning to end, hoping a fresh look might help him see something he missed the previous times he had read it. When he was done, he would do the same thing with all the notes he had taken.

The interrogation of Brent Meadows had left a bitter taste in his mouth. The man stuck with his alibi story for Richard Ellison, even after being confronted with evidence that suggested otherwise. He was obviously covering for his friend, which bothered the detective because Jack had all but eliminated Richard as a suspect in his mind. But if the man was innocent, why did he need his friend to lie for him?

Jack had missed something. He was sure of it. Whether it was in the evidence or the interviews he didn't know. But he was going to review every last detail, no matter how small, until he figured it out.

He was about halfway through the file when he decided to stretch his legs and get a cup of coffee. He took the long way to the break room, where the coffee maker was, to avoid walking by Chief Hutchins' office. He wasn't ready to give her an update and didn't want to be put in the situation of having to fake his way through a report.

The break room was empty with the exception of Officer Mendez from the night shift who was sitting in one chair with his legs stretched to another. His head was bowed into his chest which rose and fell in deep breaths. Jack crossed to fill his cup only to find the coffee pot empty. With a grumble, he dumped the old grinds, put in a new filter, and shoveled in fresh. When he hit the start button the machine whined and gurgled as it brewed. Mendez sat up with a start.

"Sorry about that." Jack's eyes remained fixed on the stream of black liquid.

"No problem," the officer muttered and slid his feet to the floor. "What time is it?"

Jack glanced at the clock above his head. "Too early for you to be here. What's going on?"

"Had to testify in court today." Mendez rose to his feet. "Didn't see the point of driving a half-hour home only to leave an hour later. So, here I am."

The coffee finished and Jack poured the fresh brew into his cup. "Here you are."

"You still working on that case?" Mendez asked. "The woman in the park?"

"I am." Jack started to leave the break room.

"Can you use a hand? I'm bored out of my mind."

"I'm reviewing the case file," Jack said. "I can use a fresh set of eyes."

"Sounds good. Lead the way."

The officer followed Jack out of the break room. The two men walked through the room toward Jack's desk. As they passed her door, Chief Hutchins called out. "Mallory!"

"Oh shit," Jack muttered. He closed his eyes, angry at himself for not taking the long way around. Taking a deep breath he opened his eyes. "Go on ahead. I have to deal with this."

Officer Mendez nodded and moved on. Jack turned and entered the chief's office, wondering how she actually saw him. It seemed to him that she called his name before he was even to her door. "What's up chief?"

"Give me an update on the case," she ordered. "Then explain to me why Detective Travis is not at his desk again."

"Well, we've run down some leads." Jack took a seat. "We've tracked down some possible witnesses and suspects."

"And?"

"And we're about the same place we were before." Jack looked her in the eyes. "Except for eliminating a couple of people from our suspect list."

Chief Hutchins stared at him. "So, you've got nothing?"

"I've got some leads to follow up," Jack countered. "I've got some theories."

"Theories?"

"Yes, ma'am."

"Nothing concrete?"

"If I had something concrete," Jack responded. "It wouldn't be a theory."

The chief glared at the detective long enough that he got the message. "Are those the leads you need to follow up?"

"Some of them."

"Is that where Detective Travis is now?"

"I honestly don't know where Shaun is." Jack sat up straight. "But you need to trust that he won't do anything that is too much for him. Keeping him tied to his desk is like a punishment. Let him do his job."

"I understand that you may have felt free to speak to the former chief however you pleased." Sharon leaned forward. "But let me make it perfectly clear. That is not the case with me."

"Understood." Jack held her gaze. "May I go now?"

"You may."

Jack stood and turned to leave.

"Oh, and Jack," the chief called after him.

He stopped, rolled his eyes then turned back around. "Yes, chief?"

"I will take your recommendation under advisement."

"That's all I ask." He left the office and caught up to Officer Mendez who was standing next to Jack's desk.

"Everything good?" Mendez gestured to the chief's office.

"Everything's good." Jack pushed a box across his desk to the officer. "Read through the notes and statements. If anything seems odd or makes you question it, let me know."

"I'm no detective," Mendez took a folder from the box. "Doubt I will see anything you didn't."

"You never know." Jack sat and picked up where he left off. "Sometimes it's just getting a fresh set of eyes that makes the difference."

The two men read every detail on every page. Jack was beginning to think he had not missed anything. He looked at Mendez, who was struggling to keep his eyes open.

The officer said, "Detective work ain't as glamorous as they show in the movies."

"No, it isn't." Jack never lifted his head.

The officer stood and reached into the box for another folder. "When you say something that seems odd, would this count?"

Jack looked up. Mendez was holding out an evidence bag with Stephanie Ellison's phone in it. The screen was on and there was a notification in the center. Jack snatched the bag out of the officer's hand. "She has two missed calls?"

"Someone doesn't know she's dead," Mendez observed.

"Or the killer wants us to think he doesn't know," Jack countered.

"Sneaky," the officer said. "But then, if we didn't know who he was, doesn't this just put him on our radar?"

"Sneaky doesn't necessarily mean smart." Jack opened the bag and pulled the phone out. Richard Ellison had provided the access code and Jack punched in the numbers to unlock it. He quickly moved to the messages and clicked on the most recent one, putting the phone on speaker.

"Stephanie," the man's voice said. "This is Kaleb Parks again. Was hoping to touch base with you. Give me a call, please."

Jack glanced at Mendez before tapping the earlier message, from an hour before. The same man's voice said, "Stephanie, Kaleb Parks here. Enjoyed our talk. If you could give me a call, I'd like to continue."

"A mystery man?" Mendez asked.

"He knows her, but not intimately," Jack said. "Though that may be what he's after."

"How do you know he doesn't know her intimately?"

"He gave his last name." Jack moved the files on his desk so he could get to his keyboard. "If they were in a relationship, I don't think he would need to do that."

"You've got a point," Mendez nodded. "But what if they met on some dating site? He might think he should make it clear who he is."

"Okay." Jack let the idea take root. "So they have a first date. He thinks they have hit it off. But now he's being ghosted. Gives his full name to be sure she knows who he is."

"Doesn't sound like our killer, does it?"

"Or he knows that eventually we would look into dating apps and his name would come up," Jack countered. "Then we're back to him just wanting us to think he doesn't know she's dead, even though he's the one that killed her."

Jack opened the call history to look for other calls from Kaleb. There were four more spread out over the week leading up to her death, but no more messages. "They haven't known each other long. No texts. Just a few calls."

"How do we find him?" Mendez asked.

Jack typed the name and searched for a criminal record. Nothing came up, not even a traffic ticket. He searched for a state ID and found two Kaleb Parks in the city. One of them was sixty-four years old. The other was forty-one. Father, son maybe? He chose the younger and searched for more information. The address was in an upscale neighborhood. Jack had investigated a domestic homicide just a few houses down, probably a dozen years ago.

It had been a nasty case. A man came home from a business trip a day early to find his wife in bed with another man. He beat the man half to death then tied him to a chair and forced him to watch as he killed and dismembered his wife of twenty years. While the husband started putting his wife's body parts in trash bags, the lover managed to break free and escape through a window, naked and bleeding. A neighbor called the police to report a streaker. When officers arrived, the husband was chasing the man through the neighborhood with a butcher knife. Some cases you just can't forget.

Kaleb had three cars, an SUV, and a pickup truck registered in his name. None of them were collectibles, leading Jack to think the man may have a family. If he was prowling dating sites, could Stephanie have found out and confronted him? A hypocritical reaction, if that were the case. Could Kaleb's wife have discovered what her husband was up to and confronted Stephanie? The possibility also existed that Kaleb was divorced. Maybe he found out that Stephanie was married and confronted her.

Officer Mendez was reading over Jack's shoulder. "You think that's him?"

"One way to find out." Jack brought up the man's number on Stephanie's phone and typed it into his own.

A man answered on the second ring. "Who is this?"

Jack took an immediate disliking to the man. "Is this Kaleb Parks on Broadmoore Drive?"

"And again, I ask," Kaleb took a deep breath. "Who is this?"

"I am calling about Stephanie Ellison." Jack paused for a second, waiting for a reaction. "Can we meet?"

"I'm not meeting a complete stranger to discuss a woman I barely know." The man did not sound panicked, but there was something in his voice. "Listen. If this is her husband, you just need to talk to her."

"This is not her husband," Jack clarified. "I'm Detective Jack Mallory. Your name came up as a possible witness in a case I am investigating. So, I can meet you somewhere, you can come in, or I can have you picked up by officers."

"Witness?" Kaleb's voice faltered. "I didn't witness anything. What's this about?"

"Mr. Parks," Jack said. "I'm not going to discuss the case over the phone. Do I need to send officers to pick you up?"

"No." Kaleb was quick to respond. "I'll come to you. Just tell me when and where."

Jack gave him the address to the station and asked that he come as soon as he could. The man agreed to be there within a half hour.

"It's definitely him," Jack said to Mendez after ending the call. "Thanks for the assist."

"I didn't do anything." Mendez looked at his watch. "And it's time for me to hit the streets."

46

Shaun Travis walked into the department and approached Jack's desk. Officer Mendez was walking toward him and nodded in greeting as he passed. The older detective was back to reading through the notes of the case when Shaun sat in the chair opposite him.

"Hutchins has been looking for you." Jack never looked up from the file he was scanning. "Where've you been?"

"Following Stephanie's trail from her last day." Shaun looked toward the chief's office. "What does she want?"

"You would have to ask her," Jack grumbled. "But before you do, check into Stephanie Ellison's phone records." He handed Shaun a scrap of paper. "See if this man was in contact with her. I know there were a half dozen calls. I want to know if there were any text messages or calls erased from her history."

Shaun took the paper and read the name, "Kaleb Parks. I'll get right on it. Who is he?"

"Possibly the last person to see Stephanie alive."

"That is something." Shaun turned to his computer. "We bringing him in?"

"He'll be here soon," Jack said. "I'd like to know everything before he arrives."

"I'll let you know what I find."

Jack grunted and returned to reviewing his notes. He had been at it for hours and had yet to find anything he had forgotten. The detective was looking forward to interviewing Kaleb Parks, if for no other reason than to have an excuse to step away from his desk.

"You said you know of six calls?" Shaun lifted his head to look at Jack.

"That's right."

"Well, that's all there are." Shaun pointed at his screen. "Six calls. No texts."

"Really?" Jack raised an eyebrow. "I thought there would be more. I was sure he had been lying about how long they had known each other."

"Well I can't tell you how long they knew each other," Shaun said. "But I can tell you they didn't start communicating by phone until about three weeks ago. Of course, that doesn't rule out meeting in person, or talking through some type of app."

"But without knowing what app, we can't get a warrant to check them out." Jack sighed.

"I can check her phone to see what apps are installed," Shaun suggested. "If I can get into the apps, I can search for conversations."

"Do that." Jack tossed Stephanie's phone to the younger detective. "But first tell me what you learned while tracing her steps."

"Okay, so, first she went to Alexandria's Boutique and buys a blouse." Shaun leaned forward like he was gossiping.

"She tells her husband she's working late and tells work she's going home early." Jack writes the information into his notes. "But she goes shopping?"

"That's right," Shaun confirmed. "The lady said she had a stain on the one she was wearing and needed a replacement in a hurry because she was meeting someone."

"Could be Kaleb Parks," Jack said. "I don't suppose the lady knew who she was meeting?"

"No."

"Where to from there?"

"Next she went to Briana's," Shaun said.

"A friend?"

"A hair salon."

"She lied to everyone so she could go shopping and get her hair done?" Jack flipped the page of his notebook and kept writing.

"The woman who did her hair said she booked the appointment with short notice, which wasn't like her." Shaun grinned like he had just spilled a huge secret. "And that she was meeting someone."

"So we've established that she was meeting someone," Jack stated the obvious. "But no one can tell us who."

"True," Shaun nodded. "But she asked the hairdresser the best way to break bad news."

"Tell me she knew what the bad news was." Jack sat up in anticipation.

"Well, no." Shaun frowned. "But she did say she thought the news was for her husband."

"And we are back to Richard." Jack underlined the last part in his notebook.

The phone on Jack's desk buzzed, and he answered. "Mallory."

He listened and continued. "Have someone bring him to interview two and sit on him until I get there."

"He's here?" Shaun looked toward the elevators. "You want me to sit in?"

"I need you to file for warrants on Richard Ellison's and Brent Meadow's phones." Jack stood. "They're hiding something and I want to know what it is."

"I'll take care of it."

Jack picked up a stack of folders and headed across the department where the interview rooms were.

47

Jack walked into interview room two with the large number of folders under his arm. He stepped up to the table and stacked everything in a neat pile.

Kaleb Parks was already there, sitting in the suspect/witness seat. From their phone conversation, Jack had decided he didn't like the man. Seeing him in his expensive suit and picture-perfect hair, reinforced that initial assessment. The man was staring at the stack of folders, as Jack knew he would. The detective also knew he would spend a good portion of the interview wondering how much of the information contained inside those folders was about him.

"Mr. Parks," Jack held out a hand. "Thank you for coming in."

Kaleb shook the offered hand and grunted. He did not want to be there and wanted Jack to know it.

"As I said on the phone, I'm Detective Jack Mallory." The detective released his grip and dropped the hand to rest on the folders. Kaleb's gaze dropped as well. "I know you are probably a busy man, so we'll try to get you out of here as quickly as possible."

"Thank you." Kaleb relaxed slightly. "You said something about me being a witness. I haven't seen anything that would be considered a crime."

"Well, I am going to ask you some questions." Jack patted the folders. "And we'll determine if you know anything or not."

Kaleb looked at the folders. "What is this about?"

"You recently had dinner with a woman named Stephanie Ellison." Jack watched the man's eyes for a reaction.

Recognition registered in his gaze. "I did. But how do you know that?"

"Can you tell me why you were dining with Mrs. Ellison?" Jack emphasized the prefix.

"Why don't you ask Mrs. Ellison?" Kaleb emphasized the prefix as well, in an almost mocking tone.

"I can get you out of here quickly," Jack said. "Or we can drag this out for hours. Why were you dining with Stephanie Ellison?"

"I was interviewing her for a position." Kaleb crossed his arms over his chest. "How is this relevant to anything?"

"An accounting position?" Jack's mind raced. Of all the possibilities, this had not been one he had thought of.

"Of course an accounting position," Kaleb threw up his arms then crossed them again. "She's an accountant. Why are you asking about her?"

"After the interview," Jack changed gears. "Did you leave the restaurant together?"

"We left the building together." Kaleb frowned. "She left in her own car."

"Did you see anyone else while you were there?" Jack continued. "Maybe someone who was paying too much attention to Stephanie? Or someone who left the parking lot right behind her?"

"Has something happened to Stephanie?" Kaleb asked. "Because I've been trying to reach her, and she's not answering."

"Did you see anyone?"

"No. I didn't see anyone," Kaleb answered. "Now tell me why you're asking about her."

"Mrs. Ellison was murdered a couple of hours after leaving that restaurant." Jack watched the man's eyes. "And you were the last to see her alive."

Kaleb sat silent for a moment. "That isn't true."

"You're saying someone else saw her after you?" Jack asked. "Do you know who?"

"Whoever killed her, obviously," Kaleb said.

Jack half grinned. "At the restaurant, the waitress overheard you calling her Steph, a nickname only those close to her use. Can you explain that?"

"The waitress overheard that?" Kaleb clasped his hands together. "That's surprising because it only happened once. I have a bad habit of shortening people's names. When Stephanie introduced herself, I called her Steph. She did not appreciate it and was quick to shut me down. I only called her Stephanie after that."

"Say I believe you," Jack uncrossed his arms and put his hands on the table between them. "Why hold an interview in a restaurant instead of your office?"

"She wanted it that way," Kaleb said. "She didn't want to be seen going into my building. In case it didn't work out."

"Did it?"

"Did it what?"

"Work out," Jack said. "How did the interview go?"

"She was a good candidate." Kaleb lowered his eyes. "I was going to offer her a job. It's a shame what happened. Do you have any idea who did it?"

"We have suspects."

"And I'm one of them?"

"You are." Jack nodded. "Until we can clear you."

"Why would I want to kill her?"

"Maybe you propositioned her and she didn't take it well," Jack suggested. "Or she learned a secret about you that you couldn't afford to get out."

"I wasn't trying to sleep with her." Kaleb defended. "I was trying to hire her."

"I only have your word that the meeting was an interview." Jack crossed his arms across his chest. "Maybe you lured her there. Maybe you planned to kill her all along."

"No."

"No one else knew about this supposed interview," Jack pointed out. "We have interviewed her family, her friends, and her coworkers. Not one of them mentioned an interview. Not even a hint that she might be looking for a new job."

"My secretary."

"Your secretary?" Jack frowned. "You're suggesting your secretary killed her?"

"No." Kaleb shook his head. "My secretary knew about the interview. She's the one who scheduled it with Mrs. Ellison."

"We can check on that." Jack wrote a note to do so.

"Please do."

Jack tapped the table with his finger. "There's one thing I don't understand."

"What is that?"

"You're interviewing a candidate for a job." Jack pulled a receipt from one of the folders next to him. He lay it on the table facing the man. "Yet she paid for dinner. Doesn't that seem odd?"

"It does," Kaleb admitted. "And I can explain."

"I'm listening."

"I went to the gym after work," Kaleb explained. "I left my wallet in my locker. It was rather embarrassing. In fact, I was trying to call her to arrange to pay her back. And to offer her the job."

"I see."

"And before you ask," Kaleb said. "Yes, I can prove it. I had my secretary draw up a contract this morning. You can ask her about it when you call to confirm the interview."

"I will." Jack put the receipt back in the folder. "That's it for now. But don't plan on leaving town for a few days while I confirm what you've told me."

"I'm in the middle of a project." Kaleb stood. "Not going anywhere."

Jack pushed himself away from the table and rose to a standing position. "Oh. One more thing."

"Yes, detective?"

"Did Stephanie, by chance, bring a laptop to the interview?"

"She did."

"Thank you." Jack picked up the pile of folders and walked back to his desk, asking an officer to see Mr. Parks out of the building.

48

A half-eaten pizza sat in its box in the center of the table. Richard sat on one side slouching in the chair, nursing a whiskey in a tumbler. The bottle sat next to the glass. Across from him, Ashlyn was drinking a beer straight from the bottle. There were two empty bottles next to her plate.

"You should never trust anyone who doesn't eat their crusts." Richard eyed the crescent moon-shaped bread on her plate.

"Is that so?"

"It is." He took a drink before continuing. "I read it somewhere."

"Where would you have read such nonsense?" Deborah asked. She was standing at the kitchen island a few feet away, working on a single slice of the pizza.

"I don't know," Richard said. "But I did."

"She knows," Ashlyn raised her beer in triumph. "You're full of it."

"I didn't say that," Deborah defended.

"But you know he is." Ashlyn pointed at her by peeling one finger away from the bottle.

"Well, you're full of it too." Richard stared down into his glass.

"I think you both have had enough to drink." Deborah walked over and took the whiskey bottle.

Ashlyn laughed, snorting beer out of her nose. Richard leaned forward and snatched the beer out of her hand, laughing as she reached for a napkin.

"You know," Ashlyn wiped at her upper lip with the napkin. "I never really liked you. Used to tell Stephanie she made a mistake marrying you."

"You didn't," Deborah turned to her.

"I know." Richard slid another slice of pizza onto his plate.

"You knew?" Both women said at the same time.

"She told me." Richard lost himself for a minute. "We didn't keep secrets. At least I didn't think so."

"Well, I think I was wrong," she confessed. "Unless, of course, you killed her."

"You know he didn't," Deborah said.

"Well, I may have been wrong about you too." He took a bite of the pizza and chewed slowly, before swallowing.

Ashlyn's eyebrows came together. "Wrong about what?"

"I always told Stephanie what an awful, miserable woman you were."

"Richard!" Deborah scolded.

Richard tried to straighten but slid back into the slouch. "But I think you were just being protective of her."

A tear formed at the corner of Ashlyn's eye. "I miss her."

"Me too," Richard sighed. He stared off into the distance. "God. Can you imagine what she would say if she could see us now?"

"She'd tell you to stop drinking," Deborah said.

"She would like that we made peace with one another." Ashlyn looked off too. "Wouldn't you, sis?"

"She wanted so badly for us to get along." Richard nodded. "I'm sorry I didn't try harder before."

"I didn't really give you the chance," Ashlyn admitted. "You know, the day she introduced you to me, I told her to dump you. I tried to set her up with a couple of guys I knew. But she wouldn't even meet them."

"I didn't know that." Richard looked surprised. "The first time we met? Why did you hate me?"

"Honestly," Ashlyn lowered her gaze. "There was something about the way she said your name."

"My name?" He sat up. "What's wrong with my name?"

"Nothing." Ashlyn looked up at him. "It was the way she said it. I knew right then that you were the one she was going to marry. I knew you were going to become the most important person in her life. And I was going to be left behind. An outsider in my own sister's life."

"It wasn't like that."

"It was." Ashlyn took a deep breath. "I see now that the reason it was like that was my own doing. I blamed you. Because it was easy. And it made me resent you more. But I was the problem."

"We both were."

She looked at him for a moment then smiled slightly. "Okay. I'll give you that."

"On that note," Deborah pushed herself away from the island. "I'm going to bed. See you in the morning."

"Goodnight, mom," Richard watched her walk toward the stairs.

"Night, Mrs. Ellison," Ashlyn called after her.

The two of them watched Deborah make her way down the hall and sat silently for a long while after hearing her close the bedroom door.

"You know, Stephanie used to threaten to take us to couples counseling," Richard said.

"You two?" Ashlyn laughed. "But you were the perfect couple."

"Oh, no." Richard shook his head. "Not her and me. You and me."

"She wanted me to go to couples therapy with you?" She frowned. "That would have been awkward."

"I think she realized that." He took a drink. "Because she stopped threatening at some point."

"I always knew she was crazy," Ashlyn said. "Always had to fix everyone. Did she ever tell you about the bird she nursed back to health when she was a kid?"

"No."

"It flew into our sliding glass door," Ashlyn recounted. "She put the thing in a box and hand-fed it until it could fly again."

"She should have been a nurse," Richard suggested.

"That was her original plan," her sister said. "But she quickly learned that while she could help people, there would also be a lot of loss to deal with. And she was too sensitive for that. Accounting was a fallback."

"Maybe we should have gone." Richard looked Ashlyn in the eyes.

"What?" She looked back at him. "To nursing school?"

"To therapy," he said. "For her."

"Now who's the crazy one?" Ashlyn smiled. "But you may be right."

The two of them sat in silence for a long while. Ashlyn was the first to break.

"I should probably be going," she said.

Richard looked at the empty bottles next to her. "You sure you should be driving? We have another spare room."

"You said 'we'," Ashlyn pointed at him.

"It's going to be a long time before I break that habit." Richard grimaced. "But the offer still stands."

"Don't you think it was weird?" Ashlyn said. "Me staying here with you, without her? Once was awkward. A second time might lead to gossip."

"I don't care if it's weird or not." Richard stood and stretched. "What I care about is you being safe. If I let you drive home after all those drinks and you don't make it, Stephanie will haunt me until the end of time."

"She would, wouldn't she?" Ashlyn smiled.

"Besides," Richard said. "Mom's here. That will make it less awkward."

She nodded and said, "Alright. I'll stay. But I need to get up early and get home. I promised my mom I would spend the day with her."

"I'll make sure you're up."

"I'll set my alarm." Ashlyn stood. "You don't have to put yourself out. I just wanted you to know I would probably be gone when you get up."

"I'll check on you just to be sure."

The two of them made their way down the hall. They stopped in front of the guest room and Richard told her where she could find more blankets and pillows if she needed them. She thanked him and they said their goodnights. Just before closing the door, Ashlyn stopped.

"You were good to her weren't you?"

"I tried to be," Richard said.

"Thank you for that." She smiled softly and pushed the door closed.

49

Detective Travis held the phone to his ear with his shoulder as he typed. He read the screen while speaking to the woman on the other end of the call. He apologized at one point for asking a question of her that was meant for someone else. It was getting late and his mind was tired.

Finally hanging up, he took his notepad and skimmed through the notes he had taken over the past hour. He typed them into his phone as he read. Three phone calls and repeated searches provided him with all the answers Jack had asked him to find.

He navigated the maze of desks between him and where Jack Mallory sat. More detectives were hovering around the department than usual. Some ignored their younger colleague, a few acknowledged him with a nod. Only one spoke as he passed. He gave each of them, in turn, exactly what he was given. He reached his destination and sat at the empty desk across from Jack.

"Hey, boss."

"Shaun," Jack snapped. "You're a detective. I'm a detective. I'm not your boss. Your boss, and mine, sits in that office over there. Call me Jack."

"Sorry. I forgot." Shaun fidgeted a minute.

"Did you need something?"

"You're lead detective," Shaun said. "Doesn't that make you the boss?"

"It makes me lead detective." Jack turned in his chair. "If it makes you feel better to think of me as your boss, then you go right ahead. But call me Jack."

"Yes, sir," Shaun said. "Um, Jack."

"Was that it?"

"No." Shaun lifted his notepad. "I checked on those items you asked about."

"That was fast." Jack leaned back in the chair, which screeched in protest. "What do you have for me?"

"Okay," Shaun lifted his notepad to read. "I checked Stephanie's phone records and found that there was no contact between her and Mr. Parks prior to the day of the interview."

"Really?" Jack questioned. "I was convinced he was lying about that."

"I spoke to his assistant and she confirmed that she did the original phone interview and also set up the face-to-face with Parks," Shaun said. "Which matched the phone records as well."

"What about the job offer?"

"The assistant said that Parks told her to type up the offer the next morning."

"Which proves nothing," Jack grumbled. "He could have asked her to write up the offer knowing full well he had already killed her."

"The gym where he has a membership was able to confirm he was there that day," Shaun said. "But they had no idea whether he left his wallet or not."

"Do you have anything that is actually useful?"

"If everything he said was true," Shaun said. "It would seem the blouse she purchased and having her hair done were for the interview."

"It would seem so." Jack turned back to his desk. "So the question becomes, who did Stephanie Ellison see after she left the restaurant that evening?"

"Was it planned? Or was it random?"

"In the morning, I want you to go visit the sister. What is her name?" Jack flipped through his notes until he found what he was looking for. "Here it is. Ashlyn Rollins. Go talk to her. Find out everything she knows about her sister, her brother-in-law, and anything she can tell you about Stephanie's friends. And enemies."

"Do we suspect the sister at all?"

Jack thought for a moment. "Everyone is a suspect at this point. Get a sense of their relationship. Get the sister's alibi. It wouldn't be the first time someone killed a family member."

50

Ashlyn woke to knocking. She sat up and looked around, trying to get her bearings. It took her a moment to realize the knocking was Richard. She was in the guest room and he, as promised, was making sure she was up in time to meet her mother for breakfast.

"Thank you!" she called out. The knocking stopped.

She threw her legs over the side of the bed and sat on the edge of the mattress for a time while she let herself finish waking up. It occurred to her that in all the years Richard and Stephanie had lived in this house, she had never stayed the night. Now she had done so twice.

Gathering her clothing from where she had draped them over a chair the night before, she dressed as quickly as she could. Checking the time told her she was running late. The alarm she had set had either not gone off or she had slept right through it. Being on time to breakfast with her mother was not going to happen. She typed off a quick text asking for another thirty minutes and apologizing. To her surprise, the reply was an uncharacteristically simple 'okay'.

She opened the door tentatively, then, seeing no one, she raced across the hall to the restroom where she tried to freshen up so she didn't look like she had just rolled out of bed. She splashed water on her face and worked her hair. When she was finished, she stared at herself in the mirror and silently promised to fix it when she got home.

Entering the kitchen, she found Richard and Deborah sitting at the table. They had a fresh mug of coffee waiting for her. She looked at it longingly. "I really don't have time."

"Take it with you." He held the mug out to her.

Accepting the offer with both hands, she cradled it close and inhaled the aromatic steam rising from its surface. "Thank you."

"Did you sleep okay?" Richard asked. "I can't even remember the last time someone stayed in that room."

"It was good." Ashlyn sipped the coffee. "But after all those beers, I could have slept on a rock."

Richard gave a half-hearted chuckle then looked down at his coffee.

"Do you want something to eat?" Deborah offered.

"No thank you," she said. "I really do have to go."

"Sure." Richard seemed confused as to what to do.

"I'll see myself out." She found her purse and started for the door. "I'll get the mug back to you."

"No hurry." It was the only thing he could think to say.

"Nice to see you, Mrs. Ellison," Ashlyn said before spinning on her heels.

"You too, dear," Deborah replied to her back.

Ashlyn left the house, locking the door behind her. Sitting in her car, she drank about half the coffee before backing out of the driveway. If she didn't hurry, she was going to be even later than the half-hour. Pushing the speed limits, she raced home and found that someone had parked in her space at the apartment complex. She cursed them under her breath and swung around to find another spot.

The elevator seemed slower than usual, prompting her to push the button a couple more times just to make sure. She considered taking the stairs but wasn't sure she was up to climbing five flights. Choosing to wait, she sipped from her coffee with her eyes focused on the elevator doors.

The chime, alerting her to the arrival of the elevator car, snapped her out of the trance she found herself in. The doors parted and an elderly couple Ashlyn recognized as residents of the building stepped forward. She waited for them to disembark. With a quick greeting, she slipped past them and inside. Pushing the button for the fifth floor she watched the doors begin to close. Just before they were sealed, a hand broke the line and the doors parted again. She only glanced at the man who stepped inside and turned away. He checked the panel, but pushed nothing, tilting his head toward the illuminated numbers above.

They rode in silence until they reached her floor where the man sidestepped to allow her to exit first. A gentleman or a serial killer, she mused. She would have found it humorous had her sister not just been murdered. Her killer was still out there somewhere. Ashlyn couldn't help but wonder if the man behind her might be Stephanie's killer and was here now to get from her what he did not get from her sister. She let out a nervous chuckle knowing how paranoid the thought was.

Turning the next corner she walked down the corridor that led to her apartment. Ashlyn glanced casually over her shoulder. The man was still only a few steps behind her. Paranoid or not, she was starting to panic. Holding her purse tight to her body, she shoved one hand inside to blindly search for her keys. A sense of relief warmed her when they were in her grasp. At the same time, he was so close, could she get inside before he was on her?

Taking an abrupt sidestep, she fumbled with her key trying to slide it into the lock. To her dismay, the man stopped as well.

"Are you Ashlyn Rollins?" His voice startled her.

"Who are you?" she demanded. "What do you want?"

"I'm Detective Shaun Travis." Shaun held up his badge. "I was hoping you might have a few minutes to answer some questions about your sister."

The relief overwhelmed her. Ashlyn let out her breath, not even realizing she was holding it. She almost laughed. With a relaxed hand, she unlocked her door and pushed it open.

"Please come in."

Shaun followed the woman into her home. She dropped her purse on the kitchen table along with her keys. Shaun continued into the living room. The decor was sparse, yet artsy. The arrangement of the furniture had a zen vibe to it. Everything was spotlessly clean, almost hospital sterile. But at the same time, there was a cozy, lived-in feel to it. It was the polar opposite of Shaun's apartment.

"Can I get you something to drink?" Ashlyn called from the kitchen. "Coffee? Water?"

"I'm good, thank you," Shaun called back over his shoulder. He was staring at a painting on the wall that was full of colored swirls entwined with a single, bold, straight brush stroke. He wondered what it was supposed to represent.

"Have a seat, detective." Ashlyn walked in with a glass of water, setting it on a coaster just before falling into the corner of the sofa.

Shaun sat in a wing-back chair directly across from her. "I couldn't help but notice your painting. Does it mean something?"

Ashlyn looked up at the colorful art piece. "Should it?"

"I thought maybe it represented the idea of maintaining a steady course through life amidst all the chaos." Shaun's hands followed the straight line and finished with a flurry of circular motions.

"Really?" Ashlyn stared at the painting as if seeing it for the first time. "I don't know about that, but I'll ask."

"You know the artist?"

"My father painted it when he was in college." She checked her watch. "I found it in their attic, and he let me have it. He never mentioned if it had any meaning. But I'll ask my mom if she knows. You said you have some questions?"

"Yes." Shaun took out his phone and opened it to his notes where he had jotted down what he needed. "Tell me about Stephanie."

"What do you want to know?"

"What was she like?" Shaun asked. "Did she have a temper? Or was she easy-going? Was she happy or sad? Was she satisfied with her life, or looking for something more?"

"Oh, so you want to know everything?" Stephanie looked at her watch then back to the detective.

"Do you need to be somewhere?"

"Pardon me?"

"You keep checking the time." Shaun pointed to her wrist. "Am I keeping you from something?"

"My mother," Ashlyn sighed. "I'm supposed to meet her for breakfast."

"Should I come back another time?"

"No." Ashlyn shook her head. "This is important. You're trying to catch who killed my sister. My mom will understand."

"Thank you."

"Stephanie was sweet." Ashlyn glanced at a photo in a frame on the end table next to her. She and Stephanie wore big smiles while hugging each other, cheek to cheek. "She wasn't the life of the party. But she was probably the reason for the party. She planned things. She wanted people around her, and they wanted to be around her. Family. Friends. It didn't matter. Everyone was welcome. Everyone was loved. And everyone loved her."

"She sounds amazing." Shaun typed more notes into his phone. "Almost too perfect. Did she have a dark side?"

"Well, you didn't want to cross her," Ashlyn laughed. "She loved you with all her heart. But if you crossed her, she may not speak to you for months."

"Months?"

"She had this friend in high school," Ashlyn grinned. "Stephanie told this girl she liked this guy named Luke. Next thing she knows, her friend is dating Luke."

"Seriously?"

"Stephanie had classes with this girl," Ashlyn said. "They were lab partners. They were in cheerleading together."

"And Stephanie stopped talking to her?" Shaun guessed.

"Eight months," Ashlyn responded. "Not a word."

"Did it end when the girl broke up with Luke?" Shaun asked.

"Nope." Ashlyn shook her head. "They only lasted a few weeks at most. But Stephanie held a grudge."

"Sounds like it." Shaun continued taking notes. "Anyone recently experience her grudge?"

"She was a lot better the past few years," she said. "I mean we all felt it to some level from time to time. But it would only be for a short time. A day or so. A week if she was really pissed. Nothing like the old days."

"What was your relationship with your sister like?" Shaun asked.

"Are you asking if she was ever mad at me?"

"Not only that," Shaun clarified. "I want to know if you were close. If you spoke every day or once a month."

"We were close." Ashlyn softened. "We didn't talk every day, but it was close to that. Was she ever mad at me? Sure. We were sisters. We fought like siblings. But we always made things right."

"What about Richard?"

"Richard?"

"Was she ever upset with him enough to not talk to him?"

"They were married." Ashlyn shrugged. "Of course, they fought. They even had times when they weren't speaking. But it never lasted long."

"You say they fought," Shaun repeated. "Was that the norm? What was their relationship like?"

"They were in love." Ashlyn smiled. "Crazy about each other. It was a finish each others' sentences kind of relationship."

"Any ongoing arguments between them?"

"You mean, like leaving socks on the floor?" Ashlyn asked. "Or the toilet seat up? Because they did. But Richard wouldn't hurt Stephanie over something like that."

"I was thinking more of the financial or affair variety," Shaun clarified.

"Oh, the big stuff," she frowned. "No. There was nothing like that. They didn't have money problems. And there was no way they would have cheated on each other."

"You sound pretty sure of that," Shaun said. "Is it possible she wouldn't have told you something that major?"

"It's possible," Ashlyn conceded. "But we talked about everything. I don't know why she would suddenly decide to not tell me something."

"It's one thing to talk about not taking the trash out," Shaun suggested. "And entirely different to talk about being cheated on."

Stephanie laughed.

"You find that funny?"

"We once spent three hours talking about infected cuticles." Ashlyn looked at her fingers. "There's not much we wouldn't talk about."

"What about enemies?"

"It's hard to imagine Stephanie would have any enemies," Ashlyn shrugged. "Everyone loved her."

"Put a little more thought into it," Shaun prodded. "Someone killed her. If there was anyone in her life capable of doing that, we need to know who."

"No one comes to mind."

"What about Richard?" Shaun asked. "Maybe he had an enemy that went after Stephanie to make a point."

"Do you really think someone would do that?" Ashlyn was shocked. "Kill Stephanie because they were mad at Richard?"

"It wouldn't be the first time." Shaun sat back in the chair. "If you can think of any names at all, it would be helpful."

"There was the neighbor."

Shaun looked through his notes. "Benjamin Johnson?"

"I don't remember his name," Ashlyn admitted. "But I know they had some trouble with him."

"We're aware of him." Shaun scrolled back to the current page in his notes. "Anyone else come to mind?"

Ashlyn sighed and stared off. After a long moment, she said, "There's Naomi."

"Naomi?"

"She was Richard's girlfriend before Stephanie," Ashlyn explained. "It was a long time ago, so I doubt it's her."

"Tell me why she came to mind?" Shaun pressed.

"From what I remember," she began. "She and Richard dated for like four or five years. I don't know if they were engaged or anything. But I do know that Brent and Wendy were not fond of her. And as I recall, she and Richard got in a fight, don't ask me what about, and they broke up. Brent and Wendy took that opportunity to introduce Richard to Stephanie, and they clicked. After that, when Naomi decided it was time to kiss and makeup, Richard wanted nothing of it. She then spent the next year or so trying to win him back. But, as I said, that was a long time ago."

"Do you know her last name?"

"I don't remember," she admitted. "And I think I heard she got married a few years ago."

"You heard?" Shaun questioned. "Was someone staying in touch with her?"

"She sent Richard an invitation." Ashlyn smiled.

Shaun finished his notes. "Anyone else?"

"Not that I can think of."

"Was it normal for Stephanie to work late and Richard to not wait up for her?"

"I know she worked late from time to time." Ashlyn took a long drink from her water glass. "But I don't know if Richard waited up or not."

"On the day she was killed, Stephanie told her employer that she was leaving early," Shaun said. "But she told Richard she had to work late. In reality, she met someone at a restaurant for a job interview. Do you know why she wouldn't tell Richard about that?"

"She wasn't always the most confident person," Ashlyn said. "She may not have wanted to have Richard asking her how it went if it didn't go well. You know, she could avoid talking about it until there was something to tell."

"Did she tell you?"

"No."

"I thought you talked about everything," Shaun said.

"Well, we couldn't possibly talk about everything." She rolled her eyes at him. "I'm just saying there were no subjects that were off limits. She probably didn't tell me for the same reason she didn't tell him. She knew I would be asking her how it went."

The detective sat silently scrolling through his notes. Eventually, he pulled a card from his pocket and handed it to her. "If you think of anything give me a call. Any detail, no matter how small, could have meaning."

Ashlyn took the card. "I will. I want you to catch whoever did this to her."

"We want that too." Shaun rose to his feet.

She stood and followed him to the door, shutting it behind him. Ashlyn was overcome by a wave of emotions. Leaning against the door, the tears started to come. It occurred to her that this was a time she would pick up the phone and call Stephanie. The thought only caused her to cry harder.

51

Jack Mallory pulled into the parking lot of Havencroft Financial Group minutes before the opening time that was indicated on the front door of the building. To his surprise, there was no one there. He waited about ten minutes before a silver Mercedes pulled in and parked a few spaces down from him. Beverly Wallis, the company's CFO, emerged from the vehicle with a briefcase in one hand and files cradled in the other arm. She made her way to the entrance.

Upon finding the door locked, she juggled her items while searching for keys in the briefcase. Triumphantly, she shifted the case to the hand cradling the files and used her free hand to unlock the door. Once it swung inward, she kicked a heeled foot into the opening to prevent it from closing and pressed her shoulder forward to push her way inside.

Jack stepped out of his car and stretched. As he approached the building, another vehicle pulled in and parked in the spot furthest from the entrance. The driver's door swung open but no one came out. Jack could see a lot of movement inside. He stopped to watch until the driver finally made their way out of the car. Kyra Strickland stood with a tray of coffee cups in one hand and a purse, a satchel, and a ring of keys in the other. She hip-checked the door to close it, then performed a contortionist act with her hand to press a button on her key fob, leading to the familiar beep announcing the lock being engaged.

She started walking across the lot until she saw Jack. The sight of the detective standing on the sidewalk between her and her destination gave her pause. She slowed, glancing around for someone to save her.

"Good morning, Ms. Strickland," Jack greeted her.

"Hello, detective," she responded in a weak voice. Her feet started working again, propelling her in a small arch around the man blocking her path. "There's no one here yet."

"That's okay." Jack followed her. "You're one of the people I'm here to see."

"Me?" The keys dropped from her hand. "What do you want with me?"

Jack bent and scooped up the keys before she could. "Want me to hold the coffees while you get the door?"

She hesitated, then held out the drink tray. He traded her for the keys and waited as she worked the lock. When the door swung free, Jack reached out and pushed it open, holding it while she entered.

Jack followed her through the opening and down the hall to the elevators. She pressed the three and stepped back to look up and watch the numbers above indicate what floor the elevator was on. The detective wondered if she always stared at the numbers, or if it was just a way to avoid looking at him.

The car arrived and the two of them took position opposite one another for the ride up. Just before they reached the third floor she reached over to take the tray of coffees out of his hand. He held on tight.

"I've got them," he assured her.

"Thanks," she muttered.

"No problem," he smiled.

The doors opened and Kyra stepped through practically sideways to avoid waiting a second longer than necessary. Although Jack waited for the door to fully open, he was right on her heels, easily catching up to her when she stopped to struggle with the entrance to Havencroft. Jack was just about to offer to help when the door swung open.

Inside, she let her purse and satchel fall to the floor next to the receptionist's desk, tossed the keys onto its surface, and turned to Jack for the coffees. He relinquished them happily this time.

"I have to take these to . . ." She tilted her head toward the offices behind her.

"Go ahead," Jack said. "I'll wait."

She walked away and was gone far longer than it should take to make the rounds of the offices. Jack started to consider that she had used a fire escape to make a run for it, which would elevate her to prime suspect status. Just as the thought formed, she returned with one of the coffees she originally had. She set the drink on her desk, her eyes focused on the detective.

"Why did you want to see me?"

"The night Mrs. Ellison was killed," Jack said. "You said that you and Chad were at Jacques' for dinner."

"Yes," she shrugged. "What of it?"

"Did you by chance see Mrs. Ellison while you were there?"

"See her?" Kyra furrowed her brow. "Was she there?"

"She was," Jack confirmed. "I take it you didn't see her. And Chad didn't mention seeing her?"

"Did he say he saw her?" Kyra asked. "He didn't tell me he saw her."

"What time do you expect Mr. Booker to arrive?"

"Chad?" Kyra pursed her lips. "He should already be here."

"Seems everyone is running late today," Jack observed.

"Mrs. Ellison always opened." Kyra blushed. "We're all trying to adjust to . . . ."

"The new norm?"

"Yeah," she nodded. "Exactly."

"What is it like for staff members who decide to move on?"

"Move on?"

"Resign to seek employment elsewhere," Jack said.

"Oh," Kyra blushed again. "You were talking about Mrs. Ellison. I thought you were asking about moving on to the other side."

"As interesting as that may be," Jack smiled. "I just want to know how short-timers are treated."

"I really don't know." She finally sat. "I don't think anyone has resigned since I've been here."

"So every employee that was here when you started is still here?"

"Yes."

"How long have you worked here?"

"Six months."

Jack laughed. "Fair enough. How about Chad? How long has he worked here?"

"Oh, he's been here a while." Kyra pulled her coffee toward her. "Almost two years."

"That is a long time." Jack tried not to sound sarcastic. "Maybe I'll ask him."

Jack moved away and stood in the waiting area watching each employee as they made their way to work and continued to the offices in the back. The few who seemed to notice him were greeted with a simple nod. Dan Fisher walked in and the forensic accountant noticed the detective right away.

"Good morning, Jack." He held out his hand. "I wasn't expecting you."

Jack shook the offered hand. "Just have some follow-up questions for a few of my witnesses. I'm surprised you weren't here earlier."

"Tried that yesterday," Dan nodded. "Waited nearly half an hour for someone to arrive. So, today I stopped for a coffee."

Jack looked at the man's hands. One held tightly to a briefcase Jack had never seen him without. The other was empty. "You forget something?"

"Damn it." Dan set his briefcase in the chair next to where Jack was standing. "Could you watch that? I'll be right back."

Before Jack could respond the tall man spun on his heels and retreated the way he had come. A few minutes later he reappeared with coffee in hand. He walked determinedly to Jack and reacquired his case. "Thanks. Can't get through the day without my jolt of caffeine."

"How are things going?" Jack inquired. "Find anything?"

"It's still a little early," Dan lowered his voice so the receptionist could not overhear. "But I have found one problem. I'm trying to trace it back to its origin."

The door opened and Brent Meadows entered. Kyra stood and greeted him. "Mr. Meadows. Glad to see you back."

"Can't stay away forever." Brent smiled. "I will have to be off for the funeral, whenever that is."

"I think Mrs. Wallis is planning to close the office that day."

"That's good." Brent nodded. "It would be good for everyone to go."

Kyra frowned.

"Everyone that wants to go." Brent corrected. "I see the detective is here."

"He's waiting for Chad."

"He is?" Brent glanced at the two men. "Who is the stiff with him?"

"That's the forensic accountant," Kyra said. "Did I say that right?"

"You did." Brent straightened. "How long has he been here?"

"Couple days." Kyra leaned closer. "They're looking at Stephanie's work."

"What are they looking for?"

"How should I know?" Kyra sipped her coffee. "Maybe they think math killed her. I know it made me want to kill myself when I was in school."

"You work in an accounting firm."

"But I don't do any counting," she smirked.

Brent shook his head and walked away. As he passed the two men in the lobby, he nodded at the detective who returned the gesture in kind.

The door opened again and Chad Booker entered. His face lit up when he saw Kyra and sank again when he spotted Jack. He walked up to the receptionist and gave her a brief hug. "What's he doing here?"

"Waiting for you," Kyra informed him.

"Me?" He seemed to panic. "What does he want with me?"

"Questions." She leaned close and whispered. "Did you know Mrs. Ellison was at Jacques' the same time we were?"

Chad's eyes went wide. "Oh, God. That was the same night. It completely slipped my mind. He's going to think I was hiding something. He's going to think I killed her."

"You knew she was there?" Kyra was shocked. "How do forget something like that? She was killed, Chad."

Jack broke away from Dan and approached the panic-stricken Chad. "Got a minute? I have some more questions."

"Not really," Chad said. "Can it wait?"

"I ask out of courtesy." Jack put a hand on the young man's shoulder and guided him toward the offices. "It's either here and now, or I take you to the station. Could be hours before you get back."

"Hours?"

Chad allowed himself to be led to Stephanie's empty office. Jack deposited him in the guest's chair and took a seat behind the desk.

"You seem reluctant to speak to me," Jack observed.

"No," Chad responded quickly. "It's not that. I just wasn't expecting you."

"Listen, I'm a detective investigating a murder." Jack folded his hands together on the desk. "And when someone doesn't want to talk to me about the case, I start to think there's a reason they don't want to cooperate. Maybe they have something to hide."

"No." Chad went pale. "Nothing to hide. You just intimidate the hell out of me."

"Well, how about I ask you my questions so you can be on your way?"

"Sure." The color started to come back to Chad's face. "Go ahead."

"The night of Stephanie Ellison's murder," Jack started. "You and Ms. Strickland were at Jacques' Bistro."

"Yes."

"It so happens that Mrs. Ellison was there as well," Jack said. "Did you happen to see her there?"

Chad stared at the detective with a blank look. "I, uh . . ."

"You what?"

The young man took a deep breath. "I saw her."

"And you didn't think to mention that when I spoke to you before?"

"Honestly?"

"Honesty would be the best way to go."

"When you questioned me before, I was completely shocked about what happened." Chad opened up. "I couldn't believe what had happened to Stephanie and I completely forgot what night I had seen her."

"It was literally the night before we talked," Jack challenged him. "You're telling me you couldn't remember one day to the next?"

"I may have had a few beers."

"How many is a few?"

"I don't know." Chad shrugged. "Enough that Kyra had to drive."

"So, it's not that it slipped your mind?" Jack questioned. "It's that you were too drunk to remember?"

"Something like that."

"But you remember now?"

"Oh, sure."

"And when you saw her?" Jack coaxed.

"Well, she was there with a man, not her husband," Chad leaned forward and spoke softly. "And she asked me . . . "

"You spoke to her?"

"Yes," Chad said. "We practically ran into one another. I was going to the restroom. She was coming out."

"And what did she ask you?" Jack prompted him to finish.

"She asked me not to tell anyone she was there."

"That's it?"

"That's it."

"Did you see the guy she was with?"

"Expensive suit. Expensive watch. Expensive haircut."

Jack stared at the accountant.

"What?"

"For a man who was too drunk to remember," Jack said. "You sure noticed a lot."

"He stood out, you know?"

"How did they act towards one another?"

"I don't know." Chad shrugged again. "They weren't sucking face, if that's what you mean."

"Good to know," Jack said. "But not what I meant. Were they cordial? Arguing?"

"Just having a conversation as far as I could tell," Chad recalled. "No drama or anything."

"Did you see them leave?"

"No."

"And you didn't have a secret crush on her?" Jack asked. "Maybe killed her in a jealous rage?"

"God, no." Chad looked terrified. "Not that there was anything wrong with her. But, no way."

Jack let him squirm for a minute before continuing. "You're familiar with the company laptops?"

"Of course."

"Are they all the same?" Jack asked. "Brand and model?"

"Similar," he said. "Some are older than others, but basically the same."

"Stephanie had a laptop at the restaurant," Jack said. "Did you see it? Did you notice if it was a company laptop?"

"Sorry." Chad shook his head. "Didn't see it."

Jack wondered how someone who noticed so much about the man she was with didn't notice the computer.

"Okay." Jack stood. "That's all I need. You're free to go hide in your cubicle."

The accountant stood and left without another word.

52

S he in?" Jack stood in front of Beverly Wallis' assistant. He knew she was in, because he had watched her enter the building just a short time ago.

The young woman picked up the phone on her desk and pressed a button. A moment later she said, "The detective is here to see you."

Jack let his eyes wander to the cheap art that decorated the walls. They were the kind of nondescript paintings found in almost any business that displayed art. None of it appealed to the detective.

"She'll see you now." The assistant hung up the phone and pointed at Beverly's door.

"Thank you," Jack mumbled. He was inside the woman's office seconds later.

"Detective," Beverly greeted him. "Any news? Have you caught Stephanie's killer?"

"Working on it," Jack responded. "I take it Dan is staying out of your hair?"

"Dan?"

"The forensic accountant."

"Oh. Didn't know his name." She seemed to ruffle. "It's never fun to have outsiders looking over your shoulder."

"Worried he'll find something?" Jack was direct.

"I hope not," she grimaced. "But it's still a little unnerving."

"I guess it would be," Jack agreed. "But that's not why I'm here."

"It's not?" She stiffened. "Then why are you here?"

"I was curious if you knew that Stephanie was on a job interview the night she was killed?"

"She was?" Beverly's eyes widened. "No. I didn't know."

"You had no idea she was thinking of leaving Havencroft?"

"None." The CFO pursed her lips. "I thought she was happy here. She's been with us so long."

"Maybe she was just testing the waters," Jack suggested.

"I suppose," Beverly said. "Guess we'll never know."

"Did Stephanie have a company-issued laptop?" Jack asked.

"All of the accountants do," Beverly confirmed.

"Do you know if her laptop is accounted for?"

"I'll find out." Beverly picked up her phone and pressed a series of numbers, then waited. She half smiled at Jack. She looked away when someone answered. "Wade. This is Beverly. Mrs. Ellison's company laptop. Do we know where it is?"

She waited, thanked the man, then hung up the phone.

"He says Stephanie's laptop is in the IT department," Beverly said. "They removed it from her office when they learned of her death. Protocol on termination of any kind."

"Is that normal?"

"I just said it was protocol."

"No," Jack corrected. "Is it normal for her to leave her company laptop at her desk when she leaves for the day? She didn't take work home?"

"Now that you mention it," Beverly shifted in her seat uncomfortably. "That is unusual. She was very dedicated to the work. She often took projects home. Does that mean something?"

"Possibly," Jack admitted. "Or it could be she knew she wouldn't have time to work on anything, with the interview and all."

"I suppose."

"One more thing," Jack made eye contact.

"Yes, detective?"

"Dan, the forensic accountant." Jack watched her face. "Dan says he has found something and is working to trace it back to its origin."

Beverly's face drained of color.

"Anything you'd like to tell me?" Jack asked. "You know. To save us some time."

The CFO shook her head slowly. "No. I don't have . . . What did he find?"

"Not at liberty." Jack dismissed her question. "But I promise we'll share when the time comes."

With that, Jack left the office. Even as he was closing the door behind him, he could hear her speaking to someone on the phone. Trying to find out what was wrong, no doubt.

53

Detective Shaun Travis knocked on the solid oak door before him and waited. His eyes followed the pattern of the inlay with interest. A combination of frosted and beveled glass created a mosaic that entranced him. He studied the design until he saw distorted shadows moving within the delicate curves and edges of the glass.

Moments later, the door swung away from him and a distressed-looking woman stood staring back at him. "May I help you?"

She sounded sad, defeated, as one might expect.

"Mrs. Rollins?" Shaun gave a friendly smile that he hoped wasn't too much for the occasion.

Stephanie's mother looked back at him for a long moment. "Do I know you?"

Shaun held up his badge. "Detective Shaun Travis, ma'am. I'm part of the team investigating your daughter's murder. I was hoping, if it wasn't an inconvenience, that I might be able to ask you some questions."

"Well, it's about time." The woman turned around and walked deeper into the house, leaving the door wide open.

Shaun stepped inside and pushed the door closed until he heard it latch. He engaged the lock before following in the direction the homeowner had gone. He caught up to her just as she was lowering herself into an overstuffed chair. She pointed at the long sofa beside her. The detective crossed in front of her and sat where she indicated.

"So you're a detective?" She squinted at him. "Seem awful young."

"I am," Shaun said. "A detective, that is."

"And you're investigating Stephanie's murder?"

Shaun nodded. "I want to say, I am so sorry for your loss."

"Thank you." Faith brushed him off. "What can you tell me? Do you have a suspect? Is it Richard?"

"I really can't tell you much," Shaun said. "We haven't narrowed it down to a single suspect just yet."

"But you have narrowed it down?"

Shaun hesitated.

"You haven't."

The disappointment in Faith's voice reminded Shaun of the time he had to explain to his mother that he had received a three-day suspension for fighting in school. His mother had been adamantly against violence of any kind, and it broke her heart. The look on her face was similar to the one he was looking at now.

"To that end," Shaun lowered his eyes to his phone where he scrolled through his notes to the last entry. He skipped a couple of lines and typed in Faith Rollin's name. "I'm here to ask you some questions about your daughter."

"Okay."

"Tell me about the relationship between Stephanie and Richard."

"What about it?" Faith asked. "You want me to tell you how he beat her and cheated on her?"

"Did he?" Shaun's head snapped up.

"Not that I know of." She shrugged.

"Then why would you say that?"

"Do you think he killed her?"

"We don't know," Shaun acknowledged. "That's what we are trying to determine. What do you honestly know about their relationship?"

"What I know is what I saw and what Stephanie told me."

"That makes sense," Shaun said. "So, tell me about that."

"When they would visit, they seemed perfectly normal and happy." A heavy sigh escaped her. "I never saw anything wrong."

"That's good, isn't it?"

"I don't know." She looked at him, almost pleading. "If he didn't kill her, then yes, it's a good thing. If he did, then I missed it. I missed the signs that may have saved her."

"What about when you and she talked?" Shaun prompted. "Did she say anything different?"

"She would tell me when they argued." Faith looked down at her hands. They were shaking. "But it was never anything major. Except . . ."

"Except what?"

"They fought about kids once." She drifted as though trying to remember.

"I didn't think they had kids," Shaun noted.

"Oh, they didn't fight about their kids," she explained. "They fought about whether or not to have kids."

"Well that's pretty major," Shaun observed. "Did one want kids and the other not?"

"No." Faith shook her head. "They both wanted a family. But she wanted to start right away. He wanted to wait."

"Who won?"

"He did, obviously," Faith answered.

"How long ago was this fight?" Shaun asked.

"Oh." She looked up at the ceiling. "Maybe three years ago."

"Three years ago?" Shaun was surprised. "Any chance they fought about it more recently?"

"If they did, she didn't tell me." Faith lowered her face to her hands. "But the way I reacted last time might have kept her from mentioning it again."

"How did you react?"

"I went off," Faith looked over her fingers at the detective. "Told her what a lousy husband Richard was being. How they were depriving me of being the grandmother I deserved to be. Accused her of being selfish for caving to what he wanted."

"That must have gone well." Shaun typed his notes quickly.

"She didn't speak to me for almost two months," Faith admitted. "Now, I'll never have grandchildren."

"What about your other daughter, Ashlyn?"

"She'll never have kids." Faith frowned. "She doesn't like men."

"She's a lesbian?"

"No," Faith corrected. "She just doesn't like men. Never dates. Never even mentions them. I think it has to do with her father's death. They were so close."

"Maybe she's just being cautious," Shaun suggested.

"Are you single?" Faith looked him in the eyes. "You're close to her age."

"Mrs. Rollins," Shaun ignored her question. "We need to move on. Can you tell me about Stephanie's friends?"

"Well there's that one girl," Faith said. "Wendy. Although I never understood what she saw in her. Nothing in common. And Stephanie was so much more than her."

"Wendy Meadows?"

"Yes." She nodded. "And that one from work. Lucy? Or Laney?"

"Lacey Novak?"

"That's right." Faith wagged a finger at him. "But I didn't understand that one either. I mean completely below her in every way."

Shaun was beginning to understand why Ashlyn never mentioned the men in her life. "Anyone else?"

"Those were the two that I met." Faith looked at a framed picture of her daughters on the table next to her. "I mean she and Ashlyn were best friends. Sisters, I know, but good friends as well."

"Can you think of any issues she might have had with Wendy or Lacey?"

"You mean other than jealousy?" Faith sneered. "They both wanted what Stephanie had. I mean she was beautiful, intelligent, successful. They all wanted to be in her shoes."

"Enough to kill her for it?" Shaun asked.

"I don't know." Faith leaned forward. "But I could see either of them doing it."

"You think they're both capable of murder?"

"You're right," Faith said. "Maybe they did it together."

"I didn't say that." It was Shaun's turn to sigh. He took a deep breath. "What about enemies. Did she ever mention anyone she had problems with?"

"No." Faith waved her hand to dismiss the idea. "Everyone loved Stephanie."

"You just suggested that two of her friends might be capable of killing her out of jealousy." Shaun pointed out. "But you don't think she had enemies? No one at all comes to mind?"

"No one."

"What about old boyfriends?" Shaun asked. "Any bad breakups? Maybe she ran into one of them and triggered him."

"Nothing like that," she grinned. "All her old boyfriends were still friends with her after it ended."

"All of them?"

"Of course."

"Okay," Shaun thought. "Maybe one of them remained friends in the hopes of winning her back. Any of them fit that description?"

"Probably all of them." Faith smiled. "Most of them attended her wedding."

"Wow." Shaun shook his head as he wrote. "Seems like that would be awkward."

"It's been a long time, detective," she said. "Too long for any of them to still be holding on to the hope she might change her mind."

"True," Shaun agreed. "But I have to ask. So, they've all moved on then?"

"Oh, yes." Her expression shifted slightly.

"What is it?"

"She mentioned one who never married," Faith remembered. "And he kept showing up out of the blue. I never really thought much of it. He seemed so harmless."

"What's his name?" Shaun pressed.

"Oh, what was it?" She looked up at the ceiling again. "Hank or Harry? No. Henry? Howie? That's it. Howard. Howard Jennings."

Shaun took the name down. "What can you tell me about him?"

"Like I said," Faith replied. "He was harmless. Just a scrawny kid that followed her around like a puppy when they were younger."

"Is that why she broke it off?" Shaun asked. "Because he was too clingy?"

"I think it was because we went on summer vacation," she thought back. "And when we returned, she met that other boy. What was his name? Oh. Mason. Mason Frey. The last boy she dated before Richard."

Shaun scribbled down the name. "And where is Mason now?"

"About two years after Stephanie and Richard started dating, Mason was killed in a car accident." Faith lowered her voice. "It was so sad. He was such a nice young man."

Shaun struck out the name. "Had Stephanie mentioned any issues at work?"

"No." Faith shook her head. "She loved that job."

"Did you know she went to a job interview the day she was killed?"

"Really?" She put a hand to her chest. "That surprises me. She always talked about taking over when her boss retired."

"Did you notice any changes in her that past few weeks?" Shaun asked. "In her personality? Or her routine? Maybe acting paranoid?"

"Nothing like that."

"Nothing like that?" Shaun asked. "Was there something else?"

"Well, we had lunch on Saturday," Faith said. "But she seemed preoccupied."

"Preoccupied how?" Shaun pressed.

"She seemed worried about something." Faith continued. "When I asked her what was wrong, she said it wasn't anything. I guess I should have made her talk to me."

Shaun wrote it down. "Don't spend too much time on what you should have done, Mrs. Rollins. You can't change it. And it will just upset you."

"I'll try."

Shaun handed her a card. "If anything else comes to mind, don't hesitate to call."

54

"How long is this guy going to be here?" Paul McIntosh walked into the conference room at Havencroft Financial Group, circled the table until he arrived at an empty chair and sat.

"What's wrong, Paul?" Nettie Huber asked. "Afraid he'll find out you're a fraud?"

Paul spun on her. "What does that mean?"

"Just joking," Nettie held her hands up. "He's got us all on edge."

"Listen, everyone," Beverly Wallis stood at the head of the table. "I called all of you together to discuss this situation."

"We called you," Victor Havencroft walked in and leaned against the wall behind Beverly.

"Yes," Beverly corrected. "We called you."

"What's going on?" Brent Meadows sat back in his seat. "Why are we here?"

"As you know," Beverly started. "Since Stephanie's death, the police have been investigating her murder. The detective talked to each of us and a forensic accountant has been combing through our finances."

"We all know," Chad said.

"What you don't know is that the forensic accountant claims to have found an issue," Beverly announced.

"What kind of issue?" Lacey Novak asked.

"He hasn't told us that." Victor pushed off the wall. "That's why we wanted to talk to all of you. If any of you know what is wrong, or have an idea, you need to come forward so we can handle it."

"So you can protect yourselves," Paul grumbled.

"So we can protect everyone," Beverly said.

A phone rang and all eyes turned to Brent. He was already looking at his phone and starting to stand. "Crap. I have to take this."

He left the room, pulling the door closed behind him.

"Does this have something to do with Stephanie's murder?" Lacey asked.

Everyone turned to her.

"What?" she questioned. "They're investigating her murder. They're looking for something tied to her murder. What if one of us killed her?"

"None of us killed her," Victor assured them.

"Could she have done something to the books?" Paul asked. "Something that got her killed?"

"That's ridiculous," Lacey argued. "She would never do that."

"You don't know that," Nettie countered. "How well did you really know her? How well did any of us know her?"

"Please, calm down." Beverly attempted to regain control of the meeting. "We aren't here to point fingers."

"Why are we here, exactly?" Paul asked.

Brent slipped back into the room as quietly as he could and retook his seat.

"Mr. Havencroft and I wanted you to be aware of the situation," Beverly said. "Because if this is serious, it could put the company at risk."

The room fell silent. If the company was in trouble, it could mean that they would all be out of jobs soon. They looked at one another.

"What are we supposed to do?" Paul asked.

"Nothing," Victor said. "Just be aware. If he asks questions, answer them. If he needs something, get it. As soon as we know his findings, we'll meet again to discuss what will happen going forward."

"Are we supposed to go back to our desks and pretend nothing is wrong?" Lacey asked.

"We're a family." Beverly looked at each of them. "This week, we lost one of our family and now we've got this to deal with, as a family. Pretend nothing is wrong? No. But continue working like our company depends on it. Okay?"

There was a mumbling of agreement in the room. The meeting was dismissed and everyone rose to leave.

"Brent, can you stay?" Victor said before the man could leave.

"Sure." Brent sidestepped to let those behind him leave. When they were gone and the door was closed again, he turned to the two bosses. "What's up?"

"You're not working on anything right now," Victor said.

"True," Brent affirmed. "Did you want me working on something?"

"I would like you to discreetly look into the books." Victor put a hand on the other's shoulder. "Try to find this problem. I would like to nip it in the bud."

"You know I'm not an accountant. And you want me to do this right under the nose of the forensic accountant?" Brent looked from one of them to the other.

"Discreetly." Victor reiterated. "You can do that, can't you?"

"He can." Beverly smiled.

"No." Brent looked back and forth. "I wouldn't know what I'm looking for. How would I find a problem if I don't even know what not having a problem would look like?"

"I told you," Beverly looked at Victor. "Let me do this."

"You don't have the time," Victor said. "He does."

"I will make the time," she said. "There's nothing more important than this."

"But the forensic accountant will notice the CFO digging around," Victor protested.

"I can use Brent to fetch me what I need." Beverly turned to Brent. "You can do that, can't you?"

"I suppose," Brent grimaced. "As long as you are specific about what it is you want."

Victor sighed. He looked from one face to the other. "It's settled then. Find the problem so we can formulate a response. Be discreet. But don't get caught. I don't want him thinking we're trying to cover something up."

55

"Thank you for coming in." Detective Jack Mallory set a stack of folders on the corner of the table and sat across from Richard Ellison.

Richard eyed the folders. "Is all of that about Stephanie?"

"About her." Jack placed a hand on the pile. "And those around her."

"Is her killer in there?"

"I think so," Jack nodded. "But we haven't quite figured out which one did it."

"And you have more questions for me?" Richard asked. "To help figure it out?"

"That's the idea," Jack said. "Shall we get started?"

"I guess so."

"Okay." Jack opened his notepad and scanned his notes. "On the night your wife was murdered, were you aware that she was having dinner with a man named Kaleb Parks?"

"No." Richard glanced at the folders. "Who is he? You're not suggesting Stephanie was having an affair?"

"Did you suspect that she was?"

"No." Richard crossed his arms. "She was always at work. Or at least I thought she was."

"She lied about being at work that night," Jack reminded him. "Maybe it wasn't the first time she lied."

"So she was having an affair?" Richard's voice cracked. "With this Kaleb guy?"

"Not with him," Jack corrected.

"What?" Richard was suddenly angry. "Why did you suggest she did?"

"I never said she was having an affair."

"What about this Kaleb?" Richard demanded. "You said . . ."

"I said they had dinner," Jack said. "Turns out it was a job interview."

"A job interview?"

"Yes."

"Not an affair?"

"Not that we're aware of."

"Why would you do that?"

Jack ignored his question. "So you didn't know she was interviewing?"

"No." Richard shook his head. "Are you sure? She loved her job. I would almost believe the affair over that."

"It was an interview," Jack confirmed. "She was going to be offered the position."

"It doesn't make sense." Richard scowled. "She loved Havencroft. She has friends there. Why would she want to leave?"

"We were hoping you could tell us," Jack said. "You said she was having a problem at work. Maybe that's why."

"A problem at work usually meant a spreadsheet didn't balance," Richard mumbled. "Nothing dramatic enough to quit over."

"Tell me about Naomi." Jack shifted the conversation.

"Naomi?"

"Your ex," Jack said.

"Oh, Naomi." Richard sat up. "What about her? I haven't heard from her in years."

"It's my understanding that after you started seeing Stephanie, Naomi tried very hard to win you back." Jack watched Richard's face.

"She did. But that was years ago." Richard looked confused. "I don't know who told you about her. But like I said, I haven't seen or heard from her in about a decade."

"She didn't send you a wedding invitation recently?"

"Oh, my God." Jack looked the detective in the eyes. "I forgot about that. But that was two or three years ago and I didn't go. I didn't even respond."

"Why would she send you an invitation?"

"I don't know," Richard said. "I mean, we dated for about five years and knew each other a couple of years before that. Maybe she thought I would want to celebrate for her. Or maybe she just wanted a gift. But the way she acted after we split ended any chance of us remaining friends."

"Suppose her marriage ended," Jack suggested. "Is it possible she decided to focus on her longest relationship? Maybe she decided to get rid of Stephanie to have a chance of getting back with you."

Richard stared, dumbfounded. "Sure she went a little crazy after we broke up. But murder? After ten years? I just . . . I mean . . . Is she even divorced?"

"We don't have a last name," Jack admitted. "We don't know. We're following every lead and this is one of them."

"Goodwin."

"Goodwin?"

"Her last name was Goodwin." Richard offered. "But that's when I knew her. I don't know what it was after she got married."

Jack jotted the name down. "We can find out. Thank you."

"I still can't imagine it would be her." Richard stared off.

"Maybe not." Richard opened one of the folders. "We'll look into it."

The detective pulled some sheets of paper out of the folder.

"The night of Stephanie's murder," Jack turned the pages and laid them in front of his suspect. "You said that you and your friend watched a game you had recorded."

"Yes," Richard was hesitant. He looked down at the papers.

"Can you explain this text?" Jack pointed. "You sent it to Stephanie at nine, saying you were going to bed."

"I . . . uh," he stammered. "Brent came over after that."

"You didn't follow up to let her know things changed?"

"I didn't think it was necessary," Richard lowered his eyes.

"You also said the two of you watched the game until close to midnight." Jack continued. "Yet, you never once texted or called your wife to see where she was, why she wasn't home. Can you explain, being so close to her, why that is?"

Richard stared down at the pages on the table. "No."

"No, what?"

"No. I can't explain it."

"Maybe I can." Jack leaned back. "I think you lied. You sent that text to your wife knowing she might not hurry home. You lied about Brent coming to your house. You convinced him to lie for you as well. What you did was follow her to a restaurant where you saw her having dinner with a man you didn't know."

"No."

"She told you she was going to work late," Jack pushed. "And here she was having dinner with another man. So, you waited. And after she came out you followed her again, but this time you got her to pull over, suggested you go to the park to walk and talk."

"That didn't happen."

"You confronted her," Jack continued. "She told you it was an interview, but she hadn't mentioned that before, so you didn't believe her. You argued. It got physical. You struck her and she went down."

"No."

"You worried she would turn you in for abuse." Jack leaned forward. "Would use this as a reason to leave you. You couldn't let that happen. So you hit her again and again."

"I didn't kill her!" Richard shouted. "I loved her. I would never hurt her."

"It's only a matter of time before we're able to prove it," Jack insisted. "It would be a lot better for you if you would confess now. The longer this goes, the less likely you will be able to make a plea."

"I didn't kill her." There were tears in his eyes.

"What are you hiding?" Jack demanded. "Something doesn't add up. You need to come clean."

"I think I need a lawyer." Richard was suddenly calm. "I'm not answering any more questions."

Jack stared at him for a long minute. "Okay. You should get that lawyer. We'll be talking again soon."

"Am I free to go?"

"There's the door." Jack pointed.

Richard slowly pushed away from the table and stood. The detective watched his every motion. As he pulled the door open, Jack stood.

"Richard," Jack said. The man turned to him. "Don't leave town."

56

"Thank you for seeing me on such short notice, Mr. Hayes." Richard Ellison sat across the desk from the criminal lawyer that his attorney recommended.

"Please, call me Gordon," the lawyer held out his hand. "I understand John Carter gave you my name."

Richard shook it and sat back. "That's right."

"What can I do for you, Mr. Ellison?"

Richard took a deep breath. "Where do I begin?"

"I've always found that the beginning is an excellent place to start." Gordon sat back. "Why don't you give that a try."

"Well, it all began when the police knocked on my door and informed me that they had found my wife."

"Found?" Gordon's interest was piqued. "Was she missing?"

"No." Richard shook his head. "Nothing like that. They found her in a park. She had been attacked." A wave of emotion hit him, and he unsuccessfully fought against the tears that were filling his eyes.

"What is the prognosis?"

"She didn't make it." He broke down, unable to hold back any longer.

Gordon had been practicing law for three decades and had watched dozens of clients fall apart over the years. Some because they were overwhelmed by the sadness and the situation that had brought them to his office. Others simply wanted to put forward the reaction they thought he expected. Gordon could usually tell the difference. But there were times, like with Mr. Ellison, when they seemed sincere, yet also just a little over the top.

The lawyer spun in his chair, snatching a box of tissues off the credenza behind him before spinning back and holding them out to Richard, who took one and mumbled a thank-you.

"I'm sorry." Richard rubbed at the corners of his eyes. "I wasn't expecting that."

"It's not entirely unexpected," Gordon assured him. "You had just told me your wife had died."

Richard nodded.

"Do you want to continue?"

"Yes." Richard wiped the tears from his eyes one more time, and seemingly, his emotions with them. "Anyway, my wife has been murdered. And I want you to understand, I did not kill her. I was home in bed when it happened."

"And you can't prove that." Gordon nodded, knowingly. Being alone was a common problem when trying to establish an alibi.

"That's where things get difficult."

"Difficult how?" Gordon raised an eyebrow.

"I'm innocent," Richard explained again. "But I have no real alibi. And my best friend knows I'm innocent. So, he kind of lied to the cops to give me an alibi."

"Kind of lied?"

"Okay. He lied." Richard's shoulders fell. "Truth be told, we both lied. He told me what he was going to do and I went along with it. He convinced me it was the best way to get the police to look for the real killer rather than focusing on me."

"But here you sit," Gordon pointed out. A lot of his clients lied about their alibis. Mostly because they had to. Telling the truth would put them at the scene of the crime.

"Here I sit." Richard looked down at the chair he was in. "The police are investigating me anyway. And they are finding issues with the whole alibi thing. I'm worried that everything is going to backfire and make me the prime suspect."

"And now you want to retain an attorney?"

"I think I should." He looked up. "Don't you?"

"Without a doubt," Gordon confirmed. "I would have told you to retain me the day your wife was found. Even the innocent need help in these situations."

"I just thought they would catch them, you know." Richard's eyes were focused on a point beyond the office they were in. "I didn't think it would come to this."

"If you retain me," Gordon said. "The first thing I will tell you is, no more conversations with the police without me being present."

"I think that would be best."

"Good," Gordon nodded. "Second. Don't discuss anything about your case with anyone. Not your friends. Not your family. And especially not to strangers. You never know when a stranger is trying to get information on you."

"Okay," Richard nodded. "I can do that."

"I would also suggest hiring an investigator." Gordon opened his desk drawer and withdrew a card. "Here's the one I use. He is rather expensive, so you don't have to use him. But use someone."

"An investigator? For what?"

"The police are about to take a deep dive into everything Richard Ellison," Gordon explained. "You need to get ahead of anything out there. You want an investigator looking into your life and your wife's life. If there are secrets to be found, you want to know what they are so they can be addressed."

"But I didn't do anything," Irritation crept into Richard's voice. "And my wife is the victim. Why would we need to look into her life? Shouldn't they be looking for who actually killed her?"

Gordon was used to anger from clients. Particularly from guilty clients. They were angry because they had been caught. Most had the idea that they had committed the perfect crime. They were convinced the police caught them out of dumb luck, and that they would be able to talk their way out of a conviction if it came to trial. Most were wrong. "The police look for the murderer. Your investigator will help build your defense."

"Can't you handle that?" Richard asked.

"I can, if you retain me."

"Then I want to retain you."

"Very good." Gordon smiled. "Now let's talk numbers. And I will require payment in advance. I hope that's not a problem."

57

J ack!"

Detective Mallory turned to the chief's office. Sharon Hutchins was standing in the doorway gesturing for him to join her. He smiled and nodded while muttering under his breath that he didn't have time to be giving updates.

He stood, took a long sip from his coffee, and walked in her direction. As he arrived he gave her another half-hearted smile. "What's up chief?"

"Dan Fisher was mugged last night." She was blunt and to the point.

"The forensic accountant, Dan Fisher?"

"You know another Dan Fisher?"

"Is he okay?" Jack thought of the man's appearance. Sure he was tall, which can be intimidating. But he was thin. It probably wouldn't take much to take him down.

"He was beaten." Sharon frowned. "Broken ribs and arm. A laceration on his head. They are keeping him for observation, but he'll recover. He was lucky."

"Doesn't sound lucky," Jack disagreed. "He looked like a businessman. Were they after money?"

"They didn't take his wallet," Sharon replied. "Just his briefcase."

"His briefcase?" Jack furrowed his brow. "So his computer and what? A bunch of papers? Did they look inside?"

"Don't know," Sharon admitted. "You'll need to talk to Dan about that."

"He was supposed to report on the Havencroft financials today," Jack thought aloud.

"Maybe someone didn't want you to hear that report?"

"If that's the case, it would suggest the killer was someone from the firm," Jack said.

"Not the husband?" Sharon asked. "Unless he knew about Dan. Is that possible?"

"His best friend works there," Jack replied. "I guess it's possible."

"You should look into that," Sharon suggested.

Jack considered telling her that he knew how to do his job but thought better of it. "I'll do that."

"I guess if it is the same person who killed Stephanie Ellison," Sharon said. "We should be grateful they didn't kill Dan."

"I'm not feeling very grateful." Jack turned. "I'm going to get back to work."

He expected her to stop him before he reached the door, but it didn't happen. Jack returned to the desk and called the hospital to see if he could see Dan. He was having his arm put in a cast, so it would have to wait.

He thought about each of the Havencroft Financial Group employees he had interviewed, wondering which among them were capable of money laundering, embezzlement, or of course murder. None were standouts. The detective's years of experience, however, had taught him that even those who seemed unlikely to be capable of doing such things often were.

Jack pulled out his notepad and started reading through his notes about the staff to see if something he had written down would strike a nerve with him, suggesting the interviewee was hiding something. Again, no one came to mind. The thought of having to sit down with each of them again was not appealing. He would need to narrow down the list. The receptionist, Kyra Stickland, for instance, was not in a position to alter financials. But since she was dating Chad Booker, who was, and they were at the same restaurant as the victim the night she was killed, he couldn't very well remove her from suspicion.

Lacey Novak was Stephanie's friend, which by definition should exclude her from consideration. However, Jack had arrested many murderers in the past identified as close friends of their victims, turning into killers in the heat of the moment. There were also those who simply placed a higher value on love or money than on friendship.

So far the only one with an alibi that cleared them of suspicion was Nettie Huber, who ironically seemed to be the only one with an actual motive. Stephanie was promoted over Nettie into the position she wanted. But her alibi, a weekly book club meeting that lasted well into the night was collaborated by more than a half-dozen women.

Victor Havencroft, owner and CEO of the company seemed the least likely to meet an employee in a dark secluded location. Yet, if Stephanie had identified him as doing something illegal within the business, he would have the most to lose.

The detective closed his notepad and stood. He was concerned with how long they had gone without a break in the case. If they weren't able to narrow down on a suspect soon, it may never happen. Jack just wasn't ready to add another unsolved to his resume. Many of those cases still haunted him, but none so much as the Brownfield Murders.

The Brownfields were a nondescript, unassuming family of five who were brutally murdered while they slept. The killer used a drug, delivered by a needle to sedate the family, then spent hours in the house, stabbing the victims repeatedly. The sight of the children was engraved in Jack's mind. One of the earlier cases Jack handled as a detective, it was his first unsolved. Despite following hundreds of leads, no motive or suspect came to light. The only things that were taken from the home were five family photos removed from the walls throughout the house. It was determined that each photo was a single portrait; one for each of the family members.

"Hey, Jack."

Jack realized that he was standing in the break room, empty coffee mug in hand. He turned to see Detective Maureen Weatherby, of Missing Persons, whom he had worked with on his last case, the one that got Shaun shot. "Detective."

"You okay?" Maureen asked. "You've been standing there for a while."

"I'm fine," Jack assured her. "Just thinking about a case. What brings you up to our department?"

"The chief," she said. "That, and you guys in homicide have the best coffee in the building."

She held up her own mug to emphasize her point.

"You come up here for coffee?"

"Almost every day." She sipped. "Surprised I don't see you more often."

"I don't like sitting at a desk too much."

"I remember that about you." Maureen pulled the carafe from the coffee maker and offered to pour. Jack held out his mug. "How have you been?"

"Not bad," he muttered. "How about you?"

"You know me," she smiled. "Living the life, looking for those who need to be found."

"Well, I should . . ."

"We should have dinner sometime," Maureen interrupted.

"What?"

"Dinner," she repeated. "I know you eat. I've seen you."

"Why would you want to have dinner with me?" He narrowed his eyes.

"I don't know. Company. Companionship. Call it whatever."

"You do know me," he said. "Don't you?"

"Not much," she said. "That's why I thought we should have dinner. Talk. Get to know one another. Nothing serious."

"If it's job advice you want, we can talk here," Jack suggested.

"You know, if you don't want to eat with me, fine." She threw up her empty hand. "Just forget it."

"I didn't say that," Jack backpedaled. "I would love to have dinner with you."

"Now you're just feeling guilty."

"Maybe. Maybe not," Jack joked. "You can find out at dinner."

"When?"

Jack thought about the case he was on. "Give me a few days and I'll let you know."

"Promise?"

"Promise."

58

Jack walked back to his desk, his eyes focused intently on the mug of coffee in his hand. Maureen had filled it to the rim, and he had already burned his fingers. At his desk, he lowered the mug and noticed that Shaun was sitting across from him.

"How long have you been here?"

Shaun looked up from his computer. "Five, maybe ten minutes."

Jack wondered how long he had been in the break room with an empty coffee cup in his hand. "What are you working on?"

"Trying to locate Howard Jennings." Shaun turned back to his screen.

"Remind me again."

"Faith Rollins mentioned that one of Stephanie's old boyfriends had some trouble letting go." Shaun talked into the screen. "So I am trying to find him so we can find out if he is still having problems with that."

"And to see if he might be the 'If I can't have her no one can' type?"

"Exactly."

"Good." Jack nodded his approval. "Listen. Do you know Dan Fisher?"

"He's the accountant, isn't he?" Shaun asked.

"Yes."

"I know of him," Shaun said. "We've never actually met. Why?"

"He's doing his magic on Havencroft," Jack informed him. "He was going to stop in today and give me his final report."

"Was going to?"

"He got mugged last night," Jack said.

"Mugged?" Shaun looked at Jack. "Is he okay?"

"He's at the hospital," Jack said. "I'm going to go find out myself when he's ready for visitors. Get this. The only thing the mugger took was his briefcase."

"The one with the report?" Shaun tilted his head. "Like they didn't want you to see it?"

"That's the one." Jack smiled.

"Kind of narrows down the suspect list." Shaun leaned back. "Should I forget about Howard?"

"No." Jack shook his head. "The financial issues at Havencroft could be completely unrelated to Stephanie's murder. One tragic crime shedding light on another less tragic one."

Shaun's shoulders fell slightly. "Guess I better get back to my search."

"How many Howard Jennings can there be?" Jack gently lifted his coffee and sipped gingerly.

"More than you might think," Shaun admitted. "But when I narrow the search to those within three years of Stephanie's age, I only have two hits."

"Two?" Jack said. "Really?"

"But only one has lived here for more than five years."

"Well there you are," Jack praised. "You should go talk to him while I talk to Dan."

"Sounds good," Shaun said. He started to pull away from his computer but rocked right back in. "Wait. I just got the phone records I requested."

"Richard Ellison's?" Jack asked.

"His and Brent Meadows'." Shaun clicked the link. "I should go through this."

Jack rolled his chair around the desk until he was next to his partner. "Let's go through them together. I'm curious if they will back up their stories."

Shaun brought up both records side by side and aligned the time stamps available. The two men leaned in closer.

"Well, now that's interesting," Jack declared.

"But what does it mean?"

"Well we know that Richard's phone never left his house the night of the murder," the senior detective said. "Which suggests he was home like he said."

"So now he's not a suspect?"

"He's not in the clear, yet." Jack dismissed the idea. "He may have left the phone to aid in his alibi."

"His alibi." Shaun looked from Richard's records to Brent's.

"Brent's phone was at Richard's house from ten until two in the morning," Jack read from the screen. He pulled out his notepad and searched until he found the notes he was looking for. "The timing is off. They said it was a three-hour game ending at midnight. He should have been there at nine. And he should have already been home well before two."

"They lied," Shaun said what they were both thinking.

"But neither phone was at the park." Jack rolled his chair back to his desk. "Were they working together? Leaving their phones at the house to show they were there while they went out and killed Mrs. Ellison?"

"That's a pretty good friend if you can convince him to help you kill your wife," Shaun said.

"I've seen it before." Jack took a long sip from his coffee. "Who knows, maybe this isn't their first kill together. But what I don't get is why the murder wasn't more organized."

"Organized?" Shaun questioned.

"Even if this was their first kill," Jack thought aloud. "They took the time to plan an alibi. They thought to leave their phones behind.

But the attack was unorganized. They didn't take a weapon. Something just seems off."

"Maybe they took a weapon but didn't get a chance to use it," Shaun suggested. "She ran and they improvised."

"Maybe the initial attack took place at Richard's home," Jack thought aloud. "He reached out to Brent in some way other than a phone call, to come help him take the body to the park."

"Only she wasn't dead," Shaun continued the thought. "So they had to finish her off there. But they didn't and they left her for dead."

"Do we have their bank records yet?"

"Not yet." Shaun shook his head. "I'll call about them."

"Do that," Jack ordered. "Meanwhile, you talk to this Howard fellow. I'm going to take another run at Meadows."

"What about Richard?"

"He said he was getting a lawyer," Jack reminded him. "We need to be ready when we talk to him again."

59

Brent Meadows sat in the interrogation room, elbows on the table, his head resting in his hands. He stared at the scratches on the table's surface. Jack had him picked up and brought in. The officers who deposited the man claimed Brent had protested the entire drive.

The decision not to invite him to come in on his own was part of a strategy to throw the man off balance. In addition, Jack now sat watching the man on the small screen in the observation room. It had been almost an hour of shuffling in his seat, staring at various points of the room, pleading with the camera, and demanding that someone talk to him or let him go.

Jack gathered his folders and entered the room where Brent waited and expressed his impatience.

"It's about time," Brent huffed. "I've been here all day. I have work to do."

"Sorry to keep you waiting." Jack put his folders on the table. "We appreciate your cooperation, you know, in the interest of catching your friend's killer."

Brent crossed his arms. "I thought we already went over everything."

"Well, as you can guess, the more we ask, the more we have to follow up on."

"I suppose."

"We just have some questions for you to help clarify statements made by others," Jack explained.

"What?" Brent's defenses went up. "What are others saying about me?"

"Follow-ups aren't always about the person," Jack clarified. "Sometimes it's about the small details that don't line up. The timelines that don't match. Usually very easy to clear up."

"Okay." Brent relaxed. "But can we get this over with? I really do need to get back to work."

"Sure." Jack smiled. He flipped open his notepad and the top folder of his stack. "Let's talk about your phone records."

"Wait," Brent sat up straight. "I thought you said this wasn't about me?"

"Timelines, Mr. Meadows," Jack assured him. "Timelines. Not you."

"What about timelines?" The man frowned. "I don't understand."

"How about I ask the questions," Jack suggested. "Then maybe it will make more sense."

"Okay. Fine."

"You and your friend, Richard Ellison, said you were at his home watching a game until midnight." Jack pretended to read from his notes.

"That's right."

"Okay," Jack nodded. "And Richard said the game lasted about three hours. Is that right?"

"Sounds right," Brent agreed.

"Okay. Good." Jack made a notation. "So that puts you at Richard's home from nine to midnight?"

"That's what we said," Brent insisted. "Why are you asking me questions I've already answered?"

"There's a problem, Mr. Meadows," Jack announced. "That's why."

"A problem?"

"Your phone records don't show you at Richard's house from nine to midnight." Jack turned a sheet of paper in his direction so

Brent could see. "It says ten to two. Why would you lie about that? I mean, the time covers Stephanie's murder. Why did you lie?"

"I didn't lie," Brent floundered. "I honestly thought it was earlier."

"You're saying you don't know what time you arrived and left?"

"I mean, not exactly." Brent shrugged. "You know, it was late, we had a few. I just got my times mixed up, that's all."

"I supposed that could happen." Jack played along. "But now I have to ask. Two in the morning and still no Stephanie. Why weren't either of you concerned enough to reach out to her? Neither of you seemed to think it unusual that she had not come home."

"Well, I left," Brent said. "Around midnight like I said. But I had to come back for my phone. I forgot it."

"You forgot your phone?"

"Yes."

"And you went back at two in the morning to get it?"

"That's what I said."

"Why did neither you nor Richard mention this earlier?"

"Because it wasn't relevant," Brent whined. "None of this is relevant. Richard didn't kill Stephanie."

"You're now saying you were only at Richard's house from ten until midnight?"

"I guess so," Brent nodded.

"I would like to believe you, Brent," Jack softened his voice. "But when people lie to me, it's usually to hide something. So, tell me what you're trying to hide."

"I'm not hiding anything," Brent rolled his eyes. "What could I possibly be hiding?"

"Maybe the fact that you helped your friend kill his wife?"

"What?" Brent gasped. "What motive would I have to help him kill her? I'm not a murderer. Richard's not either. And if he were, I wouldn't help."

"You've been friends for years," Jack pointed out. "Friendships that long can run very deep. You might do for a friend like that, something you would never do for anyone else."

"Didn't happen." Brent waved his hand between them. "No."

"Then why did you lie?" Jack asked again. "You're hiding something."

"I'm not."

"You are. Now tell me why," Jack demanded. "Or I'll throw you in jail for obstruction."

Brent stared at the detective. His phone rang and he pulled it out, hit the ignore button, and dropped it back into his pocket. Brent was tired, and he could tell Jack was only just getting started. He wasn't sure how much he could take, but he did know he had a breaking point and wasn't sure he wanted the detective to be the one to find it. He let out a long slow breath.

"Okay. I lied." Brent lowered his head.

"Why?"

"He needed an alibi." Brent talked to the table. "He was innocent with no alibi. I wanted to help him."

"How do you know he's innocent?" Jack asked.

"Because I know him," Brent said. "He couldn't hurt her. He wouldn't."

"So, Richard, a man you believe to be innocent, came to you for an alibi," Jack said. "And you didn't find that suspicious?"

"No." Brent held out his hands. "It's Richard. There's no way he did this. It had to be some random person."

"Tell me something, Brent," Jack leaned closer. "No lie. Did you ever mention to Richard that a forensic accountant was looking into Havencroft?"

60

"H oward Jennings?" Shaun stood in the hall of the apartment building he had tracked Stephanie Ellison's former boyfriend to.

The man who opened the door was tall, thick with muscle, and dressed only in a pair of jeans. The expression on his face was that of a Doberman pinscher that hadn't eaten in a few days looking at dinner. "Who's asking?"

Shaun held up his badge to a man who would have been very capable of beating his former girlfriend to death. "Detective Shaun Travis."

"Detective?" The man's stature relaxed slightly, becoming less intimidating. "What can I do for you?"

"I have questions about Stephanie Ellison," Shaun said.

"Stephanie Ellison?" The man thought. "I don't know a Stephanie . . . Oh, wait. Are you talking about Rollins?"

"That was her maiden name."

"God." Howard grinned. "I haven't heard that name in years. What brings you here?"

"Who is it honey?" a woman's voice called out. "We need to finish getting ready."

"It's nothing. I'll be right there." Howard hooked a thumb over his shoulder. "The wife. We are going to go visit her parents. Get to tell them they are finally going to be grandparents. She's very excited."

"Congratulations."

"Thanks." The man transformed from the man of steel to a cuddly teddy bear. "But really, why are you here? You said you had questions about Stephanie?"

"Stephanie was murdered, Mr. Frey," Shaun said.

"Oh, my God," Howard's eyes softened even more. "Are you serious? Who would want to hurt her? Was it her husband?"

"Your name came up during the investigation," Shaun continued. "Seems you had a difficult time letting go of the relationship."

"I'm a suspect?" Howard raised a hand to his chest. "I mean sure, I didn't want to lose her at the time. Maybe for longer than I should have. But that was years ago. I've clearly moved on."

"Can you give me a quick rundown of your movements for the past week?" Shaun asked.

"Oh, that's easy." Howard grinned. "We were hiking in the Rocky Mountains for the past two weeks."

"Two weeks?"

"Just got back this morning," he added. "Left a few days early. You know, the wife was getting sick and then the positive pregnancy test and all. Made hiking difficult and less important."

Shaun handed him a card. "Can you send me copies of your tickets, or some receipts, to the email address?"

"Sure thing, detective."

"Congratulations again."

"Tell her family I'm sorry for their loss." The large man shut the door.

61

True to his word, Richard Ellison, upon being asked to come in for another round of questions, showed up with a lawyer. Jack stood in the observation room, just as he had when Brent Meadows had been sitting in that same room earlier in the day.

Jack had been across from the lawyer before. He was good. A little arrogant for Jack's taste, but most lawyers were. The two men on the screen were leaning close together, speaking in what the detective assumed were whispers. It didn't matter at that point. As was required, the sound was shut off when only the attorney and client were in the room.

Questioning a suspect who has lawyered up was not as easy as one who thinks they can outsmart the police on their own. It wasn't like on those television shows where the lawyer sits by while the police hammer the suspect with questions. A good attorney will shut down their clients and forbid them to answer damaging questions.

Jack left the observation room. It was time to see if he could coerce any more out of Richard Ellison. A confession would be nice, but any detail that would help him finish this case would be a win.

He saw Shaun across the room and waved him over. The younger detective half-jogged to his partner.

"Get anything with . . . ," Jack scrunched his brow. "What was his name?"

"Howard Jennings," Shaun reminded. "But it was a dead end. He was out of town."

"You want to help me with Ellison?" Jack hooked his thumb toward the door. "He's gotten himself a lawyer. So this could be a waste of time. But it might be entertaining if he thinks he's smarter than his lawyer."

"Sure." Shaun followed Jack to the interrogation room and sat next to him when they were inside.

"Mr. Ellison." Jack pulled his chair closer to the table. "I see you've gotten yourself a lawyer."

"Gordon Hayes." The attorney held out his hand.

"We've met." Jack made no effort to shake the offered appendage. "About five years ago. You got Billy Mercer off on two counts of murder."

Gordon withdrew his hand. "That was . . ."

"He killed three more people before we caught him again." Jack recounted. "How does that make you feel?"

"Just doing my job, detective." Gordon got his wits about him. "You said you had questions for my client."

"We do." Jack turned to Richard. "Tell me about Dan Fisher."

"Who?" Richard glanced at his lawyer and back.

"Dan Fisher," Jack repeated the name more slowly.

"I don't know who that is." Richard glanced at his lawyer, confused.

"I think you do," Jack insisted. "Tell me."

"Detective," Gordon interrupted. "You've asked the question. My client has told you he doesn't know the man. Now, why don't you enlighten us, or move on."

Jack grimaced. It was so much better without the lawyers. "Dan Fisher is a forensic accountant who was looking into the financials of Havencroft."

"Havencroft?" Gordon tilted his head.

"The company my wife works for," Richard explained.

"And this is important to my client, how?" Gordon rolled his head back to Jack.

"Mr. Fisher was mugged last night." Jack kept his gaze on Richard. "He's in the hospital. And the only thing taken was his briefcase containing the findings from his investigation."

"Why would I . . ." Richard started.

"You think my client did that?" Gordon put a hand on Richard's arm.

"We would like an account of where he was last night," Jack said.

Gordon pulled a yellow pad from his briefcase and wrote Richard's name across the top and 'whereabouts' below.

"But why would I?"

"Richard," Gordon cautioned. "We'll discuss this later."

"Maybe your wife was skimming company funds," Jack suggested. "Maybe you knew and found out she was taking more than she was telling you. One thing leads to another and you kill her."

"That's ridiculous," Richard said. "I wouldn't kill her for that."

"I've seen people killed for less," Shaun said.

"What would you kill her for?" Jack asked.

"Don't answer that." Gordon put up a hand. "Do you have something else?"

"We need to talk to you about your alibi." Jack crossed his arms. "Need a couple of things cleared up."

"My alibi?"

"The one you lied about," Jack nodded.

"How do you know my client lied?" Gordon asked.

"It was easy really," Jack chuckled. "We checked phone records and the phone doesn't ping off the right towers at the right times."

"How can that be?" Richard asked. "I was home all night."

"And your phone suggests that might be true," Jack agreed. "But you could have always left your phone at home for that reason, while you went out and murdered your wife."

"Let's stick to facts," Gordon said. "You just said his phone didn't ping where it should and now you're saying it did."

"It isn't his phone that isn't where it should be," Jack said.

"Brent." Richard swallowed.

"Have you considered that maybe Mr. Meadows left his phone at his home when he went to Richard's home to watch the game?" Gordon offered an explanation.

"That could have happened." Jack looked at the lawyer. "But Brent's phone was at Richard's place."

"Wait." Richard's eyes rose to the detective's. "What?"

"You claim Brent was at your home from nine to midnight," Jack reminded him. "But, in fact, his phone places him there from ten to two."

"Ten?"

"We confronted him with this discrepancy and he admitted that he lied for you." Jack tapped the table. "You killed your wife, Richard. You left her a message that you were going to bed at nine. You asked your friend to come to your house at ten. That gave you an hour to go kill Stephanie and get back. All you had to do was convince Brent to lie about that hour."

"I don't understand." Richard knotted up and looked at Gordon. He clutched his chest. "I can't breathe."

"Richard?" Gordon put a hand on the man's back. "Relax, Richard. Inhale."

"Get him some water," Jack turned to Shaun.

The younger detective raced from the room.

Richard started to hyperventilate and did not resist when his lawyer physically turned him and placed hands on his shoulders.

"Richard?" Gordon squeezed. "Relax. Slow your breathing. Inhale. Exhale."

The lawyer demonstrated by taking a deep breath and releasing it slowly.

"Do we need to call you an ambulance?" Jack asked.

Shaun returned with the water and placed it on the table.

Richard held up a hand to Jack. He followed the example Gordon was setting; breathing in deeply and releasing slowly. When he lowered his hand he wrapped it around the glass, taking it and drinking half its contents. He was in control again, breathing normally.

"You good?" Jack asked.

Richard nodded.

"Getting caught sucks, huh?" Jack said.

"It's wrong," Richard said.

"Brent admitted he lied for you," Shaun said. "It's over."

"No." Richard shook his head.

"Richard," Gordon said. "I think we should stop here."

"No!" Richard snapped.

"Are you still trying to say Brent is your alibi?" Jack asked. "He came clean. He lied to help you."

"No," Richard said again. "I mean, yes. He lied. But that's not what's wrong."

"Then tell us, Richard." Jack spread his arms. "What are we missing? What's wrong?"

"Brent's phone couldn't have been at my house from ten to two," Richard said. "He was never there."

62

Dan Fisher was sitting up in the hospital bed when Jack walked into the room. A nurse was at his side taking his vitals, fingers on his wrist while the other hand held a thermometer in his mouth. He nodded at the detective and rolled his eyes.

Jack smiled. "Your wife doesn't even give you this much attention."

The nurse blushed slightly. She finished up. "Looks good, Mr. Fisher. The doctor should be in to talk to you soon."

She glanced at Jack as she slipped out of the room.

"Good to see you, Jack." Dan patted the bandage on his forehead. "You didn't have to come. Not like we're friends or anything."

"I did have to," Jack assured him. "I have to question the victim."

"Oh." Dan's smile faded slightly. "I thought . . . I mean the police were already here."

"Sure, I know," Jack said. "I could have talked to them. But, you know, I wanted to check on you, so here I am. To get it straight from the source."

"Thanks, Jack."

"Tell me what happened."

"Not much to tell." Dan pulled his arm up, along with the wires attached to it, for slack. He dropped his arm across his chest. "They've got me plugged in good."

"I see that."

"Anyway," Dan adjusted his shoulders into the pillow behind him. "I left Havencroft a little later than usual. Maybe half an hour, forty-five minutes later. Finished typing up my report before I left."

"So if they were waiting for you, they were there a while?" Jack jotted down a note. "I'll see if there are any cameras in the area."

"Good."

"So you left the building," Jack prompted. "Then what?"

"I started walking."

"Walking?" Jack frowned. "I thought you drove there?"

"I did," Dan confirmed.

"Then why were you walking?"

"I parked at a nearby strip mall," Dan said. "Stopped for coffee in the morning and decided to walk from there. I need the exercise."

"How far?"

"How far?"

"How far did you have to walk?"

"Maybe a mile," Dan said.

"And where did you get mugged?"

"About halfway."

"What happened? Did you see who did it?" Jack asked.

"Didn't see anyone." Dan touched the bandage again. "One minute I'm walking. I felt something hit my head and then I woke up in the hospital."

"So you didn't see them?"

"Not at all." Dan shrugged. "Guess they'll never be caught."

"We think whoever did this to you was after your briefcase." Jack offered. "Specifically the results of your investigation."

"You're not serious?" Dan said.

"We think they're worried about the truth getting out." The detective shifted on his feet. "It may have been their intention to kill you and steal the hard copy to keep it from reaching the light of day."

"Well thank God they failed on that first part." Dan smiled nervously. "But even if they had succeeded, they would have still failed."

The machine next to him beeped and both men looked at the flashing numbers and lines. It lasted for a few seconds before returning to normal.

"I uploaded everything as soon as I finished typing," Dan imitated taking keystrokes. "The whole report is already in the file. If that's what they were after, they never had a chance to stop it."

"Can you tell me what you found?"

"Sure. It's all up here." Dan tapped his head and winced.

63

The bank records for Richard Ellison and Brent Meadows were delivered to Shaun's desk in a manila envelope. The detective pulled the pages out and laid them side by side. There was nothing exciting. No giant withdrawals suggesting a payment for murder. No large deposits. Nothing unusual at all. Not until he went back nearly a month. Then he found activity that needed to be explained. Irregular deposits and withdraws going back at least a year. Shaun wrote down the dates and amounts before moving on.

He was looking for something that would put a suspect near the scene of the crime the night of the murder; a fast-food purchase, or gas. But neither man used their bank card that night. Nothing placed either of them near the park.

The day after, Richard made one purchase from the hospital cafeteria and nothing else the rest of the day.

Brent made two purchases. One at a grocery store near his neighborhood. The other at an auto parts store five miles from his home.

The detective spun in his chair to face a stack of boxes. The top one was the physical evidence from the case. He lifted it and set it on his desk, pulling the lid off and rummaging inside. He pulled three bags from inside and set them on his desk. Two contained pieces of taillight. The third, a piece of headlight.

Shaun picked up his phone and dialed.

"May I help you?" the man answered.

"If I give you a transaction number can you tell me what was purchased?" Shaun asked.

"Excuse me?"

"I'm trying to understand a charge on my account," Shaun lied. "If I give you the number, can you tell me what was purchased?"

"Sure." The man typed. "Okay. Give me the numbers."

He typed in what Shaun said.

"What was it?"

"Looks like a battery and alternator," the man read from the screen. "I'll have to go into a different system to tell you what car it was for."

"Not necessary," Shaun said. "Thanks."

He disconnected the call and stared at the three bags.

"What've you got?" Jack was almost directly behind his partner. The younger detective jumped.

"Oh my God, Jack." Shaun put his hand on his chest. "Give a guy a warning."

"My dad always told me that jumpy people had a guilty conscience." Jack patted his back. "Are you feeling guilty about something?"

"That's interesting." Shaun reached back into the box. "My mom said it was because I was good-hearted."

"Good-hearted?"

"You know," Shaun explained. "Good-hearted people are less suspicious of others. So when someone sneaks up behind them, they are more likely to be startled than people who expect the worst."

"So you're good-hearted?"

"If you ask my mother," Shaun grinned. "I'm a saint."

Jack laughed. "Well Saint Shaun, I know who attacked Dan."

"Well I thought I had proof of Brent's involvement," Shaun sighed. "He had made a purchase at an auto parts store. But it wasn't for a light."

"Those lights could have been there for weeks or even months," Jack said. "Doesn't rule him out."

Jack looked down at the evidence bags. "Hand me those bags."

Shaun lifted them and handed them to his partner. Jack turned the bags until he could read what the forensic team had written on them. There was a taillight from a Chevy, a taillight from a Mercedes, and a headlight from a Ford.

"Uh, Jack?" Shaun said.

"What?"

"In the interrogation room, when we were talking to Richard," Shaun said. "He mentioned that Brent's phone shouldn't have pinged at his house because Brent wasn't there."

"I was there."

"What if Richard is innocent?" Shaun asked.

"Then hearing that the friend who lied to give you an alibi was actually giving himself one," Jack nodded.

"Do you think he would confront Brent?"

"We need to go. Now."

The two men ran across the office. They raced down the stairs to Jack's car. Moments later they were weaving through traffic, lights flashing and the siren blaring.

64

Richard knocked on the Meadows' front door and waited on the porch for someone to answer. It took a moment that seemed forever.

The door opened and Wendy smiled when she saw him standing there. "Richard. I didn't know you were coming."

"Neither did I." Richard did not smile. "Is he here?"

Wendy's smile cracked as she stepped to the side. "He's in the living room."

Richard walked past her without making eye contact. Wendy shut the door and followed, noticing his tense shoulders and clenched fists.

"Richard?" she said to his back. "Is everything okay?"

He didn't respond, keeping his focus on the opening at the end of the hall that led into the kitchen and living space. He walked in and saw Brent right away. His life-long friend sat with his back to him, watching a game on the television mounted over the fireplace.

"Who was it?" Brent asked without moving.

"It's Richard," Wendy called from behind him.

Brent stood and turned. "Richard. Come on in. We can watch the game. You want a drink or something?"

"You said you wanted to give me an alibi," Richard said.

Brent froze for a moment, the only movement being that of his expression fading to concern. "About that."

"What's he talking about?" Wendy came up next to their guest.

"I had to come clean," Brent stammered. "They had it figured out."

"Who had what figured out?" Wendy insisted.

"Why was your phone at my house that night?" Richard asked.

"What?" Brent glanced at his wife, then back to his friend. "I wasn't there. That was the whole reason for helping you with an alibi."

"Your phone was at my house, Brent." There was an unexpected strength to his voice. "Tell me why."

"You lied to give him an alibi?" Wendy put her hands on her hips. "Why would you do that?"

"I just . . ."

"Come on, Brent." Richard gestured toward Wendy. "Tell her why you lied."

"What is with you?" Brent went on the offensive. "I was trying to help you."

"Help me?" Richard raised his voice. "You were trying to help me? You lied to the police. You got caught in that lie. And now they suspect me more than they already did. How is that helping me?"

"I was trying to help," Brent repeated. "It didn't work, but I tried."

"But you weren't trying to help," Richard sneered. "Not really. At least not me."

"What does that mean?"

"Why was your phone at my house, Brent?" Richard demanded.

"Will you stop about my phone?" Brent begged.

"Why do you keep asking about his phone?" Wendy asked.

"It was at my house when Stephanie was murdered." Richard turned to her. His hand raised to point at Brent. "But he wasn't there."

"What?"

"Where were you, Brent?" Richard turned back to his life-long friend. "Your phone was at my house. Where were you?"

"I was at home," Brent said. "You know that."

"I don't know that," Richard countered. "I only know what you told me. You lied to the police. Did you lie to me?"

"No." Brent looked at his wife. "Tell him. I was here that night."

Wendy looked back at him, confusion on her face. "I know you told me you were in the basement, but I didn't see you."

"Wendy?" Brent brought his hands to his face. "I'm not lying."

"If you were here," Richard asked, "how did your phone get to my house? And how did it leave?"

"I, uh," Brent looked Richard in the eyes. "I can't explain."

"You can't," Richard accused. "Or you won't?"

"Brent, just tell us," Wendy said.

"There's nothing to tell," Brent insisted.

"I'll tell you what happened." Richard stepped toward Brent. "You left your phone at my house to give you an alibi. You didn't lie to the police to give me an alibi. You lied because you needed one."

"Brent?" Wendy said. "Is that true? What did you do?"

"Nothing."

"He killed Stephanie." Richard pushed Brent.

"Brent?"

"No. Wait," Brent said. "It's me. What reason would I have to kill Stephanie? I would never."

"Then why was your phone at my house?"

"I would like to hear the answer to that."

The three of them turned to the voice. Detective Jack Mallory was entering the living room from the kitchen. Behind him was Detective Shaun Travis. Both held their weapons in front of them.

"Let me see your hands!" Jack ordered, approaching head-on, while Shaun circled to the right, cutting off access to the garage.

All three complied. Wendy froze in place. Both Richard and Brent took involuntary steps back.

"What's happening?" Wendy was frantic.

"Brent," Jack barked. "Why don't you answer your friend's question? Why was your phone at his house when you weren't?"

"Richard," Brent turned to his friend. "It's not what it looks like."

"Then explain," Richard demanded.

"I can't," Brent said again.

"You can." Jack stepped closer. "Come clean. Why did you kill Stephanie?"

"I didn't," Brent cried out. "I didn't kill anyone. I just . . . I can't. Not with her in the room."

"Me?" Wendy put her hands on her hips. "This is my fault?"

"That's not what I'm saying," Brent said. "I just can't explain everything in front of you."

"You're going to have to," Jack said. "No one is moving until this is resolved."

"Brent," Wendy snapped. "What are you hiding?"

"I didn't kill Stephanie," Brent pleaded. "I left my phone in Richard's mailbox so if Wendy checked where I was, it would look like I was there."

"And where were you?" Wendy demanded. "Where were you that you didn't want me to know? At the park killing Stephanie?"

"No." Brent closed his eyes. "I was at Tammy Mill's apartment."

"You what?" Wendy screamed. "You said that was over. You lying, cheating son-of-a-bitch!"

Wendy took a step toward her husband with her hand balled into fists. Jack intercepted, wrapping an arm around her waist, lifting her off her feet, and moving her away from him.

"You lied to the police to cover an affair?" Richard looked at his friend with pity.

"I knew when the police started looking at Stephanie's friends they might look at phone logs and they would show that I was at Richard's house. That's why I lied." Brent looked at Jack.

"You were with this Tammy Mill's?" Jack raised an eyebrow. "And she'll confirm that?"

"Yes."

"You son-of-a-bitch!" Wendy yelled at her husband. "You said you would never let this happen again. I want you out of this house!"

"Brent Meadows," Jack stepped up to the man. "You're under arrest for obstruction."

Shaun came up behind him, holstered his weapon, and cuffed him. Bewildered, Brent shook his head repeatedly.

"I didn't have anything to do with Stephanie's murder," Brent insisted. "Richard, you have to believe me."

"No, Brent," Richard said. "I don't."

65

Detectives Mallory and Travis were the first to arrive at Havencroft Financial Group the next morning. They'd had a long night and were sitting in their car drinking coffee, trying to stimulate their minds. The next car to pull into the lot Jack recognized as Kyra Strickland's. The two detectives watched as she fumbled with the items she gathered in her arms. Once secured, she locked her car and made her way to the building, keys in hand.

Jack and Shaun exited their vehicle and came up behind her just as she reached the door.

"I'll take that," Jack pulled the tray of coffees from her hand.

She was startled, but recovered quickly and unlocked the building. The three of them walked the hall and rode the elevator together without a word between them.

Inside Havencroft's lobby, Kyra did as she had done every other morning, dropping her satchel and purse to the floor and taking the coffee to the offices for whom they were intended.

While they waited, more employees entered and continued to the back. Victor Havencroft asked if they needed something when he arrived. They smiled and said they needed to ask Beverly a few more questions about Stephanie to clear up a few details. The man nodded and went on his way.

When Beverly arrived, she was surprised to see the detectives standing in the lobby. Kyra reappeared and took her seat behind the desk.

"Goodmorning, gentlemen," Beverly smiled. "Any progress on Stephanie's killer?"

"We've made some," Jack said. "That's why we're here actually."

"Really?"

"We have some follow-up questions," Shaun said. "We're hoping to shed some light on her last few days."

"Don't know how much help I will be," Beverly grinned. "But let's go to my office and see."

The three of them walked to the large corner office. There was a lovely view at that time of the morning. Jack couldn't help but look out the windows for a time.

"Uh, you had questions?" Beverly asked.

"We do," Jack turned away from the view. "You see, I've been going through my notes over and over again trying to spot that one detail. The one that would point me in the right direction. But nothing came to mind."

"Sorry to hear that." Beverly circled her desk and sat. "Does that mean you haven't caught her killer?"

"Not yet," Shaun said. "But we're close."

"Which is where you come in," Jack said.

"Me?" Beverly put a hand to her chest. "I think I've told you everything I know."

"You've told us everything you want us to know," Jack corrected. "You just left some details out."

"Like what?"

"For instance," Jack returned to the window. "That's a nice new Mercedes you have there."

"Thank you," she said. "I've worked hard for it."

"I'm sure you did," Jack said. "Earlier this week, you weren't in the office because that nearly new car was in the shop."

"Yes."

"What was wrong with it?"

"Just an oil change." She stiffened. "Nothing unusual."

"And if we told you we already checked with the auto shop about what they did?"

"Oh," Beverly jolted. "I had to have a taillight replaced. Someone hit me in a parking lot. Luckily they only cracked the cover."

"We know that's not true." Shaun dropped the evidence bag containing the piece of tail light that came from a Mercedes. "Turns out the shop you went to had its trash picked up the day before you arrived. It only took a little digging to find the light removed from your car."

"The piece we found at the park." Jack pointed at the bag on her desk. "It was a perfect fit."

"That only proves that it was the parking lot at the park where I was hit." Beverly stared at the bag.

"And what about Dan Fisher?"

"Dan who?" She looked unsure.

"Our forensic accountant who did the report on your company," Jack reminded her. "The one that was mugged before he could present me with his findings."

"That was tragic," Beverly said. "Is he okay?

"He's banged up, but okay," Shaun answered. "But the mugger took his briefcase. With the report."

"Tragic again," she said.

"Except the report was uploaded to our department files before he was mugged," Jack said. "So nothing was actually lost."

"Excuse me, what?" Beverly said.

"We know you've been embezzling from Havencroft for the past two years," Jack announced. "And when Stephanie uncovered the evidence you asked her to meet so you could explain, or maybe you were just going to tell her how you were going to pay it all back."

"I haven't embezzled anything."

"But instead," Shaun continued. "You killed her."

"What?" Beverly looked horrified. "I would never?"

"She took her work computer to that park and showed you what she had uncovered," Jack explained. "And somehow you got a hold of the computer and hit her with it. Then you kept hitting her, out of rage or fear, until she was nearly dead."

"Stop."

"You took her computer, cleaned it up, and returned it to your IT department," Jack said. "Our forensic team is checking it for blood as we speak."

"I didn't . . ."

"And then it was just you trying to stay ahead of us," Shaun said. "You did a good job of appearing above it all. Too cooperative to be a real suspect." Shaun moved to lean against her shelving. "Neither of us ever asked for your alibi."

"I was . . ."

"We know you don't have one," Jack interrupted. "And then comes Dan. He's not easily swayed. He's a numbers man. Doesn't care for chit-chat. Just wants to get the job done. And he does."

"So you followed him to his car that night and attacked him the first chance you got."

"Me?" Beverly pleaded. "How could I have hurt a grown man?"

"Show her, Shaun," Jack said.

Shaun moved slightly and pointed to a photo of her receiving her black belt. "It wasn't too hard to take Dan down, was it?"

Beverly sat silently. "You can't prove I embezzled anything."

"Oh, yes." Jack smiled. "That report you stole. Well, it turns out the file was uploaded to our department computer. You didn't stop the report, you just added another charge to your list."

66

S o, I hear you got your killer." Detective Maureen Weatherby sat across from Jack in the restaurant she had chosen.

"We did," Jack confirmed. "She's going away for a long time."

"Can you share the details while we're waiting for our food?"

"Not much to share." Jack shrugged. "We got her into the interrogation room and she cracked like an egg."

"She confessed?"

"To everything." Jack nodded. "She started embezzling from the company almost two years ago. Then Stephanie found out and confronted her. The night of the murder, she asked Stephanie to meet her to talk through what she had found."

"And she agreed?" Maureen asked.

"She did," Jack said. "But Beverly knew almost immediately that Stephanie wasn't going to change her mind. She knew then she was going to have to kill her."

"That poor woman." Maureen sighed. "I still can't believe she agreed to meet in that dark park."

"They had known each other for years," Jack said. "They were friends and co-workers. Stephanie had no reason to think she was going to hurt her. But once Stephanie showed her what she had found and that she had to report it, that's when Beverly snapped. She yanked the laptop out of Stephanie's hands and hit her with it. She went down but started crawling away. So Beverly kept hitting her, to finish her off."

"Brutal." Maureen sipped from her water. "Especially being friends."

"She left, backed into a bench breaking out a tail light, then drove home," Jack said. "The next morning she reported to work as if nothing had ever happened."

The waitress came with their food and the two detectives ate and made small talk.

"This is nice," Maureen said when they were nearly finished.

"It is," Jack agreed. "We should do it again."

"I would like that," she smiled.

The waitress came back by with their check. "Any dessert?"

"No, thanks," Jack said. Then he looked at Maureen. "Unless you wanted something."

"No." She smiled again. "I think we can cover dessert on our own."

Jack looked at the woman sitting across from him. "We should go."

They stood and Jack threw a fifty on the table to cover the meal and a tip. He put his arm around Maureen's waist and the two walked out into the night.

THE END

Thank you for reading!

Dear Reader,

I hope you enjoyed reading **Dog Walkers** as much as I enjoyed writing it. At this time, I would like to request, if you're so inclined, please consider leaving a review of **Dog Walkers**. I would love to hear your feedback.

Amazon:

Goodreads:
https://www.goodreads.com/author/show/18986676.William_Coleman

Website: https://www.williamcoleman.net

Facebook: https://www.facebook.com/williamcolemanauthor/

Many Thanks,

William Coleman

Other novels by William Coleman:

THE WIDOW'S HUSBAND
PAYBACK
NICK OF TIME
MURDER REVISITED
THE CONTRACT
DOG WALKERS
FIRST FRIDAYS

Made in the USA
Las Vegas, NV
12 May 2024

89861015R00184